From Paris, with Butter

A NOVEL

Christine DeSalvo

Published by Foxglove Press

FROM PARIS, WITH BUTTER. Copyright © 2025 by Christine DeSalvo

Hardcover ISBN: 979-8-9999399-2-0
Paperback ISBN: 979-8-9999399-0-6
Ebook ISBN: 979-8-9999399-1-3

Contents

Chapter 1

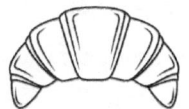

J ack had been fiddling with the box in his pocket all evening. Before the first course of caviar and iced consommé had been brought out, he was chewing his bottom lip.

When the scallop ravioli was served, a sweat had broken out on his brow, and by the time the final course—a pair of strawberry meringues—was unveiled, it must have been clear to everyone in the restaurant what he was planning to do.

I had eaten the meringues many times and knew that they were the closest to perfection egg whites and sugar could aspire to, but poor Jack didn't touch his. He was actually wringing his napkin between his hands as he looked despairingly out the window.

Maybe that was understandable. The view from Le Jules Verne was, of course, unparalleled. Michelin-starred, internationally-renowned, the preferred dining establishment of politicians and celebrities and royalty the world over, the restaurant occupied perhaps the most-coveted patch of real estate in all of Paris.

The City of Lights has no lack of beautiful places, but only one restaurant is situated on the second level of the Eiffel Tower. Through the floor-to-ceiling windows, diners could view the lacy metal of the Tower just outside and, beyond that, Paris stretching itself to perfection until it melted into the horizon. No wonder Jack was dazzled.

Come on, Jack, I thought. Don't make me wait all evening. The sun was setting and, as it dipped another centimeter, its rays struck the Tower and set the metalwork ablaze with golden light. This was the perfect moment.

Thankfully, Jack realized it, too. Wrenching his gaze from the view, he turned back to the table and smiled. In a smooth motion, he reached into his pocket and brought out a small, ivory box. I was grinning even before he opened it.

Inside was a gold ring set with a shining oval diamond.

There was a soft sound as his chair slid over the plush carpet, then Jack was bent on one knee. Without realizing it, I had brought my hands to my face. I was shaky with happiness.

There was just the smallest wobble in Jack's voice as he spoke. "Ava, you make me the happiest man in the world. I don't want to go through life with anyone except you. My love, will you marry me?"

There was a fraught moment when the lovely girl who'd been sitting across from Jack all evening—and looking a bit nervous herself—seemed too stunned to speak. She brought a hand to her own face, as if making sure she was still in the real world. Then she broke into a smile, two dimples appearing on her cheeks.

"Of course," she said breathlessly, and I had a moment of pure delight.

A smattering of applause broke out across the restaurant. As soon as Jack slipped the ring on Ava's finger—a perfect fit—I was there at the table, a bottle of champagne in my hands.

"A drink to celebrate?"

They grinned at each other, then at me, and Jack reached out to clasp my hand.

"Yes. And thank you for all your help planning this," he said. "I would have made a mess of it if I'd tried to do it on my own."

"It was my absolute pleasure," I said, pouring the champagne into two flutes. They wanted a photo, naturally, so I took several, kneeling to get the angle just right. When I left, they were happily whispering, their heads bent close together.

I checked on my other tables, refilling glasses and making sure no one had been waiting too long for their next course. My head was spinning pleasantly by the time I slipped inside the staff room to catch my breath. Yasmine was already there, checking her dark, glossy hair in a mirror.

She turned to me. "How'd it go?"

"Perfect," I said, sagging against the wall as I let my breath out. "When he called to make the reservation, he said he wanted to propose right at sunset, so I paced the courses slower to time it right."

Yasmine smiled. "You'll get an invite to this wedding too, I'm sure. You must be breaking some kind of record, Margot. How many is this for you now?"

"How many what?" I asked distractedly. I was remembering how happy Jack and his girlfriend—fiancée—had looked.

"How many engagements have you seen here?"

I always kept track. If I thought about it hard enough, I was confident I could pull up a memory of each one.

"One hundred and eighty-seven," I said with a smile.

Chapter 2

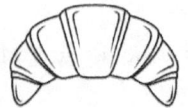

"Thank you! Oh, thank you so much," Ava said as she hugged each person she passed on her way out of the restaurant at the end of their meal. She was nearly as bubbly as the champagne she'd drunk.

The French are not generally considered huggers (why hug when you can kiss?), but I hugged her and Jack tightly as they left.

Jack had been particularly nervous about the proposal going well, and he and I had traded emails back and forth for weeks going over the details: when he should pop the question, the precise bottle of champagne I'd bring for them to toast their engagement, where he and Ava could go for a celebratory nightcap afterward...

To see everything turn out so well for them made me feel as jubilant as the newly-betrothed couple. It always did.

Pulling off a successful engagement gave me such a high that I'd become the restaurant's de facto engagement coordinator, spending as much time working through details as the proposers wanted, and pulling out all the stops when they arrived at the restaurant.

My coworkers good-naturedly ribbed me for all the unpaid time I devoted to proposals, but each one was a guaranteed moment of happiness for me. The fact that Le Jules Verne was one of the most popular proposal spots on the planet had been a major reason I'd applied for a job here five years ago. Engagements always made me giddy. If I couldn't experience one myself, at least I could work in a place full of happy couples.

"Your sixth course," I said to a Canadian pair as I placed two slices of plum moelleux cake with blackberry sorbet and lightly sweetened cream in front of them. "How did you enjoy the cheese selection?"

The man threw his hands up in mock despair. "Why can I understand your French perfectly, but as soon as I ask anyone else in Paris for so much as the time, they lose me immediately?"

I smiled, not mentioning that I was speaking particularly clearly, the way I always did when diners spoke to me in careful, hopeful French.

"I read my phrasebook so many times, but every time I say even two words in French, the person either doesn't understand, or they comment that I have an accent," the man continued, exasperated. "I know I have an accent! I'm from Toronto!" He took a bite of blackberry sorbet and groaned with pleasure.

"That's just the French being French," I reassured him. "We love commenting on accents. What have you been trying to say?"

I pulled out my notebook and wrote out phonetically the phrases he and his partner had been struggling with. When they were able to repeat them back with a decent grasp of the pronunciation, I declared them ready to take on the country.

"You're speaking wonderfully. Anyone who claims to not understand you now is being purposefully difficult. Which will probably happen! But at least you know it isn't your fault."

At my next table, the madrileños I was serving had already spent a week in France. The man wanted to see more art, but his wife had clearly had her fill of museums. She actually shuddered when he pulled out a guidebook for the Louvre. When I brought out their final course, they asked my advice on how to break their impasse.

"The Musée Rodin," I said firmly. "Just the gardens. It's full of some of the most famous sculptures in the world, but you'll be outside in the sun with flowers and fountains around you." When her husband, after a moment's hesitation, accepted that suggestion, his wife heaved a sigh. She mouthed silent thanks to me before draining her wine glass.

"I haven't spilled a single thing today," Colette, our newest server, whispered to me as she bounced between her tables.

As I took a table's empty plates, I noticed that Leïla, another server, was deep in conversation with a grand-looking couple from Moscow, the woman absolutely dripping with jewels. I couldn't understand what they were saying, and I feared trouble was brewing, but then the man laughed, and Leïla—who generally spent her shifts terrified she'd ruin everything, despite diners loving her for her sweetness and brilliant language skills—let out a small laugh herself.

The kitchens were whipping up courses perfectly, the waitstaff flitted gracefully between tables, and no one asked for last-minute substitutions or turned their nose up at the wine pairings Paul, our sommelier, suggested. It was one of those perfect evenings where all the guests were happy.

Which, of course, meant something had to go off the rails.

At the front of the main dining room, I noticed Luc gesturing for me. Luc had been initially hired as a server, like the rest of us, but after spilling two trays in a week (including a deeply unfortunate incident involving the mayor of Brussels and a tureen of roasted garlic soup), he'd been moved to the front of house position. It suited him much better. Despite his joking demeanor (and poor balance), he was meticulously organized and kept all the reservations running smoothly.

"Your guests for table eight," Luc told me when I reached him, indicating a couple standing at the restaurant's entrance.

It was a youngish man and woman. She looked to be mid- twenties, he maybe half a decade older. She had a pale face framed by short, feathery hair. She was standing perfectly still, taking in the restaurant and giving off an unmistakable aura of *je ne sais quoi*, that ability to appear interesting and confident without doing a single thing.

Her partner was harder to pin down. The man was partially backlit, but there was enough light to see that he was tall and thin, with muscular arms. He was wearing a dark suit, beautifully tailored. His face was in shadow, but he had a head of unruly blond curls.

"*Bonsoir*," I said, going to them. "Welcome to Le Jules Verne. I'll show you to your table."

The man stepped forward so that I could see his face. It was thin with prominent cheekbones and an aquiline nose. In the light, he was even more attractive than his partner. Not just attractive; there was something about him that held the eye. Distinguished, my grandmother would have called him.

His eyes, a vibrant hazel, looked me up and down. For some reason, his gaze made me feel off balance. Like I'd stepped on a floorboard that unexpectedly wobbled.

"Please follow me," I said again, giving myself a little shake to regain my composure.

I led them to their table, held out the chair for the woman, and placed their menus before them.

"Our sommelier will be along in a moment, but let me describe the first course. It's caviar and iced conso—"

"What kind of caviar?" the man asked, cutting across me.

"Osetra caviar," I said, smiling.

"Where is it sourced from?"

If he had waited ten seconds I would have answered all his questions, but sometimes people were eager. "Lake Kardjali in Bulgaria. It was harvested just a few weeks ago," I added with a flourish.

"What's the mercury content?"

I paused, momentarily stumped. I couldn't remember the last time a guest had asked a question about a dish that I couldn't answer. I'm not sure it had ever happened, actually.

The woman placed a hand on the man's arm. "It's fine."

"No, I want to know." He turned back to me, his gaze piercing. Now that he was in the light, I could see his eyes were nearly golden. "The mercury content?" he repeated.

"I'm...not sure, Monsieur." Admitting defeat left a sour taste in my mouth. "Let me ask the kitchen. The sommelier will be right along."

In the kitchens, one of the sous chefs and I squinted at a tin of caviar, but there was no indicator of mercury levels anywhere on it. At least that meant I hadn't missed anything.

"What will you tell them?" the sous chef asked.

I was busy running internet searches on my phone. When I found the information I was looking for, I wrote it neatly on a piece of paper, including the source, and brought it over to the table.

"This is what I could find," I said, back to feeling in control. "Lake Kardjali itself is free of mercury, so I'd expect the mercury levels in the caviar to be negligible."

The man stared at the scrap of paper, a stray curl falling over his forehead as he bent his head low.

"Fine," he said shortly, as though he'd lost some kind of bet. "We'll accept a spoonful's worth of caviar."

"Of course, Monsieur."

Keep looking happy, I reminded myself as I picked up his plate. Fortunately, half a decade as a server had taught me to look cheerful no matter how I felt.

If I could maintain a perfectly delighted expression when a diner brought a tuna and mustard sandwich into Le Jules Verne and then asked me to microwave it as though I was her personal assistant and this was not a restaurant that served its own food, this would be a piece of cake.

I caught a glimpse of my expression in the kitchen mirror.

Flawless.

Dismissive guests, who made it clear they saw me as little more than the vessel that brought them food, were something I was well used to. The same was true with whatever demands they came up with.

This man might think he was being special by specifying the number of tablespoons of caviar he was willing to eat, but he had no idea that, in the last month alone, I'd dealt with guests who'd variously requested: no food warmer or colder than lukewarm temperature, cheese that was pure to pale white only (a color wheel had been helpfully provided), and someone who had insisted that they could have any sort of artificially-flavored maple syrup but couldn't touch a drop of the real stuff. All had been pleasantly accommodated. (The last request had been especially easy as Le Jules Verne's head chef regarded maple syrup as "poison designed for babies and idiots" and refused to ever include it in his recipes.) This was child's play.

When I explained the next course, the cold strawberry soup, the man asked curtly about pesticides. I was able to assure him the strawberries were entirely organic. I even pulled out the official certification I had put in my pocket in anticipation of this question. He glared at me as though I was presenting his death warrant.

That was the odd thing. For every course he had questions: how had the salad greens been washed, was there dye in the cheese rind, what exact beekeeper did the honey we used come from? And every time I answered, he only appeared to get angrier.

"Is there a specific concern you have, Monsieur?" I finally asked, after the fifth such demand for information. "If so, I might be able to give you more guidance."

"Just answer the questions I ask you," he snapped. For the first time that evening, my smile dropped. His partner blushed, all her earlier confidence and composure gone.

With an effort, I smiled again, crinkling my eyes so it looked genuine. "Of course, Monsieur. I'm happy to answer any questions you may have."

But the man wasn't paying attention; he was now staring intently at my shoulder.

"You have something there," he said, pointing a long finger.

I glanced at my shoulder. Stuck to my dress was a tiny, miniscule crumb.

"Yes, uh, thank you," I said, flicking it away as I tried to hide my annoyance. How obnoxious, both that the man should point it out and that I should have a crumb on me in the first place. I prided myself on always appearing put together. Had the crumb been there all day?

Again, this man was knocking me off balance. The only thing for it was to keep the courses coming until they finished their meal and walked out of Le Jules Verne, hopefully to never return.

"Your next course," I said a few minutes later, setting the plates before them. "Steak à la tartare with cured egg yolk, truffle cream, and—"

"No." The forcefulness of the man's voice stopped me cold. "Take it back."

"Monsieur?" I'd seen some foreigners blanch at the idea of eating raw beef, but this couple appeared thoroughly French. They'd probably eaten steak tartare before their first teeth had come in.

"We're not eating that," the man said. His partner was looking down at her clasped hands, but I could see that she was blushing even harder now.

The man glared, those golden eyes burning into me. "Why is this so difficult for you?"

I blinked. No one, not even sour old men who walked in with baseball caps and cargo shorts took this much offense to steak tartare.

"I'm sorry, Monsieur. Perhaps you could go over again what you're hoping to avoid—"

"You know, you're really a terrible server."

My smile, which I had kept so carefully affixed throughout the whole interaction, slid off my face.

Who was this man? He sits there in his stuffy suit and messy hair, deriding every dish I bring out, as though Le Jules Verne doesn't post its menu online for diners to read before they decide to visit.

Who was he to decide what kind of server I was? For the last five years, the only thing that had really mattered to me was doing this job well.

Did he know how many hours I spent studying the ever-changing menu so that I could answer any question I was asked? Did he know this job was at the forefront of my thoughts, every day, from morning until night? Did he know how many calls I'd taken from nervous guests, wanting their proposal or birthday or anniversary to go perfectly, and how I'd listened to every detail and then done everything in my power to make their wishes come true? Did he know how many weddings I'd been invited to by guests grateful for the help I'd given with their engagements? Did he know that, this very evening, I'd called in a favor to get two of my diners' tickets for Giverny when the website said they were booked solid?

Of course he didn't. He didn't like the steak tartare, and that was enough for him to turn his nose up at my entire career.

"Monsieur, this doesn't seem to be the place for you," I said, my voice polite but steely. "Why don't I pack up the rest of your meal—the courses that you want—and then we can all enjoy the rest of our evening in peace?"

As soon as the words left my lips, I regretted them. I hadn't raised my voice or even said anything especially rude, but to essentially tell a guest to leave went against everything I believed as a server. My job was to help people have one of the great dining experiences of their lives. I wanted every diner at Le Jules Verne to leave several orders of magnitude happier than they had been when they'd walked in. Despite the man's irrational and never-ending demands, I hadn't done that here. And I hated him for making me feel like a failure.

The man's feelings seemed to match mine. "Are you throwing us out?" he asked, his voice as quiet and hard as my own.

At the moment, my deepest wish was for this man to leave and never haunt Le Jules Verne's dining rooms again, but I blanched at actually saying so outright. "Of course not," I said smoothly. "It's your choice to stay or leave. I only suggested it because the meal doesn't seem to be what you expected."

There was movement behind me, and I quickly looked around at the other tables. None of the diners seemed to realize anything was amiss, although Leïla was looking at me anxiously. But the man gave a sharp intake of breath, and my attention jolted back to him.

"*Not what I expected?*" he repeated.

"Margot." Luc was behind me, whispering in my ear, but I ignored him.

The man leaned forward, across the table. "I called ahead, informed the woman I spoke with that my sister had a compromised immune system because of cancer treatment, and I was assured the menu would be modified for us. Then I arrive here, and I get saddled with a server who doesn't know the first thing—"

His partner—sister—was dragging on his sleeve now, trying to get him to quiet down. Behind me, Luc was mirroring her.

"Margot, I forgot. I'm so sorry," he whispered, his voice strained. "The Roches, they requested modifications to the menu. Their dishes are waiting in the kitchen."

Luc was still speaking, but his voice was dimmed, as though it was coming from very far away. I couldn't even tell him to speak louder. All I could do was stand still as a wave of humiliation washed over me.

This man had a sick sister and had decided to treat her to a nice meal. He'd done the right thing by calling in advance and asking for menu modifications, then we'd dropped the ball and—even worse—I'd tried to force them out. I'd taken what was meant to be a positive, perhaps healing, experience and made it terrible.

In my entire career, I'd never felt so embarrassed.

"Monsieur, Mademoiselle, please accept my deepest apologies," I began, my voice faint from the blood pounding in my ears. "There was a miscommunication with your request. You should have received modified courses, and it's beneath Le Jules Verne's standards that you did not. We're bringing out your first corrected courses now—" I glanced at Luc who took off nearly at a sprint. "Your meal will, of course, be on the house.

"Now," I said, struggling mightily to resume my cheery demeanor, "Is there anything I can get you? Anything at all?"

Chapter 3

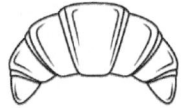

The man continued glowering, but his sister, looking paler than ever, smiled. "We're fine. Thank you for your help."

The rest of the meal crawled along. I brought out the (correct) courses, smiled so hard that tears pricked the corners of my eyes, and did everything I could to try to right this meal. But it was already ruined, and the three of us were simply going through the motions miserably. My shame was almost overwhelming.

The woman seemed especially embarrassed, even though she had no reason to be. She picked at her food and seemed close to tears.

After a few minutes, her brother stopped glaring at the tablecloth and made an effort to lift her spirits. He spoke too low for me to hear, but he seemed to be making little jokes. It was enough to eventually coax a smile out of her.

The woman tried to pay at the end of the meal, but her brother and I both waved her card away. They were some of the final guests to leave, and when I finally made it to the staff room, the story had already spread.

"Margot, you did nothing wrong. I do worse every day, honestly," Leïla said.

"It's my fault; it's entirely my fault," Luc said, head in his hands.

I patted his shoulder. "It's alright. Everyone makes mistakes."

I certainly had.

"Here, they're testing desserts in the kitchens, and I made sure to save some for you," Yasmine said, pushing a plate of profiteroles at me.

I took a profiterole and squeezed it gently between my fingers until the outer shell gave a satisfying crackle. I tried to smile at Yasmine, but I knew she wasn't fooled. When you've worked with someone practically every day for the past five years, it's hard to hide your feelings.

"Don't feel bad, Margot. That man was so rude to you, he deserved every-thing you said to him," Colette said, elegantly stretching her legs. She'd trained for years as a ballerina, but a skiing accident had ended her career.

She wasn't the type to stay down for long, though. She'd interviewed at Le Jules Verne while still on crutches and was now taking courses in costume design when not at work. She held out her empty wine glass to Paul.

"He was rude," Paul agreed, "Although he had excellent taste in wine." He poured the rest of a Loire Valley Cabernet Franc into Colette's glass, stifling a yawn.

Paul and his wife had welcomed twins a few months ago, and I could tell from the dark circles under his eyes that the babies still weren't sleeping through the night. But Paul's tiredness hadn't affected his work in the slightest, and he was renowned as one of the best sommeliers in Paris. He had Le Jules Verne's thick wine menu practically memorized.

Yasmine bit into a profiterole, not smudging her lipstick one centimeter.

"Yours are better," she said as she licked a fingertip. I smiled, knowing she was trying to lift my mood.

"I'm serious, Margot. The profiteroles you made for my birthday had a better flavor."

"She's right," Luc agreed. "You could teach the pastry team a thing or two."

Knowing they were complimenting me to try to bolster my self-esteem only made me feel worse. I gulped down my glass of wine and mindlessly chewed a profiterole (OK, maybe it was a little spongy). While my coworkers were still deep in conversation, I made my excuses and hurriedly put on my coat.

For one of the only times in my life, I couldn't wait to leave work.

***

A waft of cool air greeted me as I stepped out at the base of the Eiffel Tower. I drank it in with long gulps. As I walked, I replayed the entire evening in my head, ruminating over how I could have handled the situation better.

Luc had dropped the ball, and the man had been rude, no doubt, but part of my job was dealing with rude diners. I should have spoken up sooner, tried to get clarification on what exactly they could and couldn't eat. It had been a long day, and I'd been missing key information, but that was really no excuse.

I should have never lost my patience, never made even the vaguest suggestion that they should leave.

I trudged home miserably. The woman's pale, unhappy face kept flickering through my mind. The key point of pride in my life was that I was an exceptional server, that diners I met had a better experience than they expected and left happier than planned. That hadn't happened tonight.

With a sigh, I undid my chignon, letting my hair flutter in the breeze. I looked around, trying to take my mind off work. The tourist crowds had broken up, but there were still couples strolling together and parents pointing out the Eiffel Tower's sparkling lights to their sleepy-eyed children.

My apartment was located in Paris' 15th arrondissement, on the left bank of the Seine River and not far from Le Jules Verne. I preferred to walk to and from work every day that I could, especially on an evening like tonight, when Paris' sultry summer heat lost its edge and became soft and pleasant in the dark.

I crossed the river into the leafy, elegant 7th arrondissement, one of the poshest areas of the city. As I walked, I passed glowing street lamps and grand old buildings with wrought iron balconies and vines creeping up the stonework.

Paris, truthfully, is not always one of the best-smelling places in the world (its charms lie in other areas), but tonight the air was filled with the delicious scents of honeysuckle spilling out of neighborhood window boxes and the duck confit an elderly couple was sharing at the one of the restaurants still open at this hour.

That restaurant was all aglow, as though there was a spotlight focused directly on this tiny slice of the world. The man and woman were both white-haired and impeccably dressed, he in a dark suit, she in a cornflower blue dress with a silvery shawl draped over her shoulders.

She pulled the shawl off and folded it carefully as the man cut the duck, both of them concentrating on their tasks. The man raised his head as he passed her the larger piece, and a smile of pure contentment passed between them. It made something in my chest twist painfully.

I crossed the invisible line into my own 15th arrondissement and turned down a narrow, slightly shabby side street. On the corner was my building. Peering into the darkness, I saw a familiar figure sitting on the entrance steps.

My landlady, Madame Blanchet, sometimes suffered from insomnia and claimed night air was the only cure for it. In her arms was a thick blanket. I knew that Bijou, Madame Blanchet's little white dog, would be snuggled inside, having no problems with sleeping himself.

"Bonsoir, Madame. Trouble sleeping again?"

"Hello, Margot. Yes, another night spent awake," Madame Blanchet said, sounding not a bit bothered. "At least if someone decides to drop a bomb, I'll see it falling and know my end has come."

I had long stopped being nonplussed by Madame Blanchet's dark pronouncements. Instead of trying to convince her that she need not spend her night as an air raid warden, I smiled and bent to scratch the bit of Bijou's ear that stuck out of the blanket. "Would it help if I made you a cup of tea, Madame?"

"And miss a night like this? No chérie, but it's kind of you to offer. By the way, my sister has a new research assistant working for her. From Corsica."

I bit my tongue, knowing where this was going.

Madame Blanchet nodded. "He's *quite* smart, my sister said, and has a home overlooking the sea in Corsica. She showed me a photo, and he's not handsome, but you know how high the prices are for waterfront property these days. Just turn the lights off when you're with him and make sure you're facing the sea." Madame Blanchet stifled a yawn behind an elegant hand. "I'll invite him over sometime so that you two can meet."

Ever since I'd moved into this apartment half a decade ago, Madame Blanchet had been setting me up on dates. They were always unequivocally disastrous.

There'd been one who'd shown up drunk, another who'd scooped out his crème brûlée with his hands and shoveled it into his mouth, one who'd asked for our server's number while still on the date with me, one who'd stalked out of the restaurant when I'd admitted that I liked (actually loved) crappy fast food, and, most recently, a man who had behaved atrociously all during dinner, then announced he was heading to the airport to spend two weeks in Greece. I'd ended up spending half a month watching his parakeet because I didn't trust that he wouldn't let the poor thing starve.

I'd gone into each date with high hopes but, eventually, even my hopelessly romantic self had to admit Madame Blanchet was the world's worst matchmaker.

Since then, I'd made a solemn promise to myself that I'd do whatever it took—fake an illness, sign up for an intensive yoga retreat, make an international move—to avoid any future suitors she suggested. I was still finding parakeet feathers stuck in my clothes.

"I'm quite busy with work these days," I said, tucking Bijou back into his blanket, "But thank you for thinking of me, Madame."

I wished Madame Blanchard and Bijou a pleasant evening and was about to head inside when she called me back.

"I forgot to mention, chérie, but you have a new next-door neighbor. He finally got his things up from Provence. I'll invite you all over for wine and brie so you can get acquainted."

"Oh, don't go to too much trouble for my sake," I said, immediately deciding to decline until I could meet this new neighbor myself (in case this turned into another matchmaking scheme). "And try not to stay up too late, Madame."

"Of course not, but if I get accosted, make sure they bury me in my yellow silk gown." Madame Blanchet settled back against the steps.

The 15th arrondissement was one of the better addresses to have in Paris (and one of the best to have in the world, in my opinion). This remained true even though my building had seen better days, and perhaps better centuries.

The stairs squeaked atrociously as I went up them, but it was a comforting sound, the same way the dust-encrusted lamps and faded satin wallpaper lining the stairwell were comforting.

I flicked on the lights of my tiny, worn apartment. In the yellow glow, I saw the landscape paintings I'd hung in brass frames, the row of herbs growing on the windowsill, my pale lavender couch, and the bouquet of dahlias I'd arranged in a glass vase that morning. Pushed against the wall was my little dining table, one chair coated lightly with dust.

It was late, but I wasn't tired. Going to the fridge, I pulled out the sheet pan on which I'd laid a neatly rolled-out rectangle of dough that morning and set it on the counter. Then I made myself a cup of tea and took it to the deep window seat.

From there, if I leaned in the right direction, I could just make out the Eiffel Tower. Most people wouldn't like seeing their workplace from their home, but it always made me happy to see the Tower.

I sipped my tea, forehead pressed against the cool window glass, as I waited for the dough to lose its chill. I baked something nearly every day, and this morning I'd woken up and known immediately that I wanted to make baguettes. The stock I always kept in the freezer (for bread-related emergencies, of which there are many in France) was nearly depleted.

Once the dough was ready, I began the familiar pattern of shaping it into oblongs.

As I worked my way through the steps, memories of learning to bake with my mother, my grandmother, and—in a few sepia-tinted memories—my great-grandmother, flowed through my mind. They made my heart thump painfully.

It was late by the time I'd dimpled the top of the baguettes, and the city's lights shone out against the night. It was one of the rare moments Paris was very nearly silent. The revelers had finally stumbled home, and the early risers—the bakers, the street sweepers, the shopkeepers—were still in their beds, savoring the final hours of sleep before they began a new day.

I loved being awake at these times; it made me feel as though I was the only one awake in the entire city, that Paris flaunted its charms solely for me at this hour.

But there was something...

Barely perceptible sounds emanated from the apartment adjoining mine: the clatter of pans being placed on the counter, the staccato sound of a knife pressing against a chopping board. I slid my baguettes into the oven, then sat at my table.

As I sipped my now tepid tea, a parade of scents permeated my apartment: onions, beef, rosemary.

My new neighbor must be making dinner, although it was a very late one. I wondered what had delayed his meal. Through the wall, I heard the muffled sound of female laughter.

Ah. Cooking for his partner. This was Paris, after all. If a person stayed up late, it generally wasn't to work on their taxes. I pictured a generically attractive couple curled together on a couch as they waited for their meal to finish simmering.

I sighed heavily, sending little ripples racing across my tea.

When the timer went off, I pulled the baguettes out of the oven and smiled for a moment as I appraised their golden crusts. I set them on a cooling rack, where they'd remain until one became my breakfast tomorrow.

Tired now, I decided to run a bath. I poured in a generous amount of lavender bath salts then slipped into the scented water.

Leaning back, I again went through all the nice things that had happened today. Every time the image of the man and his sister wormed its way into my head, I flicked it away.

I soaked in the bath until the water grew cold.

Chapter 4

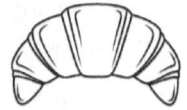

The rain was coming down in sheets by the time I got to work the next afternoon.

Rain always put diners in a bad mood. They got cold, their nice clothes got wet, their hair turned flat or frizzy, and they complained about not being able to see the view of Paris they'd been promised.

The staff at Le Jules Verne was used to providing perfection, but even we couldn't control the weather. (Although, after one endless month of rainy days and damp, sullen diners, Luc had attempted an anti-rain dance in each of the three dining rooms. It hadn't worked—and it'd taken days for the smell of burnt sage to dissipate—but no one could say we weren't devoted to our guests.)

I and the other servers darted around, taking dripping umbrellas and damp coats, making sure the bathrooms were kept stocked with a pile of fluffy towels, and cheerily assuring guests that the city's lights sparkled even more beautifully in the rain. We were well-practiced at lifting spirits, and most of the guests, once enveloped in the restaurant's serene opulence, shook off their disappointment.

"Paris in the rain, what could be more romantic?" they said to each other, smiling as though it was a secret they'd been let in on.

There were always hold outs, though, people who arrived at the restaurant mad or seemingly hoping to get mad. There was a couple like that this evening. I had known they'd be difficult from the moment they'd walked in. It was something in the way they held themselves, as though readying for a fight. They were gorgeously attired, and, despite appreciating elegant fashion when the wearers weren't making my job a misery, I'd silently dubbed the couple the Peacocks.

The Peacocks were at one of Yasmine's tables, and her smile hadn't even slipped when they'd dumped their sopping umbrellas in her arms. From the corner of my eye, I watched as my friend passed back and forth from their table to the kitchens, looking a little more harried each time she went by.

I was grateful for my own guests, who were happy and obliging, listening raptly as I explained how the different parts of each course played against each other and where our ingredients were sourced from.

One of my tables was an older couple from Edinburgh who'd come to Le Jules Verne years ago while honeymooning in Paris. Each time I checked on them, we traded stories of what Paris had been like back then, how the restaurant scene had changed, and, yes, it was magical when anyone could just walk under the Eiffel Tower, wasn't it?

"Is this the right time to visit Giverny?" the woman asked. "I've been wanting to go for years."

"It's the perfect time," I assured her. "The water lilies are blooming and—"

Raised voices abruptly cut me off. Immediately, every staffer at Le Jules Verne turned toward the source of the outburst.

It was like a tableau at the Louvre. Madame Peacock was sitting with her arms crossed, glowering at Yasmine. Monsieur Peacock had half-risen out of his seat, one hand gripping his chair, the other pointing at my friend. As for Yasmine herself, her face held a mixture of indignation and apprehension.

I gave my table a reassuring smile, then made my way to Yasmine as quickly as possible without looking hurried. The voices picked up again.

"We pay all this money, and you're telling me my wife has to take whatever is on her plate and be happy about it?" Monsieur Peacock shouted, his words slurred. "I can go to McDonald's and tell them to take the pickles off my burger, but I can't do the same here?"

He rose fully from his chair and swayed on his feet. "Overblown tourist trap," he sneered, gripping his chair with both hands now. "And the tower's swaying, too."

Plastering a smile on, I stepped firmly in front of Monsieur Peacock.

"Good evening, Monsieur. How may I help you?"

Monsieur Peacock appeared momentarily confused by the appearance of a second server. His head swiveled between me and Yasmine. Madame Peacock, however, beamed at me.

"My dear," she said, not breaking her smile. "There's been a silly little misunderstanding. I didn't like the sound of the next course; scallops don't agree with me. I remember last time we were here—we've been here several times—we had the most delightful lobster ravioli. It was on the menu last time; I'm sure the chef still knows how to make it, but *that* woman—" she shot an ugly look at Yasmine, "She said we couldn't make substitutions, even though this meal is costing us a pretty penny."

Internally, I heaved a sigh. I remembered the ravioli; it had debuted a little more than two years ago (although it had been made with langoustine, not lobster).

I smiled at both the Peacocks. "I'm so sorry," I began, and I watched their faces contract into frowns. "We ask for dietary restrictions when making a reservation, but it's not possible for us to make an entire course substitution the day of. I loved that ravioli, too," I said, turning to Madame Peacock, "But I'm afraid we don't have the ingredients here to make it today."

"Ridiculous," Monsieur Peacock fumed. He was standing right beside me, and I smelled the wine on his breath as he glared at Yasmine. "This place is going to the dogs. The food is bad enough, but now the staff isn't even from France?"

I heard Yasmine's tiny, sharp intake of breath. Mechanically, I smiled again.

"Have my colleagues been gossiping about me?" I asked, lightly, like we were all sharing a joke. "It's true I was born in Austria, but no matter how many times I ask, the chef still won't put schnitzel on the menu!" My laughter rang out across the silent restaurant.

"None of the rest of the staff hold it against me, though. Even though they were all born in France." My smile danced the line between friendly and ferocious. "Every. Single. One." I gave the Peacocks a final glance, then grabbed Yasmine by the shoulder and turned away.

In the privacy of the staff room, I seethed while Yasmine watched.

"Don't let it get to you," Yasmine said, following my progress as I paced back and forth. "Those comments stopped bothering me years ago."

"It's just that it's *wrong*," I spat. "You *were* born in France, you're a native speaker, you've lived your whole life here. What more do they want?"

Yasmine smiled sardonically. "You know. They want their vision of a Parisian waitress, not a Franco-Algerian." Her face hardened. "This is why I can't wait to get out of here."

Ever since I'd known her, Yasmine's dream had been to go into the hotel industry and eventually open her own inn. After talking about it for years, she'd finally saved enough money to enroll in a hospitality program and make her dream a reality. She was applying widely, and her top choice was the prestigious EHL Hospitality Business School in Switzerland.

"When I have my own hotel, I'll just throw out anyone who speaks like that," Yasmine said, her eyes blazing. "Right on the street, I don't care if it's midnight. No more being polite and crawling back to see if they're enjoying the dessert course."

"Colette will take care of their table; don't worry about that," I said, waving my hand as though brushing the problem away.

"I never understood why you love this job so much," Yasmine said softly.

I smiled. "Because I'm a hopeless romantic who lives for making people's wildest proposal dreams come true. It makes it easier to forget about the bad apples. Now, come on. I bet Paul will take pity on you and give you a glass of champagne before you head back out there."

The Peacocks had refused their desserts and made a great show of announcing that they wouldn't be leaving a tip—which may have hurt servers in some parts of the world, but not in France, and certainly not at Le Jules Verne, where staff was compensated quite decently.

The rest of the service had gone by smoothly enough, with all us servers making apologies for the distraction and offering extra meringues on the house.

After final diners had left (on their own time, of course. The staff at Le Jules Verne would rather impale themselves on the top of the Eiffel Tower itself than hurry a guest along), I was about to shrug on my coat when Le Jules Verne's imposing head chef appeared in the dining room. Immediately everyone froze, except for Luc, who actually dove under a table.

I'd been standing in the middle of the dining room, so there was nowhere for me to hide. Taking long, heavy steps, Chef Jean-Baptist La Croix planted himself directly in front of me. I was centimeters from his clenched fists and bloodstained apron. He seemed to blot out the evening's feeble light.

"I've created a new chestnut soup," Chef La Croix declared, taking the same tone I expect a dictator would use to announce the construction of a new nuclear warhead. "I need taste testers. You will come," he said, pointing right between my eyes, "And you," he said to Yasmine.

"Hurry up," he added, as Yasmine and I slunk together behind him. As I walked past, Colette reached out to clasp my hand, as though I was being shipped off to war.

Towering, with a baritone voice and a formidable gaze, Chef La Croix was the kind of personality stories always swirled around. I heard a new one nearly every week: that even as a student he'd been so intimidating that it'd been *he* who'd struck fear into the august teachers at Le Cordon Bleu rather than the other way around. That he'd turned down the chance to be the private chef to the Sultan of Brunei at a salary of five million euros a year because he would have had to bow to his new boss. That he'd served as a cook in the military before becoming a restaurant chef and, during one particularly intense firefight, had climbed out of the bunker and shouted at everyone to be quiet while he iced his cinnamon rolls (and quiet had duly ensued).

"Sit down," Chef La Croix said once we were in the empty kitchen. It wasn't immediately clear where he meant, so in my nervousness, I took a seat on the floor. Chef La Croix raised an eyebrow.

"The kind of people we hire these days," he grumbled, but he didn't suggest where I could sit instead. Nervously, Yasmine folded her legs and sat on the ground beside me.

"Take it," Chef La Croix said, pushing bowls of soup into mine and Yasmine's hands. "And have out with it. What's wrong with it? There's something flat in the flavor."

Even in my terror at being so close to Chef La Croix (well, his feet) I was curious about this new dish. I took a spoonful of soup and let it rest on my tongue before swallowing. "It's excellent," I squeaked, admiring the velvety texture, the layers that built on each other.

"I agree," Yasmine piped in.

"Yes, I know," Chef La Croix growled impatiently. "But it's short of perfect. It's missing a layer."

I took another taste and frowned, trying to frame my thoughts in the way that would cause the least amount of rage from Chef La Croix. I didn't even consider trying to sugarcoat it. The only thing that elicited Chef La Croix's wrath faster than unwarranted criticism was unwarranted praise.

He turned toward me, eyes boring into mine.

I quailed under that gaze. "Well, I, um...

"Spit it out," he growled.

I quickly swallowed a mouthful of hot soup. Chef La Croix watched impassively as I choked for several moments, my tongue scalded.

"I...I thought at first it needed fresh herbs, but I think the soup's flavors are too light for that. It'd be overpowered." I swallowed again, this time from nerves. "Maybe an herb-infused olive oil, drizzled over just at the end?"

Chef La Croix took a spoonful of soup from his own bowl and swallowed it. There was an alarming moment of silence.

"Ye-es," he said slowly. "Perhaps chives or even tarragon if I can keep it light enough. That's not a useless idea." He gave a tooth-baring grin that was known to strike terror into the heart of every cook at Le Jules Verne. I returned it with a wavery one of my own.

"How did the strawberry soup go over with the diners?" Chef asked, naming the chilled starter that had debuted over the summer.

"Accolades all around," I quickly replied.

Then, because she apparently had a death wish, Yasmine added, "One table said they found it a little oversalted."

Chef La Croix, who had closed his eyes as he sipped another spoonful of soup, immediately snapped them open. "Who said that?" he demanded. He stood, looming over us as his face darkened. "Were they British? I've told you, I don't want to hear their complaints. A country that has built its cuisine on the back of boiled cabbage does not understand properly seasoned food. They live in eternal jealousy of us, this kind of behavior is to be expected of them..."

I was shaking in my boots, and even Yasmine looked to be regretting her burst of honesty. Chef La Croix continued in this vein for quite some time until a rap on the door rescued us.

Our savior, a cheery delivery man, stepped in. He brought with him several rounds of Reblochon, the soft Alpine cheese that was an integral component of the salad currently starring as the third course on Le Jules Verne's menu. Chef La Croix opened the boxes and lifted the cheeses out, taking care to smell each one and weigh it in his hand.

"Yes, much better than the crumbling piles of garbage they tried to give me last time," he murmured, setting the cheese in a neat row. The delivery man held out a form to sign, and Chef La Croix dashed off a florid signature.

The man glanced at the signature, then looked again more closely. "Monsieur La Croix?" he read.

I knew what was coming,

Chef La Croix's face darkened. "Yes. That is my name."

The delivery man grinned, and I silently willed him to just bid us farewell and take his leave.

But they never could.

The man looked between the signature and the chef, who was positively glowering by now. He pointed at Chef La Croix. "You have the same name as the bubbly water drink?"

"Get out of my restaurant!" Chef La Croix roared, the noise echoing around the kitchen. "And never, ever mention that abomination of a drink in my presence!"

The man fled without looking back.

Chef La Croix turned to me and Yasmine, still looking thunderous. "Do you have anything to add?"

"No, Chef," I said meekly.

"See you for the dinner service, Chef," Yasmine added.

"Don't speak of this to anyone," Chef La Croix said, as though we'd just overheard a state secret. "Now, get out."

As we fled to the elevator, I could still hear Chef La Croix in the kitchens, muttering dark oaths about the atrocities of sparkling water.

Once outside, Yasmine and I breathed in the warm evening air.

"I hope Chef doesn't work himself into too much of a state," Yasmine said, smoothing her hands over her cherry red blouse. The color made her glow under the streetlamps. "You all take work so seriously, I swear. One of these days everyone at the restaurant is going to drop dead of a collective stroke."

I smiled. Yasmine liked to make a great show of being above it all while the rest of us agonized over every little detail at Le Jules Verne, but I knew that, despite her blasé air, she cared just as much about getting things perfect. She'd worked at Le Jules Verne even longer than I had and was the best server I knew.

"What have you been baking?" she asked.

I dug around in my purse. "My creation from this morning," I said, handing her a little paper box.

Yasmine lifted the lid, and the scent of parmesan and pastry wafted out. Inside, nestled like golden-brown eggs, were a quartet of gougères, savory cheese puffs. I was always hard on my baking, but even I could admit these looked gorgeous. They were buttery and cheesy, with a crisp, golden crust and a sprinkling of parmesan and black pepper across the top. When I'd taken them out of the oven this morning and tasted one, it was so light it had practically dissolved on my tongue.

Yasmine pulled a gougère out and bit into it, her eyes closed. "Oh, Margot. These are delicious," she said, shutting her eyes as she chewed. She took a second and appraised the glossy cheese puff as it rested on her palm. "You played around with the recipe. It's better now."

"It's not traditional, but I added a bit of cheddar to contrast with the Gruyère," I said, pleased Yasmine had noticed. I'd spent hours tinkering with the ingredients, creating so many batches that even Madame Blanchet—a great devotee of my baking—eventually pleaded that she couldn't take any more off my hands.

"You should bake professionally," Yasmine said, picking up one of her favorite topics. "Or at least sell these on a streetcorner so the masses can enjoy them, too."

I shook my head at her praise but couldn't help but smile.

We turned the corner onto the Boulevard de Grenelle. The street was full of stately apartment buildings crowned with ornate balconies and flower boxes spilling over with red and pink geraniums. Linden trees lined the boulevard on either side.

Beyond them was the edge of the small, elegant Square Nicole de Haute-clocque which was so perfectly manicured it reminded me of a jewel box. The sun had just slipped below the horizon, and everything was so still and quiet we might have been walking through a landscape painting hung in the Musée D'Orsay. *Paris At Dusk,* I would have called it.

"Margot," Yasmine said. The sound of my name jolted me back to the present.

"Sorry," I said, "Lost in thought. Did I tell you the Chilean man, Mateo, emailed again? Now he's thinking about having us bring out the engagement ring with the dessert course. He's worried that if I put it in her champagne glass there's a chance his girlfriend will drink it without noticing."

Yasmine smiled as she shook her head. "How do you still get excited over each engagement? I would just tell him to toss the ring at her and be done with it."

"Oh really? You wouldn't just drop it in the soup bowl?"

"Look, that was *one* time, and like I told everyone, it was an accident. That girl had me taking pictures of her for nearly half an hour while she twirled her pasta like an idiot. My arm got tired, and her phone just *happened* to fall into the soup tureen."

"Right. Of course," I said solemnly. "It could have happened to anyone. Now, most people might not have laughed hysterically—to the point that you collapsed to the ground and Luc started taking bets on whether you'd pee yourself—as the girl plunged her arms into the soup to fish her phone out, but that's why you're such a good server, Yasmine. You really make each meal your own."

I looked slyly at Yasmine, and we burst into laughter on the street.

"I'll be so glad when I'm out of there," Yasmine said, still grinning. "No more running around with rickety trays, or serving people for seven courses, or dealing with their unhinged dietary restrictions. God, Margot, do you know what I'm going to do if another person walks in and tells me they're severely gluten intolerant then flips out when we give them a substitution for bread?"

"All I know is they should probably get a very good protective case for their phone."

"Advice I would give anyone," Yasmine agreed, nodding sagely.

At the next street corner, Yasmine peeled off toward her apartment. She waved as she popped the final gougère into her mouth.

I reached my building and stepped inside. When I opened the door to my floor, I was immediately greeted by the scent of roasting chicken.

Another late dinner for my new neighbor, I thought idly. Just as I reached my door, the one next to mine—my new neighbor's—swung open. Out stepped a man.

A wall sconce was out (again), so the man was mostly in shadow. It wasn't until he took a step toward me and a blond curl fell across his forehead that I stopped with a start.

"No," I breathed. "You are not my new neighbor."

But the insufferable man from the restaurant, the man with the cancer-stricken sister, the man who'd driven me to one of the worst days of my professional life, had indeed just stepped out of the apartment next to mine.

What had I done to deserve this bad luck? It must have been something in a past life. I couldn't think of anything I'd done in this existence to warrant this kind of negative karma.

The man recognized me at the same moment. If I hadn't been overwhelmed with horror, his wide-eyed shock would have made me laugh.

We stood in the dim hallway, appraising each other.

This is your chance to make things right, I told myself. *You'll figure out his favorite dessert, bake it for him, and move past the entire incident at the restaurant. You should be grateful for this opportunity.*

Well, that was a bit of a stretch. But, still. At the very least, he would never again catch me being rude.

Forcing a smile, I stuck out my hand. "You must be my new neighbor. I'm Margot Delcour. I live right next door. What a coincidence for us to meet again."

The man gave no sign of reaching for my hand, but I wasn't giving up that easily.

"I'm glad we were able to sort out the confusion at Le Jules Verne, and I hope you and your sister enjoyed the rest of your meal," I said, smiling wider despite the awkwardness. "Madame Blanchet said you just moved in."

Silence. Yawning, endless silence.

"You're from Provence?" Smiling even wider, I gave a double thumbs-up, which indicated the level of desperation this hellscape of a conversation had put me in.

"I'm from Aix," he said slowly, as though each word pained him.

Despite the man's obvious lack of desire for a conversation, I would consider it a moral failing to not learn anything about this person with whom I'd now be sharing a (poorly-insulated, sometimes rat-infested) wall. And if my new neighbor thought he wasn't giving me enough to work with, conversation wise, then he was quite mistaken.

I had once waited on a table of born-again Buddhists on a silent retreat, and by the end of dinner I not only knew their names, home countries, and general life goals, I'd also counseled two of them through relationship troubles they were struggling with. This was child's play.

"I love Aix," I said, beaming widely. "I used to go on holidays there with my grandparents. It's most beautiful at the end of summer, don't you think? When it's cooled down a little and the lavender is all in bloom."

This was an excellent opening to many potentially fascinating conversational paths of the man's choosing. He took none of them.

Straining a little now, I plowed on. "You must be an excellent cook. I'm always smelling something delicious when I get home from work."

The man's face darkened. "No," he said shortly. "I don't cook. You must be smelling my takeaway meals."

I knew enough about cooking to know that takeaway food didn't smell like a meal simmering for hours, the flavors slowly building on each other. Even at *this very moment* I could smell the chicken currently roasting in his oven.

A little smirk played across the man's face. "I do takeaway mostly these days. I've had a hard time finding a restaurant that meets my standards."

Touché.

I took stock of what I'd learned about this man. My new neighbor was glowering, impatient with the service industry, excellent at holding grudges, and a compulsive liar about cooking. Excellent.

When the previous occupants of his apartment—two cousins extremely dedicated to their Daft Punk tribute band—had moved out, I'd thought things could only go up from here. Instead, the universe had tossed something even baffling my way: a man who lied about roasting chicken.

What could cause such a twisted personality? Was he breaking a ritual fast and didn't want to get caught? Had he signed a blood oath to PETA that'd he'd only ever make vegan food and was now regretting it? It was nonsensical.

The man was edging sideways, clearly trying to get around me.

"Please," I said, trying one last time to right this ship. "I must have missed your name."

The man paused. "I'm Laurent Roche." He sounded perplexed, as though he couldn't understand why I'd ever need that information.

He was right. Neighbor or not, I had no intention of speaking to this Laurent Roche again. Looking away, I stepped aside so he could move past me.

Chapter 5

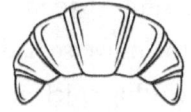

Laurent Roche was sautéing onions. I smelled them the moment I woke up. Inhaling, I stretched luxuriously. It was late morning, and my bedroom was full of daylight. I always liked keeping the curtains open as I slept, so that I awoke in a pool of sun.

I wondered what would become of the onions. Would they be the star ingredient in a soupe à l'oignon? Tucked into a quiche? Mixed into a ratatouille?

Oh, but that's right, he doesn't cook. Well, let him keep his eccentricities. If a person wanted to cook up a storm, then fervently deny it, I wasn't going to stand in his way.

I got up, ran a bath, combed a conditioning treatment into my hair, then slipped into the warm water and let all the tension of the previous day melt away. When the water was tepid, I stepped out, then applied my face serums and blow-dried my hair. I put on a black dress (the staple of my wardrobe even before working at Le Jules Verne), and slipped my mother's emerald ring onto my finger.

I opened the windows, and my lace curtains fluttered gently in the warm morning air. As I prepared a late breakfast of earl gray tea and a raspberry lemon scone, I mentally ran through the day's schedule.

Tonight, Mateo would be proposing to his girlfriend, Anna. From his home in Santiago, he'd emailed us several times to make sure every detail was set. I spread a thick layer of blackberry jam across my scone as I reviewed my notes.

Mateo had asked for customized menus with a message celebrating his and Anna's third anniversary. A standard request. Furthermore, he'd asked for a second set of menus to arrive with dessert, after he'd proposed, that congratulated the newly-engaged couple.

He'd also mentioned how he would very much like a photo of him proposing and that he hoped we might make that happen. To be helpful, he'd included a minutely-detailed description of how he expected the proposal to go, from the course during which it would happen, to exactly how he'd pull his chair out and get down on one knee, to the words he'd open with: "My dear Anna, if there's anything these last three years had taught me..."

He'd even included a drawing, complete with two stick figures, a table, and a diamond ring, so the photographer would know just how to frame the shot.

Mateo had offered to pay for these services, but the request had been politely, but firmly, declined. The proposal team at Le Jules Verne (i.e. me) would be more than happy to help make his dreams a reality.

When I arrived at work, preparations for the dinner service were already in full swing. There was clanking and grumbling coming from the kitchen, Paul was looking over a new shipment of wine, and Yasmine was calling out instructions to Colette and Leïla while Luc thumbed through the list of the evening's reservations.

Standing in the doorway, I watched them all for a moment, swelling with happiness that I got to be part of this every day. My private moment of pleasure over, I made my way to where we kept personalized menus. Yes, there were Mateo's, both copies. Just the way he'd asked.

There were multiple high-rollers today, and even though a British reality star wanted to get a photo standing in an open window (for the lighting), and an ambassador from Asia was put out that we were no longer serving the pea and watercress soup he'd enjoyed last spring, a server was always there to resolve the issue and extol the virtues of the new summer menu/remaining fully inside the restaurant.

Midway through my shift, Luc motioned for me to come over.

"Mateo and Anna," he said, indicating a well-dressed couple who were holding hands. Mateo attempted to smile, but his nerves got the better of him and it turned into a queasy-looking grimace.

I beamed at them. "Welcome to Le Jules Verne," I said in Spanish.

I brought them to one of the restaurant's choicest tables, right by the windows. I went to pull out Anna's chair, but Mateo, in a spasm of chivalry, darted past and pulled out his girlfriend's chair himself.

He overdid it somewhat and nearly toppled the chair (and himself). A moment later, he was alright, helping Anna into her seat while panting slightly. I gave him a bracing smile.

"Your menus," I said, once Mateo was in his seat. "I hear you're celebrating your third anniversary tonight. My deepest congratulations." Anna and Mateo beamed at each other.

I worked my way around my tables, bringing out new courses and making sure water and wine glasses were filled. Mateo looked paler every time I stopped by. His plan was to propose after the fifth course (the infamous steak tartare). In my pocket bumped my phone so I'd be ready to take a photo at a moment's notice.

Everything was progressing smoothly, and I had just brought Mateo and Anna the steak tartare when there was a commotion on the other side of the room. I turned toward the noise. There, not far from one of my tables, was a man bent on one knee. In his hands was a sparkling ring.

His dinner companion gasped, flung her arms around her new fiancé, and promptly burst into tears. The other diners applauded, smiling at the couple's joy. I smiled too, but a lump was rising in my throat.

Many people gave Le Jules Verne advance notice that they were planning to propose, if only to help get the details right, but it certainly wasn't required. Rogue proposals weren't a problem.

Except today, when we had another proposal planned just minutes from now. Even someone who didn't particularly care what others thought would feel silly pulling the same move the restaurant had just seen.

I swung back toward Mateo's table. Anna was smiling and clapping for the newly-engaged couple, but Mateo looked devastated. I could see the curve of the ring box in his jacket pocket. He was glancing around now, as though the answer to what he should do next would appear on the restaurant's walls. His fingers fluttered to his pocket, then dropped limply to his lap.

Looking at Mateo, my heart broke. Anna was speaking animatedly to him, but he barely mustered a nod as he stared at his empty hands. All those careful plans, ruined.

No, I decided, the force of my conviction startling me. *No one's proposal is going to be ruined. Not tonight.*

When I brought Mateo and Anna their sixth course, the plum moelleux cakes, I explained the dish, how it'd been composed, and where the blackberries and sweet cream had been sourced from. Anna seemed delighted and had already grabbed her spoon, but Mateo only looked on listlessly. Which wasn't surprising; he thought he'd have a fiancée by now.

But he still would, very soon, if I had anything to do with it.

"Oh, and one other thing," I said. "Because you're celebrating your anniversary, our chef wanted to know if you'd like to enjoy your dessert on our terrace. It's rather small, but the view is the best in Paris, I think." Mateo raised hopeful eyes to me. I gave him the shadow of a wink.

Anna was thrilled to go, and as she and Mateo hurried to put on their jackets, I grabbed their dessert plates.

"Right this way," I said. As I led them through the back of the restaurant, I passed Yasmine, who raised her eyebrows in confusion. I didn't even break my stride.

The terrace was less of a terrace and more of an outdoor landing where staff members took their smoke breaks. Diners weren't technically allowed, but that didn't trouble me at all. I'd been the perfect server for half a decade now. Le Jules Verne would allow me this.

I hadn't lied about the view. When I opened the door onto the terrace, Anna gave a little gasp of happiness. Just centimeters away was the Eiffel Tower itself, sparkling with light. Looking entranced, Anna reached out a delicate hand to touch it. Mateo turned to me, his hand in his pocket.

"Thank you," he mouthed.

Just as I closed the door, I heard him speak. "My dear Anna..."

The door had a single, small window, positioned above my head. I held my phone up to it and prayed the photos I was getting fit Mateo's framing specifications. I stayed outside the door, smiling at my coworkers as they rushed back and forth, most doing a double take over their shoulders.

After a few minutes, there was a soft knock on the other side. I opened the door and ushered in Mateo and Anna. Despite looking a bit chilled, they glowed with happiness. On Anna's finger was a shimmering diamond with an emerald set on each side.

"Oh, what a beautiful ring," I told Anna. "The emeralds set the diamond off perfectly. They're my favorite stone," I said, showing her my own emerald ring. Anna was too overcome with happiness to speak, but she smiled at me.

Anna and Mateo's radiant happiness stirred something in me, wistfulness or longing, I'm not sure. Whatever it was, I pushed it down. This was their moment. It wasn't the time for me to conduct a self-assessment of my emotional state.

"I think the photos came out well," I said, showing Mateo my phone.

As Anna held tightly to her new fiancé's hand, I sent Mateo the photos before ushering the couple back into the dining room. "I wish you both so much happiness," I said, smiling.

I checked on each of my tables, then slipped into the staff room. There, I took a moment to soak in the perfection of the evening, of proposal plans not being ruined, of everyone leaving happy after all. I gave a little shiver, then opened my eyes. Time to get back to work.

Chapter 6

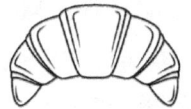

"Oh, damn."

I was walking home after work and, as I dug around in my purse, my fingers had brushed a small box.

I'd spent much of yesterday making macarons–in two flavors no less–as a gift to Yasmine for completing her hospitality school applications. Although I'd made several thousand macarons in my life, I'd wanted these to be perfect.

And they were, with smooth, glossy shells and a crisp exterior that gave way to a chewy inside. I'd dyed them Yasmine's favorite colors, gold and purple, and created two fillings: champagne and vanilla plum. I'd put the six most perfect ones into a box, intending to give them to Yasmine after work, but in the rush of the day they'd lain forgotten in my purse.

Cautiously, I opened the box. Of course. They were squashed now.

I was already downcast when I approached my building. The scene that greeted me when I turned the corner didn't improve things. On the side-walk—blocking the way into the building, naturally—was my new neighbor/eternal enemy, Laurent Roche, president of the Brotherhood of Furtive Cooks.

He was wearing another expensive suit and looked like he'd just stepped out of a fashion magazine. Congrats to him. At his feet were a polished briefcase and two grocery bags. He was on his phone, barking out sentences about mergers and deadlines.

Rather late for a business call. He must think he's terribly important.

Monsieur Roche's telephone call gave me the perfect excuse not to greet him. Instead, I tried to edge by as inconspicuously as possible. Just as I thought I'd slipped past, there was a sudden tug on the back of my coat. Startled, I spun around to see what had stopped me. It was Monsieur Roche, holding me back like I was a puppy trying to make a break for it.

"Excuse me," I said, taking a large step away from him so that he had to break our connection. *What a rude person.*

I turned to the building again, but Monsieur Roche shook his head to stop me. I stared at him with my I-hate-you-but-I-can-still-look-polite expression I'd perfected during my time at Le Jules Verne until he ended his phone call.

"You can't go in there," he said, pocketing his phone. "There's been an accident."

"An accident?" I repeated, startled. "Is anyone hurt?" I stood on my toes, trying to look into the building. Just then, a fire truck turned down our street, its lights flashing.

"No one hurt," Monsieur Roche said shortly. "Madame Blanchet was performing a séance?" He broke off, looking momentarily perplexed.

"Yes," I said, nodding. "She hosts séances often." I'd been invited multiple times, but I'd firmly told Madame Blanchet that incense gave me headaches.

"Well, she was hitting some pipes in the bathroom with a wrench to activate the spirits or whatever she said, and she ended up knocking a pipe loose. We've been told to vacate the building while they check for water damage."

I frowned, annoyed that I had to rely on this man for any information. "Where are Madame Blanchet and Bijou?"

"Is Bijou the dog? Madame Blanchet is at the café around the corner," Monsieur Roche said, indicating the direction. "Half the building is with her. The dog was in her purse when she left."

"I'm glad everyone is alright," I said, watching firemen descend upon the building. Monsieur Roche was back to looking at his phone and wasn't paying me attention. Yes, ladies and gentlemen, we have a very important businessman right here.

"I'm going to join them," I said. I looked at Monsieur Roche, feeling awkward. "Do you...want to come along?" I asked, even though I couldn't imagine this wet blanket of a person adding enjoyment to any gathering.

Fortunately, he shook his head. "Still have work to do." He lifted his bags from the ground. One tipped, spilling its contents. Out rolled two onions and a sack of potatoes.

I looked at the groceries for a moment, knowing I should just help him and go on my merry way.

But I chose chaos.

I reached down and grabbed the sack of potatoes. "These are some lovely potatoes you bought."

Monsieur Roche took them roughly from me and shoved them back in the bag.

"What are you going to cook with them?" I asked, the picture of innocence.

The thick eyebrows furrowed. "I don't cook," he said, as though I'd just accused him of something unspeakable. Then, perhaps realizing it might be odd for an avowed non-cook to be seen with a bag of raw potatoes, his face colored. It made him look nicer. More human.

"The potatoes are for decorative purposes," he said, as though that was not a completely insane comment to make.

"Decorative purposes?" I repeated, enjoying this more and more. I'd never met anyone who was such a compulsive liar while simultaneously being so bad at it.

"Yes," Monsieur Roche said, looking decidedly flustered now. "The uh...rural ambience reminds me of home."

I nodded as though he'd just made a brilliant remark. "Fascinating."

I was about to make another comment when the expression on Monsieur Roche's face stopped me cold. He looked drawn and anxious.

"Please," he said, actually pleading. "I...I just need to get back on this call now." He seemed so stricken that I knew any further jokes would only be cruel.

I suddenly felt bad. Presumably, if he was making such bizarre lies, there had to be a reason behind it. Even workaholic sticks-in-the-mud deserved their secrets.

Trying to make up for my jibes, I dug around in my purse and pulled out the little box.

"Here," I said, holding it out. "They're macarons. In case you need something for dessert. Um, I usually bake something to welcome new neighbors, but I'm not sure what you like, and this is all I have on me, and I'm sorry they're crushed, but I think they'll still taste alright..." Now I was the one stumbling over my words.

"Anyway, have a good evening."

I shoved the box into Monsieur Roche's hands. His fingers instinctively curled around it before he seemed to register what had happened. I turned toward the café and was gone before he had time to muster a thank you or tell me he didn't actually want damaged baked goods from crazed women he didn't know.

That was really *the last time I spoke to Monsieur Roche,* I promised myself as I walked into the café. Bijou ran up to me, begging to be picked up. *No point in continuing that torture.*

Chapter 7

I spent the next morning browsing the markets in St. Germain, picking up tomatoes, apples, and anise. My favorite cheesemonger was there, and although I was well stocked, I chatted with him, discussing the new Camembert he was expecting and sampling the slivers of different varieties he pressed on me.

Afterwards, I went for a stroll along the Quai de la Mégisserie and popped into several of the small flower shops, their greenery spilling into the streets. At the final one, I purchased a gorgeous bouquet of pale pink Japanese anemones. The owner wrapped them up for me in brown paper.

I returned to my apartment in the afternoon. As (terrible) luck would have it, Laurent Roche was just stepping out of his own apartment. I gave a brief nod, then went to unlock my door as quickly as possible. Out of the corner of my eye, I saw him pause.

"Mademoiselle Delcour?" He said my name like a question. To be honest, I was surprised he remembered it.

"Yes?" I turned to face him, wondering what I could have done to annoy him this time.

"Your macarons. The ones you made. They were very good." Monsieur Roche's brow was furrowed, as though he couldn't quite believe he was saying something nice to me. That made two of us.

"Oh. Thank you."

He was still frowning, his golden eyes glimmering beneath his brow. "Good food deserves to be complimented."

He spoke as solemnly as if he was giving a sermon at a graveside. If I hadn't been caught so off guard by his praise, I would have laughed at his seriousness. I half expected him to start intoning a hymn next.

Monsieur Roche's politeness quota for the day apparently met, he gave me a stiff nod and started to close his door.

"Hey," he said, pausing with the door nearly closed. He was speaking to someone inside. "You should still be napping."

I'm not sure what I was expecting to appear—a child? A tousled lover?—but it certainly wasn't the small, scruffy gray cat that appeared in the doorway. The animal meowed forlornly, showing a pink mouth.

Sighing, Monsieur Roche picked up the cat and held it to his chest.

"You have a cat?"

Something strange was happening with my emotions. As I watched the little creature butt Laurent under the chin, I suddenly remembered my own childhood cat. His name was Jacques.

We only had him when I was very young, but I remembered him sitting on the countertop as my mother taught me how to laminate dough for croissants, his glossy black fur dusted with flour. Every night he'd slept in my bed, his warm little body curled at my feet.

We couldn't take Jacques with us when we'd left Paris, and I'd been devastated to leave him with our neighbors. For years after that, I'd begged my mother to adopt a new cat, but she (rightly) said we moved too often for a pet. Eventually, I gave up, and Jacques faded to the back of my memory. Funny how that happens.

Jolting me back to the present, Laurent looked up just then and smiled—actually smiled—at me.

His teeth were slightly crooked. Despite the world's growing preference for perfectly straight, perfectly white rows of teeth, I still preferred an imperfect smile.

And Monsieur Roche's certainly did wonders. His smile transformed him from a scowling, solemn office drone to an actual human who looked like he might crack a joke at a posh restaurant then raise an eyebrow when you burst into laughter and the other diners glared.

"This is Minerva," he said, stroking the cat, who began to purr as he ruffled her fur. "She's incredibly spoiled. I found her poking around trashcans for scraps as a kitten, and now her favorite food is coq au vin, cooled to just above room temperature."

He looked down at his little cat and smiled again. I did not think him a man for dimples; his carved features suggested stone and ice more than any hint of softness, but a dimple he had, right on his left cheek. It made him—was it possible?—ever so slightly adorable.

I made a split-second decision. It was the dimple that made me do it. That and how much he clearly loved his cat.

"Monsieur Roche, would you like to come over some evening for dinner? I'm not as good at cooking as I am at baking, but you'll be able to give the takeaway shops an evening off." I laughed a little, the joke not landing quite as I wanted to.

The smile slipped from Laurent's face, and he was back to being all angles and hard lines. He and Minerva both blinked their golden eyes. "Well..." He brushed a stray curl from his forehead. "That's possible, although it might be difficult to find an evening that fits our schedules. Work takes up a lot of my time."

I blinked. What an odd thing to say, especially for a Frenchman. It was nearly unpatriotic. I had never known a fellow countryman to decline an open dinner invitation due to busy schedules. Half the country would probably be willing to cancel their plans and sit down to a meal right this very moment if promised decent wine and a fresh baguette.

Monsieur Roche was staring at his shoes, which had been burnished to a high sheen. "I'll look into it," he said finally, his tone suggesting that he'd rather be eaten alive by vultures than spend another minute considering the idea. "I should go now."

Still not meeting my eyes, Laurent Roche gently placed Minerva back inside. He shut the door and slipped past me. In another moment he was on the street, walking quickly without looking back.

***

"He what?" Yasmine said, eyebrows raised high. "No, tell the story again, you must have told it wrong."

It was several hours later, and the Le Jules Verne staff was sitting together for a glass of wine before guests began arriving for dinner service. I had only meant to tell Yasmine about my run-in with Laurent Roche, but it was nearly impossible to say anything in private at the restaurant. The rest of the servers had quickly come over to listen.

"And I thought the rejection I got last weekend from the guy at my gym was brutal," Luc put in.

"It wasn't a date. It was just a neighborly invitation," I said.

"Even worse," Luc declared. "There could be all kinds of reasons for turning down a date, but when it's just a dinner invite, you know it's only because he hates you."

"He told you that he was too *busy?*" Paul repeated. "This is not a Frenchman. Are you sure he's not some Brit or American in disguise?"

"Maybe he doesn't like eating in other people's homes," Colette said as she applied lipstick. "My grandmother was a picky eater, and she only liked food she made herself."

"Oh," I said, realizing something. "He did try my food, actually. I had extra macarons, and when we met, I thought I'd do something nice, so I gave them to him. He told me he liked them, but..."

In my head, I replayed my conversation with Laurent. What had I been thinking? He was a posh businessman who was probably used to dining in Paris' best restaurants every night. And I'd forced half a dozen sad, squashed macarons on him.

How pathetic. He probably felt bad for me. That's why he'd complimented me. Like a parent accepting an inedible creation from their child but not wanting to break their heart.

Oh, God. This was a low point. I'd rather go back to him communicating only in scowls.

As I sat, staring into the void as my coworkers debated what could make a man turn down a dinner invitation, Chef La Croix came in and bellowed at us to get ready for the first diners.

Last night, after dinner service had ended, Chef La Croix had given me a loud and public dressing down for letting Mateo and Anna onto the terrace. He'd achieved impressive feats of theatrics ("And if they'd fallen off the Tower, Margot, what would have happened then? You would have gone straight to jail, and I wouldn't have shed a single tear over you."), and I'd made sure to look appropriately cowed. He gave me an extra stern look this evening. I managed to plaster on my sunniest smile in return, but my heart wasn't in it.

Dinner service started off poorly, with a guest handing me a napkin dripping with snot and telling me to get them a new one.

"Things can only go up from here," I told myself as I scrubbed my hands under scalding water in the staff bathroom.

"I have news for you," Yasmine said as we passed each other in the kitchens.

"If it's that table seventeen still wants yellow mustard instead of Dijon, I already told them we don't have any," I responded. *And the next time they want yellow mustard, they should try a ballpark.*

"No, not about work. Well, it's work, but not *this* work," Yasmine said enigmatically, then rushed off.

An hour later, we passed each other again. "You know that charity my mom is part of? The one that helps refugees get settled in France?"

"Of course," I said, looking around the kitchen for paper napkins because one of my tables "didn't like how cloth napkins felt."

"They're having their annual fundraising gala this spring. Food, drinks, auction, live music, the works."

"Yes? You want me to go with you?" I guessed, taking the two plates a sous chef held out to me.

"No, their pastry chef just dropped out. I told them you'd be great for it."

I nearly dropped the plates. "Wait, what?"

But Yasmine was already gone.

"Yasmine, absolutely not," I said later, as we guzzled water during a quick break.

"Why not? You're a fabulous baker."

"Only for fun," I said quickly. I remembered Monsieur Roche and his firm refusal of a home-cooked meal. "And maybe not even for that."

"Margot, come on. You bake all the time. I have no doubt you'll amaze them."

I shook my head. My fingers clenched around my water glass. "I don't have a certified kitchen space or—"

"You'll use theirs," Yasmine cut in. "And I know you already have your commercial baking license. I heard you mention it to diners once."

Merde.

That had been a throwaway remark I'd immediately regretted. Not because it wasn't true—I did have my commercial baking license—but because I hated to remember the time during my life when I'd gotten it.

"Just think about it," Yasmine said.

I didn't need to think about it. The idea sent a knot of panic twisting in my stomach.

I forced a shrug, keeping my voice light. "Yasmine, I just don't think I'm up for it." I saw her open her mouth to argue and took the chance to escape. "Sorry, I have to run. Table three is waiting for their next course."

I got through the rest of my shift by thinking of nothing else than bringing out courses, explaining the food, and refilling water glasses. At the end of the night, I tried to slink out, but Yasmine caught me before I'd taken two steps from the staff room.

"Margot," she said, frowning. "Why don't you want to do this? You're always willing to help me with anything."

I fiddled with my coat sleeves. "I just don't want to."

It wasn't exactly a lie.

Yasmine studied me. For a second, I thought she was about to push. Instead, she softened. "Margot, they're desperate. Seriously, just do your best, and they'll be thrilled with whatever you bake. It's for a good cause."

I shook my head, but she kept going.

"Look, why don't you just come to an orientation meeting with me? No pressure. If you still don't want to do it, I'll never mention it again for as long as I live."

I shifted uncomfortably. But Yasmine was right; just attending a meeting wasn't stressful. Or it shouldn't be. And I was perpetually a sucker for good causes.

"Will there be free food?" I asked warily.

"Mountains of it," Yasmine said, crossing her heart with her index finger.

I hesitated a moment longer.

"Alright," I sighed. "Just the meeting. That's all I'm promising."

Yasmine clapped her hands and kissed me on both cheeks.

***

Thus, that weekend, at an hour when I was usually still sleeping or lazing about in bed, I found myself walking into an aging office building, wondering why I had ever agreed to this.

"The culinary team is meeting in room 24," Yasmine said, leading me firmly by the arm as though I might abscond at any moment.

Which, to be honest, had been on my mind.

"Yasmine, I appreciate your confidence in me, but this is a terrible idea. Everyone else is going to be a professional."

"Not at all. My mother told me half the sous chefs are still in school or only work in kitchens on the side. Plus, the only reason you aren't a professional is because you haven't gone to pastry school. You'd blow them all out of the water."

My stomach churned. "I only promised I'd go to this meeting. Nothing else."

"I know," Yasmine said serenely. "And we'll stuff our faces after the meeting's over. Come on, the room's right here."

I wanted to say something more, to impress upon Yasmine that there was really no chance that I'd ever end up as pastry chef for this event, but she was already dragging me into the room.

Well, she'd realize I was serious when I didn't change my mind.

As I entered a room filled with tables, I was still half-distracted as Yasmine led us to a pair of empty seats. It wasn't until I had settled into my chair that I remembered my manners and turned to greet the person seated on my other side.

The man's head turned, and I found myself looking into Laurent Roche's gold-flecked eyes.

Chapter 8

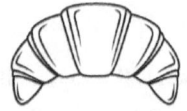

I was caught so off guard that, before Monsieur Roche could utter a word, I'd stood up again, grabbed Yasmine's arm, and dragged her to a new table at the back of the room.

"What is your problem?" Yasmine hissed.

"That's my new neighbor," I whispered, jittery from his surprise appearance. "You remember, from the restaurant."

Yasmine immediately stopped frowning at me and craned her neck forward, trying to get a view of Laurent. I was hunched as low as humanly possible in my seat, but I could still see him turning his head in confusion. I ducked lower, my head now nearly level with my knees.

"Oh, wow. I didn't notice how hot he was when he was being an ass at dinner. Look at those arm muscles," Yasmine whispered, blatantly ogling him.

"Keep your shirt on," I muttered. "He's a misanthrope who lies about cooking."

"What's his name again?" Yasmine whispered.

"Laurent Roche."

Yasmine flipped through the papers she held, but just then, a woman went to the front of the room and rapped her hand on the table for attention.

Reluctantly, I sat up. She introduced herself as Fatima, head of culinary services for the gala, and dove into the logistics of the event. As she spoke, my attention kept flicking back to Laurent.

What was he doing here? Monsieur Roche, who claimed never to cook, who was the epitome of the finance bro cliché–what was he doing at a culinary meeting for a charity event?

"Let's introduce everyone," Fatima was saying, and I turned my attention back to her. She began to read off her list. For each person on the culinary team, she said their name, job they'd have at the gala, and a sentence or two about their background.

Since my only credentials were "longtime waitress at the esteemed Le Jules Verne" I felt awkward again when it was my turn, despite the people nearby giving me friendly smiles. No matter what Yasmine said, everyone else seemed to be a professional.

At least wondering about Monsieur Roche gave me a distraction from my anxiety. His name was last on the list, and by the time Fatima got to it, I was almost bouncing in my seat with curiosity.

"Finally, our head chef is Monsieur Laurent Roche. He recently moved here from Aix-en-Provence, where he was head chef at the Michelin-starred Les Champs D'Or."

My mouth dropped open.

This was certainly new information.

I looked intently at the back of Laurent's head, the only part of him I could see from this vantage point.

He used to be a *chef*? This made his cooking denials even weirder. Possibilities rocketed through my mind. Had things ended badly in Aix and he was trying to put his past behind him? Was he in some sort of witness protection program that required him to take on an entirely new career and never mention his old one?

But then why was he volunteering as head chef at a charity event? What the actual hell was going on with this man?

I don't consider myself a particularly lucky person (No one who has accidentally dropped a fork on a diner's head, then watched as said fork bounced off the diner's head, hit the man's (full) glass of red wine, which itself then shattered onto the hapless diner's lap, could consider themselves lucky), but sometimes the universe cuts me some slack. This was one of those times. (And yes, that man had his meal fully comped.)

As Fatima discussed how the chefs would be working together, two women sitting at a table in front of me bent their heads together.

"Laurent Roche. You remember him, right?" one woman whispered. My ears perked up.

"Of course. His mother was one of my closest friends growing up. I didn't know he lived in Paris now," the other whispered back.

Lacking any shame, I elbowed Yasmine to get her attention.

"He left Aix when his restaurant closed and his relationship ended," the first woman said. "Did you know his girlfriend left him for a coworker? Very messy. He came to Paris for a new start."

"What?"

The word hissed out of me involuntarily. As the women turned my way, I stared straight ahead and acted as though I was deeply enthralled by Fatima, who was now discussing bathroom locations for the gala. Ah, yes. Fascinating *and* important to know.

My outburst seemed to have distracted the two women though, and they didn't pick the conversation back up.

As Fatima continued, now on the subject of dishwashing policies, my mind reeled. So Monsieur Roche was a former chef, and at a Michelin-starred restaurant no less. They didn't give those stars out like candy.

And he had a tragic dating history to boot. Well, we had that in common. Next time we met in the hallway we'd have to compare notes. Then I could see if Laurent had also been tricked into a blind date with a person who'd tried to pressure him into a perfume-related pyramid scheme that also sounded vaguely like it might be human trafficking.

But you're not going to talk to him again, I reminded myself. *Because he's a curmudgeon whose only hobbies are secretly cooking and lying about secretly cooking.*

My lack of focus must have been obvious because Yasmine elbowed me in the ribs. When I turned her way, she tilted her head toward Fatima, indicating I should be paying attention. She was right, of course. I was here to fulfill an obligation to her, not go on a side quest digging up my neighbor's mysterious background.

Fatima clapped her hands together. "This is an excellent time for a break. Take a half hour, enjoy some food, then the culinary team will reconvene and begin putting together a menu."

I was the first to stand. Pulling Yasmine behind me, I shot through the doors and into the bustling main room. It was filled with the scent of freshly-brewed coffee and baked goods laced with honey. Momentarily caught up in the crowd, I looked around for some place to go, my fingers still wrapped around Yasmine's wrist.

"The bathroom is down that hallway," she said, pointing. We made a beeline for it. As we did, I reached out my free hand and grabbed one of the honey pastries. For research purposes.

As soon as I pulled the door shut behind us, I turned to Yasmine.

"Did you hear that? That neighbor of mine who keeps *swearing* he doesn't cook—even though I smell him making dinner every night—is an actual chef!"

"*Was* a chef," Yasmine corrected. "You told me he's some sort of businessman now." Yasmine shook her head in mock disappointment. "Poor man. All those career struggles and not one person told him his path clearly lies in modeling."

"Yasmine. Focus."

"Oh I am. Did you see the way that suit fit him?"

I raised an eyebrow at my friend, but she kept on, undaunted.

"I'm telling you, Margot. This is a gift from the heavens. This is karma rewarding you for being nice to that woman who tried to bring her pet snake into the restaurant last month. Get yourself a hot hookup, girl. Just leave before he gets weird about making you breakfast."

I snorted. "Ah yes, just what I always dreamed of. A fling with a compulsive liar who only cooks with the door locked and the drapes drawn."

"You can't be too picky, Margot."

I rolled my eyes and took a bite of pastry.

The universe most definitely *was* on my side today because, not only was the pastry delicious, but just then the bathroom door swung open. In walked the two women who'd been gossiping about Laurent earlier. They stood in front of the mirrors, reapplying their lipstick.

For a brief moment, I considered taking the mature, aloof route and not asking them about Laurent.

But of course I wasn't going to do that. I had to live next to this man, after all, and I should know who my neighbor was. It was definitely not just because I wanted to hear some good gossip.

"Pardon me," I said, going up to them. They both turned and smiled. "I was sitting near you during the meeting, and I couldn't help but overhear you talking about Laurent Roche. Do you know him? He just moved next door to me."

The women said nothing for a moment. I had a sudden, panicked thought that I'd overstepped, but then the women turned to each other, then back to me, and the floodgates opened.

"Living next to you? How lucky!" the older of the two said, clasping her hands together.

"Has he cooked for you?" the other asked.

"Is he seeing anyone?" the first woman asked, looking hopeful.

I had to tell them that I knew practically nothing about my new neighbor, and he'd hardly spoken at all to me.

"I gave him a few macarons, but I'm not sure if he liked them," I admitted.

As one, the women pressed their hands to their chests, aghast.

"Didn't like your macarons! But I'm sure they were lovely."

"You look like an excellent baker."

"Did he thank you for them, at least?"

It took several minutes for them to come down from that affront and answer my questions about who, exactly, Laurent Roche was.

"He's a Provençal," the older woman said, a little sniffy in the way Parisians always are about people who come from places other than Paris. "From one of the little towns near Aix. That's where his restaurant was, and it was very well-received, too. It was quite a shock when it closed."

"Why did it close?" I asked.

"I'm not exactly sure," the woman admitted. "I heard a rumor about money and also that his girlfriend wanted him to quit. I saw them dining at La Table de Pierre Reboul once," she added, smiling at the memory. "Her dress was pale pink silk. Gorgeous."

"Yes," the first woman said, seemingly intent on being the one with more information to share. "But then she left him anyway."

"And for one of her *coworkers*," the other woman stage-whispered. I swung my attention back to her, feeling like I was attending the French Open.

"Tragic, isn't it?" the first woman said, looking delighted.

"Do you know what he's doing in Paris?" I asked, trying to digest all this information.

Both women shook their heads. "I haven't heard a thing. But it's promising that he's volunteering at this event. At least we know the food will be excellent. What is he like now?"

I wracked my brain, trying to think of anything I knew about Laurent Roche besides his grouchy demeanor and inability to admit he cooked.

"His shoes are always so shiny," I finally said.

The younger woman nodded. "He was like that as a child, too. At church, his sister came in looking like she'd just been dragged through the woods, but Laurent was always perfectly turned out. He's always been very charming too, even when he was a boy. Make sure you don't lose your head over him."

I assured the woman she had absolutely nothing to worry about on that front.

Chapter 9

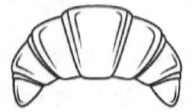

"Are you warming up to the idea of being their pastry chef?" Yasmine asked as we exited the bathroom.

"Sorry, Yasmine. Especially not with my neighbor also volunteering. If that's not a sign from the universe that I shouldn't do this, I don't know what is."

Yasmine rolled her eyes, but she *had* promised that I wasn't beholden to anything more than attending this meeting.

"Just keep thinking about it," she said. "I need to sit in on the decorating meetings with my mother now, but I'll call you tonight. Remember, you still have time to change your mind!" she called as she hurried off.

I waved her off, then decided that, if I was going to feel bad, I might as well feel bad and be well fed.

I busied myself with taking a sample of every food that was being passed around. By the time I'd circled the room twice, making sure I hadn't missed anything, my plate was piled high with kebabs, couscous, fruit, and pastries.

The meeting room was, thankfully, empty, so I sat down to enjoy my feast in peace.

At that moment, Monsieur Bad Times himself had to walk through the door. I gave him a curt nod and turned back to my food. I had three pieces of baklava on my plate, and no one, not even Laurent Roche, was going to ruin a single bite of it.

Except that, apparently, he would.

Although there were plenty of empty tables, he took the seat directly across from me. I didn't even glance at him.

I bit into my baklava, trying to savor the crispy phyllo dough drenched in honey, but the dark cloud of misery that was Monsieur Roche kept distracting me. His mere presence made me jumpy, and when I went to reach for my coffee, I accidentally knocked it over.

Of course, it spilled all over my neighbor.

He swore and stood up with a start, his suit jacket wet.

"I'm so sorry," I gasped, pushing all my napkins toward him and running to get more. When I returned, Monsieur Roche was blotting his soaked jacket, looking more aggrieved than ever.

He turned those golden eyes on me. "Every time we meet—which is disturbingly often," he began, taking the napkins I passed over, "I'm more and more surprised that Le Jules Verne employs you as a server. How many diners have you spilled drinks on?"

"This was an accident, and that's none of your business," I said, nearly snarling with embarrassment. How did this man always catch me at my worst?

I had all these sharp retorts ready, about how I knew his girlfriend had left him and his restaurant closed, but now I was, again, caught on my back foot. (And the answer was two. Two diners I'd spilled drinks on in five years, which wasn't a bad record at all.)

I paused in wiping the table to see Monsieur Roche smirking. "You know, you're more interesting when you're annoyed," he said. "I knew that sunshiny attitude you had at the restaurant was just an act."

Now that was a bridge too far.

"I'll have you know," I said, speaking slowly to remain calm, "that I am a very happy person. *Exceptionally* happy. And I love my job. As long as the diners aren't acting like asses."

Whoops, that wasn't very sunshiny.

Monsieur Roche grinned wider. "No, I can tell. You might be able to hide it most of the time, but you're a grump like me. I bet you curse under your breath at slow walkers, too."

I glanced up, startled, then immediately returned to cleaning the table. "You're incorrect, Monsieur. I love slow walkers. I adore them. They allow me to slow down myself and appreciate the, uh, beauty of my surroundings." I smiled radiantly, just for good measure.

Infuriatingly, Monsieur Roche shook his head. "Protest all you want, Mademoiselle Delcour. But I know a fellow grouch when I see one. I just hope you're able to make it through the gala without wrecking someone's meal."

I was still sputtering for a response when the door opened and Fatima and her assistant sailed in.

"All ready to get back to work?" Fatima asked cheerfully.

"Absolutely!" I chirped, smiling my widest smile. Then I sat down and rage ate the rest of my baklava as the others filed in. Not once did I look at Laurent Roche.

By the time I was finished eating, I was fully resolved to see this gala through. I hadn't felt this motivated to do something in years. Let Monsieur Roche smirk and make his snide comments. I'd show him just how competent I was. And I'd do it with a smile.

"Let's start throwing out ideas for the menu," Fatima said once we were all seated. "We want it to have a cohesive theme, nothing too restrictive, but we don't want a series of disparate dishes, either."

"The theme should be classic French dining," a sous chef sitting to my left said. "Escargots, Crêpes Suzette. The kind of food our grandparents knew they'd be served when they attended a dinner party. I'm sure everyone here knows how to cook those recipes, and it'll give immigrants an experience they wouldn't have had before."

As I inwardly blanched at the idea of making hundreds of Crêpes Suzette (so much alcohol, so many flames), a woman sitting on my other side shook her head.

"Isn't that tone deaf? The gala is to raise money for this organization that supports immigrants from around the world, and we're not serving a single dish they'd recognize?"

"We're welcoming them to our country," the man insisted. "That includes sharing our culture and our food."

"No one wants to go back to the stale dinner parties of the 1950s," the woman retorted.

"Have you polled them? What were the results?"

"Alright then!" Fatima's assistant cut in. "Let's compromise. What if, every other course, we switch between French and international fare?"

Everyone paused to consider the idea. I wasn't fully convinced

"Ye-es," the woman began. "Something like kofta kebabs followed by vichyssoise?"

"That could work," the man conceded.

Laurent Roche's eyes flickered to mine. It lasted only a fraction of a second, but it was enough for me to understand that I wasn't the only person who thought following the strong, spice-forward flavors of kebabs with the delicate flavors of a potato and leek soup was a terrible idea.

Fatima's assistant loved it, though. "Wonderful! Perhaps we could have the rest of the event follow the switches in the menu? You know, when we bring out a French dish, it's served on porcelain from Sèvres, and we'll have the band play something by Edith Piaf. And when we bring out, say a dish from Algeria, we'll switch the serving ware, and have the band play an Algerian song, or maybe we could even bring in a mandole player?"

I knew enough about the restaurant world that I could see the gala quickly spiraling out of control if we attempted that many changes throughout the night, but others were nodding along.

Out of the corner of my eye, I saw Laurent Roche smirking in my direction again. As if he knew exactly how doubtful I was feeling about this idea. Well, I'd show him.

"I think it's a wonderful idea," I said to the woman. She beamed.

"No, it's a terrible idea," Laurent said. "It's much too difficult to pull off, and the final result will be chaos."

I rolled my eyes at his pessimism. No one needed to know I secretly agreed with him.

His comment set off another round of arguing, which only paused when the door opened and a woman swept in. All of us turned toward her.

She was the kind of person who probably regularly brought conversations to a halt when she walked into a room. She was tall and elegant with blonde hair pulled into a chignon. The forest green dress she wore lightly skimmed the floor as she came toward us. I'd seen enough expensive clothes from my time at Le Jules Verne to have an excellent eye for them. Despite the dress's simple cut, I could tell it was made from high-quality fabric and had been tailored to fit her exact size.

"Ah, Sabine, I'm glad you found the time," Fatima said, pulling out a chair for the woman. "Everyone, this is Sabine, our event coordinator. She's very busy overseeing all the parts of the gala, but she wanted to drop in and see how the menu was coming together."

"I'm sure it's coming along wonderfully," Sabine said. Her voice was smooth, and a little deeper than I expected. When she smiled, her red lips parted to reveal two rows of perfect white teeth.

Sabine sat down and the argument resumed. But this time, Laurent didn't speak up. He sat silently, glaring at his hands again. That meant Fatima's assistant was able to spin her ideas without pushback. By the time she mentioned alternating fire breathers and can-can dancers between every course, I knew I had to step in.

"What about a fusion?" I suggested. "Instead of switching between French and international food, we have every course combine both?"

"How?" one of the sous chefs asked.

"It could be anything," I said, thinking fast. "Like lamb chops crusted with fennel and cumin or chickpea cassoulet, or croissants with a baklava filling."

There was a pause, and I looked around anxiously while everyone considered my idea. Maybe it was too out there?

But then Laurent spoke up: "I think that's an excellent suggestion." I looked at him for just a second before turning to see Fatima nodding in agreement. Monsieur-Know-It-All must think the back-and-forth cuisine idea was even worse than I did to publicly compliment me.

That set off another flurry of chatter as people began discussing what dishes they could make. Rough ideas were drawn up, and another meeting was set to finalize them. I glowed a little that my idea seemed so popular, but then I noticed Sabine staring at me. She didn't look happy.

After the meeting ended and people began filing out, Sabine stood in front of me, blocking my way to the door.

"What's your name?" she asked. She was smiling, but there was nothing friendly in her face.

"I'm Margot Delcour."

She flipped through her files until she came to the page she wanted.

"You're a server?" she said, raising an eyebrow.

"I am," I confirmed, wondering why she'd taken a sudden interest in me. Perhaps she had a secret hatred for fusion dishes and now saw me as the enemy?

"Do you really think you're up for baking everything we need for the gala?"

How obnoxious. An hour ago I was dead set against doing a single thing for this event, and now, once I'd decided to volunteer, I had people pushing back? Even worse, she was voicing my own fears.

Of course I don't think I'm up for baking everything you need for the gala! I wanted to cry. *I'm an absolute wreck; just last week I forgot to poke holes in my éclairs, and when I tried to pipe in the pastry cream, the steam trapped inside caused them to explode like little pastry grenades.*

But she didn't need to know that.

"I think I'm prepared. I'll certainly do my best." I smiled extra sunnily, just because I knew it set people like her on edge.

Sabine stared at me a few moments longer. "Well, we'll see," she said ominously. She turned on her heel and left.

Chapter 10

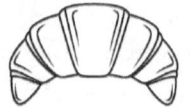

"**Y**ou'll do it? Margot, you're amazing!" Yasmine gripped my face between her hands and kissed me on each cheek. "What made you change your mind?"

I shrugged. "I decided I should challenge myself. That, and my life's work is now to prove to my neighbor that I'm competent at something."

"I support your obsessive need for validation if it means the gala gets a pastry chef."

Yasmine was staying to make an inventory of past gala decorations, so I took the opportunity to head out before Monsieur Roche popped out from behind a corner or something.

The day was crisp but bright, with the scent of fall just coming in on the wind. I decided to get dinner in the Latin Quarter.

When I told Parisians that my favorite part of Paris was the Latin Quarter, they generally looked as though I'd just suggested we get coffee at Starbucks (i.e. horrified to their very soul). The Latin Quarter, they insisted, was too crowded, too touristy, too...overdone.

I didn't have time for that kind of negativity. The whole point of the Latin Quarter was for it to be filled with people. The bookshops, the cafes, the grand buildings, the tiny, winding streets: none of them would mean anything if they were empty.

So I always smiled when I saw it busy, even if the people were loud, blocked the sidewalk to take photos, and tried to pay for their gelato with American dollars.

I strolled past the Cathedral Notre Dame which was happily swarming with people. Growing up, I'd always preferred the nearby Sainte-Chappelle church, with its stained-glass windows that were so beautiful they looked like sheets of jewels pounded flat. But after the terrible fire Notre Dame had suffered, I, like every other French person, had catapulted Notre Dame to the top of my best beloved and most cherished of places.

A woman near the entrance was playing guitar and singing, and doing a beautiful job of it. I took a seat on one of the benches and let the crowds part around me while I looked at the old church. The restoration had been done so well.

Past the cathedral, I walked for a few minutes until I found the place I was looking for: one of Paris' quintessential cafes, with a crowd of small tables outside, chairs all turned so they faced the sidewalk. I slipped past them, though, and asked the hostess for a seat inside.

"A good idea on a day like today," she said, looking at the leaves being battered around by the wind. Once seated at a corner table, I ordered a glass of Alsatian Riesling, flinty and bone dry. The waiter recommended the roast chicken with hazelnuts, so that was what I ordered, along with a baguette and some homemade butter.

Leaning back into my chair, I took out the battered notebook I used for recipe ideas and everything else that needed to be jotted down.

I was actually doing this. I was going to be the pastry chef for an actual event. And things hadn't even gone terribly yet. The team had agreed on my idea for fusion recipes, and now it was all up to me to come up with the desserts for the gala. This was the fun part.

Flipping to a blank page, I began making a list of recipe ideas. Macarons with a cardamom filling? Petit-fours topped with jalebi and a dusting of chopped pecans? Madeleines flavored with rose water?

I scribbled wildly, filling several pages with ideas. Now that I was committed (both to the gala and to proving Monsieur Roche wrong), I didn't want my work to be anything less than my best.

When my food came out, my heart lifted at the sight of it. The chicken was hot and crackling, the dark meat sliding off the bones. The hazelnuts swam in a garlic sauce surrounded by heaps of caramelized onions. I spread a thick layer of butter across the baguette and bit into the velvety, still-warm bread.

It was nearly dusk when I put down my pencil and swallowed the last sip of wine. After complimenting the server on the food and paying for my meal, I stepped back outside. The sun was setting, but the wind had dropped, so it was still pleasant enough to walk.

The street lamps blinked on as I walked along the Seine. It was the tail end of golden hour, and all of Paris appeared burnished to a high sheen. In the rich light, even the peeling paint on the buildings, even the lopsided sign advertising cheap cigarettes, even the bits of trash skittering along the road looked beautiful and as though they were meant to be here.

I reached my building and climbed the stairs to my floor. The light was still out in the hallway, so I didn't see the little package in the gloom until I nearly stepped on it. There in my doorway was a tidy parcel, small enough to fit in my hand.

Perplexed, I brought it inside and opened it up under the fluorescent light of my kitchen. I pulled back the paper to discover a thick piece of quiche. How odd.

I leaned in closer. The quiche was cleanly cut, nicely browned on top. I sniffed, taking in scents of onion, spinach, and pork lardons. There was a crispy bit of pork sticking temptingly out of the filling. I broke it off and popped it in my mouth, letting it melt on my tongue. Delicious.

I flipped the quiche over. The crust was cooked nicely, not soggy or under-baked. I broke a piece off and tasted it.

Eh. Not much flavor, and the dough had been overworked. I went to pinch off another piece, then froze.

What was I doing? Eating food that had been abandoned on my doorstep by who knows who? What if it was trash that had fallen out of a garbage bag? No, it'd been too nicely wrapped for that.

What if it was poisoned? Frantically, I tried to make a list of potential enemies. The guy from the winter I'd declined a second date with because he'd been rude to the waiter? The diner from last week who'd been inordinately angry when I was unable to magically whip up a side of macaroni and cheese (which was not on Le Jules Verne's menu and never would be)? My cousin Timothée for that time I'd trounced him at tennis in front of all our relatives when we were teenagers? None of those warranted murder by quiche.

Right??

With rising panic, I pawed through the quiche's wrappings. There, tucked into the paper, was a notecard, neatly folded in half. I opened it, hoping for a pleasant greeting (or at least an antidote recipe).

Instead, I blinked in surprise. The note was written in elegant cursive, although the effect was somewhat marred by a splattering of grease across the card.

Mlle Delcour, just wanted to get your opinion. -Laurent

Oh. Well, then.

I read the note several times despite understanding it perfectly. Unconsciously, I'd begun to eat the quiche again. It really was delicious, despite the crust.

Maybe Laurent Roche didn't actually despise me? Maybe he was simply having a bad day every single day that I'd seen him? Maybe our run-in today had thawed some of his frostiness?

I read the note through again. He wanted my opinion on his food. This Michelin-starred chef wanted my opinion. I took another bite of quiche. Well, I'd give it to him. But I'd provide it along with a gift.

My mother had always impressed upon me the importance of having fresh bread available for whenever unexpected guests dropped by. I hadn't baked anything today, but, fortunately, I had a round of pain de campagne sitting in my tiny freezer. It only needed to be thawed and warmed. I took it out.

It was such a small thing, a single scribbled sentence, but I was strangely excited. It was as though my entire perspective had been shifted back into alignment. Laurent Roche didn't hate me after all.

I was hugely impatient for the bread to thaw, so I sliced the loaf to hurry things along. Once it was ready, I spritzed it with a bit of water, then put it in a hot oven for a few minutes so the crust was crisp and golden.

Now, what to write back? Something clever, but not too clever, lest he think I was trying hard. I pondered it while the bread cooled on the rack, then ripped a page from my notebook and dashed off my message.

Quiche: excellent. Crust: store-bought? -Margot

I tied twine around the sliced loaf and tucked the note in, then went and stood in front of Monsieur Roche's door.

Here, I encountered another conundrum. It was late, nearly midnight. I would normally never consider bothering someone at this hour. But if I didn't knock, Laurent probably wouldn't notice the bread until morning, when it'd no longer be at its warm, fresh-from-the-oven peak of deliciousness.

I never liked giving people food that was less than its best, and the stakes felt unusually high here.

Obviously, the sane thing to do would have been to wait until morning to do the baking, when I could have left the bread at a normal hour. But no, in my eagerness to respond, I'd cooked through the night, like a flour-dusted Dracula.

I stood in the darkened hallway, shuffling from foot to foot as I tried to decide what would be the least-bizarre course of action. I had just decided to leave the bread in the doorway and was bending to lay it down when the door swung open.

I came face-to-face with a pair of shiny shoes. Very shiny shoes. They were so shiny I could see my reflection in them. I looked scared out of my wits.

Slowly, I lifted my head. Laurent stared down at me. He'd ditched the suit jacket I'd drenched with coffee and was now wearing a polo shirt with a perfectly-starched canary yellow apron over it. There was a smudge of flour on his cheek, which I swear only enhanced his cheekbones.

I can only imagine how I appeared, crouching in his doorway with my floury clothes and hurriedly pinned-up hair. Probably like a sewer troll who'd decided to take a stroll in the aboveground world and be really creepy about it.

I scrambled up quickly. "Hi! I mean, good evening? Why are you up so late?" I demanded, as though I wasn't just as wide awake as he was at this hour.

Laurent had taken a half step back when he'd opened the door—probably because he hadn't been expecting to find his neighbor skulking in front of it—but he recovered quickly.

"Good evening," he said politely, as though this was a completely normal meeting we were having. "I was just about to take out the trash."

"Oh. Well, I saw the quiche you left. I wanted to give you this." I thrust the pain de campagne at him. "I made it."

Laurent put the trash bag down so he could take the bread. "Thank you," he murmured, turning the loaf in his hands. "And a note?"

He flicked it open, and I died a thousand deaths as he read it. Why had I tried to be funny? Why hadn't I just written 'thank you' and left it at that? That would have been perfectly acceptable and not make me want to sink into the earth now.

The gold in Laurent's eyes shone in the dark hallway.

"You think the crust was store bought?" The corner of his mouth quirked up. "That's possibly the most offensive thing one could say to a chef."

"I was just trying to, you know, make a joke," I said awkwardly, back to cringing embarrassment. "It wasn't terrible. But also, still not that great," I added, physically incapable of lying about subpar pastry.

Why am I like this?

Laurent stared at me for a second, then a grin slowly spread across his face. His eyes crinkled with laughter. Gone was my mysterious, closed-off neighbor, and in his place was this man who seemed to actually find me amusing.

"Pastry was always my weakness in culinary school, and my lack of practice seems to have compounded the issue." He shrugged, still smiling. "I appreciate the feedback."

"I had to leave the meeting today quickly," he continued, "But I wanted to ask…Well, normally I wouldn't do things this way." He stopped and rubbed the back of his neck, suddenly looking as awkward as I felt.

"I know I ought to offer to make the meal," Laurent continued, "But most of my kitchen tools are still buried in moving boxes. Even Minerva has been turning her nose up at my attempts at cooking right now. Also, you did offer earlier, and I'm afraid I might have been rude in declining and perhaps this could make up for that transgression…" Laurent trailed off.

He was actually babbling. What was making this man so nervous?

Laurent took a breath and seemed to pull himself together. "What I'm trying to say is that, if your offer still stands, I'd love to come over for dinner."

I blinked at him, completely lost for words. Was this…? Did he want…?

"But I thought you hated me." The truth was out before I realized I'd said it.

Laurent's eyes went wide. "Hate you?"

"All you do is grumble at me and insult my abilities as a server. Plus, you keep pretending you never cook."

Laurent blushed under his tan. The color contrasted nicely with the blond hair now flopping in his eyes again. He cleared his throat uncomfortably.

"Yes. Well." He cleared his throat again. "To start, I grumble at everyone. But I *was* unspeakably rude to you at Le Jules Verne. It was a stressful situation for me, and I realized too late the mix-up was entirely not your fault. Even if it was, I should never have behaved the way I did. I apologize, unreservedly.

"And today I was only joking around. It's very clear to me that you're an exceptional server. I hope you didn't take it seriously," Laurent said, sounding chagrined. "And as for the cooking...That's a low point, even for me."

His mouth quirked up and he spread his hands in front of him the same way I did when everything was falling apart and there was nothing to do but accept it.

"I lied about cooking because I really *haven't* cooked in over a year. I packed it all away when I closed my restaurant. Cooking caused...quite a few problems in my life. I think I didn't want to admit I was back at it because I was afraid those problems might return. I certainly didn't consider how stupid it'd be to lie to my own neighbor about cooking.

"I also didn't realize quite how porous these walls are. Do you know that I've smelled every delicious thing you've baked since the day I moved in? You did something with chocolate last week, and I could barely finish my work memos I was drooling so much." Laurent smiled, still looking sheepish. "What I'm trying to say is that I've behaved terribly since the moment we met. The quiche was my small attempt at an apology."

He stood in front of me, looking hopeful and embarrassed.

I raised an eyebrow. "Does this mean that the next time I smell you roasting chicken, you won't try to claim you've never so much as touched an oven before?"

"On my honor," Laurent said solemnly as he crossed his heart. "In the interests of full disclosure, I made a frozen pizza for dinner tonight. That alone should tell you I've blown past all thresholds of shame."

"Oh dear. Your situation is even more dire than I thought." I grinned at Laurent. I knew very well what it was like to look back on decisions made during the worst time in your life and wonder what the hell you'd been thinking.

"Does Thursday work for dinner?" I suggested, naming the next evening I had off from work. "Seven o'clock?"

Laurent grinned again. "I'll be there."

"Excellent. I'll be making kebabs, followed by a delicate vegetable soup."

Laurent laughed. As his eyes crinkled again, I realized how happy it made me to make him laugh. It so completely changed his entire personality.

"I was terrified what kind of menu we were going to end up with for a while there," he admitted. "Your idea was brilliant."

"It's not that brilliant," I said, shrugging. "My mother used to be a pastry chef. She created these amazing recipes that combined French pastry techniques with desserts of all the exotic places she visited. She had one for a tarte tatin with figs and rosewater that people went crazy for."

"Well, I'm just glad you saved all the gala's guests from double-fisting Beaujolais and mint tea the entire night."

"I should probably take this out now," he added, picking up the trash bag (which did indeed have a pizza box sticking out of the top). "Thank you for the bread, Margot. I hope you enjoy the rest of your evening."

As though I was going to do anything other than sit on my couch and run through this conversation in my head a thousand times.

Chapter 11

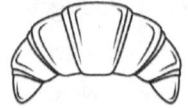

"He's coming over for *dinner*?" Colette squealed. It was the evening after I'd run into Laurent and had my entire worldview thrown into disorder.

"Is it a date?" Yasmine asked.

"Just a platonic, neighborly meal," I said.

Eyerolls all around, which I chose to ignore.

"Did he seem like he was flirting?" Yasmine pressed.

"I don't think so?"

"But he said he wanted to have dinner with you. And he baked you a quiche," Colette said firmly, as though that settled things.

"He baked *a* quiche and gave Margot a slice," Luc corrected.

"But still, to have dinner at someone's house, that's no small thing," Colette insisted.

"Did you kiss? Hug? Shake hands?" Yasmine asked.

"No. He was, well, holding a bag of trash."

This stumped even Colette, and there was a moment of fraught silence. I wasn't even sure what to think myself. Laurent Roche was, despite his apologies, still a snobbish grump. He wasn't a good dating prospect, even if he had a cute cat and looked like a catalog model (Yasmine's opinion, not mine).

"In any case, it doesn't matter if it's a date right now," Paul said, speaking up from where he sat in the corner, sorting through newly-arrived shipments of wine. "Anything can *become* a date, even if it doesn't start as one. The question we should be discussing is: what is Margot going to cook?"

This sent everyone into a flurry of suggestions, but before I had any time to consider them, the elevator dinged and it was time to get to work.

It was the first day of Chef La Croix's fall menu, and menu switch days were always chaotic. We had to learn all the details about the new courses to relay to guests, the kitchens had to get the timing of them just right so no diner had too long of a gap between courses, and sometimes, even when we did everything right, a guest had a meltdown because they were expecting last season's menu, even though Le Jules Verne made this information very, *very* clear.

I pushed any thought of Laurent out of my mind and stepped into the dining rooms feeling like a soldier heading into battle.

But, tonight at least, every diner at Le Jules Verne seemed pleased with the menu. As they should be. I'd tried it myself weeks ago, when the kitchens had been doing a test run, and every course had been perfection.

As the evening wore on, the other servers whispered suggestions of what I could make Laurent each time we passed each other.

"Broiled swordfish," Colette said, balancing a platter of empty wine glasses. "Easy, but impressive."

"Absolutely do not serve a man fish on the first date," Luc said, passing in the opposite direction. "The main course should be roast chicken."

"No chicken, no fish," Yasmine said later, carrying out a pair of chocolate mousses. "A sophisticated chef will only appreciate red meat. And don't try making any Provençal specialties," she added, stepping aside as the kitchen door swung open and Colette blazed in, looking harassed. "You'll never be able to make them as well as his mother."

As the evening progressed, the suggestions kept on coming.

Duck confit.

The scallops with a citrus reduction that had been a standout from last year's summer menu.

Baked Camembert.

Chocolate soufflé.

"No make *this*," Colette said, passing by with a plate of bucatini pasta with chive lemon sauce. "Every time I bring a plate of it out, I want to bury my face in it."

By the end of the shift, my mind was reeling with suggestions. The staff meal we had at one of the empty tables didn't make things any clearer.

"You need to keep the menu simple," Yasmine said.

"No, you need to impress him," Colette insisted.

"What about a vegetarian meal?" Paul suggested.

"Oh, Margot, have a baked potato bar. They're all the rage now," Luc said, although he might have been trolling.

They jumped from one idea to another, and by the time Colette and Luc started concocting a French/Mexican menu, I was so overwhelmed that I didn't even bother telling them their idea of putting escargots in tacos was objectively appalling.

Suddenly, a shadow loomed. Everyone went silent.

Standing over us was Chef La Croix. There were bloodstains splattered across his apron, and even though I knew (??) they were from cutting short ribs for the menu's fourth course, they made him look even more frightening than normal.

When he spoke, his voice was low and quiet.

"Is someone in need of a menu?"

I'd never heard a more terrifying sentence. No one moved for several seconds. I would rather serve Laurent one of his frozen pizzas and torpedo the dinner than have Chef La Croix learn I needed his help.

Then, Yasmine pointed a traitorous finger in my direction.

Chef La Croix's gaze snapped to me. I gulped. The bloodstains really weren't helping him appear more approachable.

Chef La Croix's eyes narrowed. "Come with me, Margot."

As I stood to leave, I took a final glance at my coworkers. They stared back as though I was headed for the gallows.

Chef La Croix led me to the kitchens, past the long counters where two sous chefs were putting ingredients away, over to a dimly-lit back corner. From a cabinet, he pulled out two small stools and set them on the ground.

"Sit," he ordered.

I immediately sat. He settled himself across from me.

Somehow, he appeared even more intimidating hunched on a tiny stool.

"Explain it to me."

I gulped, then started talking. I told him about my new neighbor and the predicament I'd landed myself in when I'd impulsively invited him over for dinner before learning he was a Michelin-starred chef who had likely surpassed me in cooking skills before he could write his own name.

Chef La Croix listened carefully, his brow furrowed and his dark eyes never leaving my face. He only spoke after I had petered into silence.

"His name is Roche? And his restaurant was in Aix?" he asked. "I know of him. You'll need to introduce us sometime."

I nodded, although I couldn't imagine a more nightmarish scenario than my terrifying boss meeting the neighbor I was sort-of-very-much-hoping I was planning a date for.

Chef La Croix went silent, and that made me nervous, so I began listing some of the suggestions the others had given.

"Colette suggested beef tartare, but Yasmine said to do crêpes, and Paul thought—"

"No," Chef La Croix said, cutting across me. "I heard their ideas, and they are all terrible."

"Oh." I'd actually thought Yasmine had been on to something with the crêpes, but never mind.

"The menu," Chef La Croix began, eyes boring into me, "needs to be food that you love. Food you love to cook and food you love to eat. If you don't love it, anything you make will be *garbage*!" He banged his fist into his other palm with the final word, and I nearly fell off my stool.

"Understand?"

I nodded quickly.

"Good. Now, what did your family cook when you were growing up?"

The question caught me off guard. "Oh, I can't really think of anything," I began, but then the memories started coming thick and fast.

Waking up to the scent of baking bread and knowing that, when I sat down at the kitchen table, my mother would have a croissant spread with Nutella waiting for me. Living in Alsace, in the northeastern corner of the country, with its bountiful orchards and vineyards. I'd go apple picking, and my grandmother would turn my haul into a tarte tatin with puddles of sugar and melted butter swimming among the fruit. Gorging myself on jiggly, creamy blanc-manger coco when my mother and I lived in Martinique. Carefully slicing apples for a pie in

Washington DC and beaming with pride when my mother told me what a good job I'd done.

Chef La Croix sat silently as I poured out the stories. If he noticed me getting teary-eyed, he didn't say a word about it. When I was done, he pulled out a ratty notebook and a pencil stub.

"Now, this is what you're going to make." He flipped open the notebook and began to write, explaining the reason for each course and how I should go about cooking it.

When he finished, he tore the page out and handed it to me. I took it as though it were a precious object. Which it was.

I could not have come up with a better menu if I'd dedicated a year to it. It was all food I was deeply familiar with, all food I'd grown up with and, yes, all food that I loved. It was heavy on my Alsatian background and played to my strengths as a baker. It was impressive but not overly so. It was elevated, but still comforting. There it all was, written in Chef La Croix's loopy cursive.

Entrée: Saltfish acra (Fried fish fritters, generally served with a spicy sauce, and a favorite dish from the year my mother and I lived in Martinique. Chef La Croix had been delighted when I'd mentioned it. "A perfect start to the meal. It's exotic, but not strange. It's light, but not insubstantial.")

Salad: Arugula with fig and goat cheese ("A standard, but it's a standard because it works," Chef La Croix had said. "People like food they know, especially after a dish they're less used to. This is familiar and a lighter contrast to the other courses. Go heavy on the black pepper.")

Main course: Tarte flambée (The crispy pizza-esque flatbread that was a specialty of Alsace. It's my favorite food in the world and thus merited an instant spot in Chef La Croix's menu. I'd made it probably a hundred times over the years and could practically do it in my sleep. According to Chef La Croix, it was essential that I feel confident in a dinner's main course.)

Dessert: Tarte tatin (A pastry with fruit, often apples, caramelized in butter and sugar before being baked. "I could recommend no other dessert to an Alsatian," was all Chef La Croix had said.)

I read the menu through twice, then looked up at Chef La Croix. "It's perfect," I breathed, tears pricking my eyes again. I nearly reached out to clasp his hand.

It was a good thing I didn't because Chef La Croix had resumed looking terrifying. He raised a disdainful eyebrow. "Yes. I know. Now get out of my kitchen."

I hurriedly obeyed, the precious paper still clutched in my hands.

Chapter 12

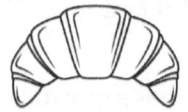

The days flew by in a flurry of work and grocery shopping until Thursday arrived, clear and sunny. I slept in late, then had hot chocolate and buttered toast on the balcony as I watched Paris go about its morning. Then it was time to get cooking.

I'd created a minutely-detailed cooking schedule, structured so that I could get most of the work out of the way before Laurent arrived. It'd been years since I'd gone more than two days without baking something, but I couldn't remember the last time I'd made dinner for another person. Having most of the meal done beforehand would make me feel more confident.

Slightly more confident.

I started things off easy by making the salad dressing. I went about it carefully, taste-testing throughout the process to make sure there was a perfect balance between all the ingredients: olive oil, blood orange balsamic vinegar I'd gotten specially, Dijon mustard, honey, minced garlic, and salt and pepper.

It took a bit of effort, but I was pleased with it by the time I decanted it into a glass jar and put it in the fridge.

Next, I prepped the apples for the tarte tatin, peeling, seeding, and quartering them. They got placed in the fridge as well to dry out a bit so the tart wouldn't get soggy. It was a trick my mother had taught me.

After that, I made the puff pastry. The frozen brands at the store were usually pretty good, but I absolutely could not serve Laurent store-bought pastry after my jibe at his quiche. Plus, I always found the process of pastry-making to be soothing.

Methodically, I went through the steps: grating the slightly-frozen butter, mixing it with flour, adding just the right amount of water, and kneading it into dough.

It was late afternoon by now, and I nervously ran through the recipes again and triple-checked that I had all the ingredients. Once that was sorted, I realized that I should probably put some effort into my appearance, too.

I flailed around my closet for a few minutes before deciding on a burgundy dress that had always served me well on previous dates. (Not that this was a date. Maybe.)

A half hour before Laurent was due to arrive, I brushed my hair, leaving it down since I always wore it up for work, and did my makeup, choosing a subtle mauve lipstick. Then I put the radio on to my favorite jazz station, lit the unscented candles I had decorating the table, and stood back to survey my work.

"I think this might actually go alright," I said. I decided that my nerves were due to the rarity of me hosting dinner and not because the dinner was for Laurent Roche in particular.

I'd meant to have the saltfish acras finished just before Laurent arrived, but their prep took me longer than expected. I'd never actually made acras before, but I'd watched our neighbor in Martinique teach my mother, and then watched my mother make them many times herself. It had seemed quite straightforward, but I was slow to chop everything. By the time there was a quiet knock on my door, I had the batter ready and oil heating, but I hadn't fried any of the fritters yet.

I went to open the door, aware that I was sweating slightly and my hair was likely frizzing about my head. On the other side stood Laurent, wearing slacks and a button-down shirt and looking again like he'd just stepped away from a photoshoot. In his hands were two bottles of wine.

His mouth quirked. "I figured I was safest with both a white and a red."

I laughed, some of my nervous energy dissipating now that Laurent was actually here. We stepped toward each other to kiss on each cheek. A shiver ran down my back as his warm skin pressed against mine.

I ushered him in with greetings and small talk questions about his day, opened the bottle of red to let it breathe, then opened the white wine and poured us each a glass.

"To store-bought pastry," Laurent said, and I laughed and clinked my glass against his.

"I meant to have the first course ready," I admitted, "But I still need a few minutes."

"Not to worry," Laurent said, looking into the mixing bowl with professional interest. "What are we having?"

"Saltfish acras. The recipe is from Martinique."

Laurent's face lit up. "Acras? Wonderful. I had an offer to work in the Caribbean several years ago, but I turned it down to stay in Europe. I read up on the food, though."

We went to the stove together, where the pan of oil was still heating.

"Do you do a lot of frying?" Laurent asked as I scooped out a mound of batter.

"No. When I lived in the United States, a group of us tried to make Monte Cristos, but I wasn't in charge of the frying part." I held a hand over the oil to try to judge the temperature.

"Do you have a deep fryer thermometer?" Laurent now sounded slightly concerned.

"Oh, no," I said breezily. "It's been heating for a while, though, so I'm sure it's hot enough."

"Yes, but—" Laurent started. At the same time, I dropped a spoonful of batter into the oil, and the very wise warning he was probably about to give was cut off as my kitchen exploded.

Honestly, I don't know what I was thinking. That the oil would reach the optimum temperature and just stay there, despite being over a burning flame? That deep fry thermometers were a quaint extravagance and not a deeply-essential tool when cooking in oil? That frying wasn't at all as finicky as baking?

The pan of oil had sat, half-forgotten, on the stove, getting hotter and hotter until it was roughly comparable to the surface of the sun.

At least Laurent and I had the intelligence to drop to the ground. That spared us from the worst effects of hot oil splattering in every direction, although some of it still got in my hair.

There was an unholy sizzling sound, and a billow of smoke rose from the pan. That set the fire alarm wailing.

Gallantly, with one hand shielding his face from the jets of burning oil still rocketing across my kitchen, Laurent stood and quickly moved the pan to the back burner before turning off the stove. He then sprinted across the room to open the window and began opening closets, presumably to find a broom to turn off the alarm.

I remained crouched on the kitchen floor, shell-shocked by how quickly this meal had devolved into a disaster/potential arson event. By some miracle, I was still clutching my wine glass. I took a gulp.

A knock at my door roused me from my stupor. There was Madame Blanchet, an utterly terrified Bijou whimpering at her side.

"Any problems, Margot?" she asked, smiling benevolently.

"Not at all," I said, speaking loudly to be heard above the fire alarm. I smiled, trying to look as though I hadn't just nearly burned the building down. "Just a little kitchen mishap."

The alarm suddenly cut out, and a wave of black smoke rolled over us. I did my best to stifle a cough. Like the tiny traitor he was, Bijou sneezed three times in succession.

"Well, you enjoy yourself, ma chérie," Madame Blanchet said, politely suppressing a cough of her own.

"Oh, is Monsieur Roche here too?" she asked, as a frazzled-looking Laurent appeared, clutching a broom in a death grip. "Are you two having dinner together? How lovely," she said as another black cloud of smoke briefly enveloped her head. "Don't worry, I won't tell anyone what's been going on," she added as she left.

Which meant the entire building would know about it by tomorrow.

I closed the door behind Madame Blanchet and turned to face Laurent.

The sudden silence, now that the fire alarm had stopped blaring, felt oppressive. I was acutely aware that my dress was crumpled, my face was flushed, and my hair was dripping with cooking oil. Laurent looked hardly better with his clothes greasy and wrinkled.

We stared at each other, both panting slightly.

Laurent cleared his throat. "I think the oil might have been just slightly too hot."

Just then, a glop of oil plopped from my hair to my shoulder, and the absurdity of it all was too much. I looked around my formerly-pristine kitchen and started laughing to cover my embarrassment. I kept on laughing as my stomach ached and I gasped for breath, until I had to lean against the counter to prevent myself from toppling over.

It must have been obvious to Laurent how close my laughter was to turning into tears because he came over and patted my shoulder awkwardly.

"Don't worry, it all turned out alright," he said.

"We haven't even started dinner!" I wailed.

"Well...yes, that's true," Laurent conceded. "How about this: I'll get my deep fry thermometer, uh, and maybe take a quick shower. Then we can resume." Laurent smiled bracingly. "It's just a slight delay."

After checking that oil was no longer exploding across the kitchen, he left. I half-expected to never see him again.

Nevertheless, as soon as the door closed behind Laurent, I sprang into action, quickly wiping down the kitchen and blowing out the candles (I wasn't risking any more fire-related mishaps this evening).

I checked the photo of my mother that hung over the counter and heaved a sigh when I saw it was unscathed. I pressed the glass briefly with my fingertips, then went to take a shower. That got rid of my nicely-styled hair and makeup, but at least I wasn't dripping cooking oil anymore.

I put on a new dress and combed my wet hair but didn't have time to do anything else before I heard Laurent's knock.

Greeting him was even more awkward than it had been the first time. We appraised each other, damp and fresh-faced, until Laurent raised his hand, showing the thermometer he held. "Want to give it another try?"

I was tempted to just throw the towel in on this whole dinner and ask Laurent if he had any more frozen pizzas lying around, but I figured I couldn't send him away without providing a single bite of food. We stood together by the stove, and there Laurent taught me the very important skill of measuring oil's temperature before you drop food into a searing vat of it.

"I can't believe I never thought to check the temperature," I said, laughing to cover my embarrassment.

"It happens to everyone," Laurent said. "You should have seen the disasters I made my first few months at culinary school."

Once we'd hit the optimal temperature, I dropped in spoonfuls of batter. This time they did not explode but only sizzled enticingly and turned a pleasant golden brown.

"I think they're excellent," Laurent said, once we'd sat down to eat the acras. "Beautifully flavored."

I tried one. It tasted alright, but the texture was off, maybe because the batter had sat on the counter for such a long time before I'd started frying.

Laurent was highly complimentary of the fritters, and the salad too, which I'd brought out at the same time since it was so late and I was starving. I thought I'd done a good job with the salad, but even a perfect green salad is still just a green salad. It could never really impress a chef of Laurent's caliber.

That meant it all came down to the main course, the tarte flambée. I'd made the dough before Laurent had arrived, and it had rested longer than it was meant to, but I thought it was still salvageable.

Laurent poured us each another glass of wine, the red this time, and we went into the kitchen. There, we made stiff small talk as I spread the dough onto a baking sheet, trying to get it as thin as possible so it'd have the traditional cracker-thin crust.

I mixed together fromage blanc, crème fraiche, salt, pepper, and a tiny grating of fresh nutmeg, then spread it across the dough. After sprinkling bacon lardons and thinly-sliced onions across the top, I put it in the oven (which I had made triple sure was set to the correct temperature).

Tarte flambées don't take long to cook, but Laurent and I struggled to fill the silence.

It was mostly my fault. I was so anxious about the food I had already ruined and the food I was sure I was about to ruin that I could barely pay attention to what Laurent was saying. I was on my third glass of wine now, every atom in my body screaming out against the awkwardness of this evening.

Laurent had been excruciatingly polite all evening, but in the way you would be to a boss or distant cousin. He had probably decided I was an idiot after the debacle with the cooking oil and was counting the minutes until he could return home and make his own palatable dinner.

He seemed nervous himself, straightening my row of spices and aligning my cookbooks so each spine was perfectly perpendicular to the counter. Or maybe he just thought I was a slob on top of being a terrible cook.

I tried to hide my relief when the timer went off and I could pull the tarte flambée out of the oven. In my anxiousness to move dinner along, I forgot to check the bottom of the crust the way I'd done every other time I've made this recipe. I didn't realize it until we were sitting down to eat.

"It's underbaked," I said, letting the piece I'd just taken a bite from drop back onto my plate. I ducked my head so that Laurent couldn't see the color rising in my cheeks.

He was, again, full of compliments, but we both knew it was a less-than-stellar rendering of tarte flambée. This was supposed to be the showstopper of the meal.

Tired and demoralized, I gave up even trying to force conversation. Instead, I went back into the kitchen to wait for the tarte tatin to finish baking.

Just this final course and this meal would be over. Then I could go back to giving Laurent polite, formal greetings when we occasionally passed each other in the hallway.

Dinner had been a full-blown disaster and the conversation even worse, but, for some reason, the thought of this being the only time I ever really spoke to Laurent depressed me.

The timer buzzed, jolting me from my reverie. I pulled the tarte out and set it on the counter. While I waited a few minutes for it to cool, Laurent came over and tried to get a conversation going about our hobbies, but it fizzled out. I wanted to ask him about cooking and running a restaurant, but I was too embarrassed to even mention food after this subpar meal I'd served him.

As soon as I judged enough time had passed, I inverted the tarte from the skillet onto a serving platter, so that the apples were now on top. I leaned in closer to appraise my work.

It looked good. It looked beautiful, actually. I'd taken my time to carefully arrange the apples, and now they spread across the pastry like a glossy golden flower. It smelled good, too, the caramel mixing with the scent of crisp apples and buttery pastry.

"That looks wonderful," Laurent said, peering over my shoulder.

I cut us each a slice and topped them with a dollop of freshly-whipped sweet cream. Without waiting for Laurent, I grabbed a forkful. Pausing with the bite of tarte right before my lips, I wished with everything I had in me that it would taste alright.

I took a bite, trying to discern any flaws. Too much sugar? Too much salt? Underbaked crust?

But...no.

I glanced at Laurent. His eyes were closed, and his fork dangled limply from his hand as he chewed slowly.

I stared at him as the seconds ticked by, awaiting his verdict. He was wearing a new button-down shirt, and this one also stretched tightly over the thick muscles in his arms. He had the sleeves rolled to his elbows, and I saw a shiny pink scar on his forearm, probably from some long-ago cooking mishap. I took in his dark blonde eyelashes and his carved cheekbones, which moved slightly as he chewed. His hair was beginning to dry in the heat of the kitchen, returning to its usual tousled state.

Finally, Laurent opened his eyes. He smiled at the tarte, then at me. His mouth quirked, and I thought I'd get another half smile, but he kept going, his grin stretching wider and wider until he was laughing in delight.

"It's perfection on a plate."

With that, the floodgates opened.

With me so relieved at one of my recipes finally working out and Laurent no longer pressured to drown me in compliments to make me feel better, we suddenly had a thousand things to talk about.

He wanted to know exactly how I'd made the tarte, what other things I'd learned to cook from my mother, how I'd liked living in Martinique, what my favorite dish from Le Jules Verne was, how I'd gotten my puff pastry to come out so light and airy, and on and on and on.

I poured us each a new glass of wine, then pulled him back into the kitchen where I made a new puff pastry right then and there.

"The trick is to use light, even strokes to roll it out. Then you want to do book folds, turning it ninety degrees after each fold," I told him.

"Hold on; I need to write that down."

Laurent pulled out his wallet and opened it to reveal a small leather notebook.

Seeing it made me smile. "I keep a notebook on me, too. For recipe ideas and such." I laid mine next to Laurent's. Mine was quite a bit more battered than his (which was, of course, in pristine condition), but seeing the two little notebooks together filled me with an inexplicable happiness.

"I can't go anywhere without mine," Laurent admitted.

"People always tell me to just use the notes app on my phone, but it's not the same."

"Absolutely not," Laurent agreed. "Plus, what if there's an extended power outage? The phones will lose power, and we'll be the only ones with scrawled ideas for (Laurent flipped through his notebook) Japanese duck à l'orange and some concoction of celery and scallops that I had a dream about but now sounds horrifying."

He turned his notebook to a blank page and, in perfect, tiny handwriting, copied out what I'd told him about making puff pastry. As he wrote, I looked at what else was visible from his open wallet. There was his ID, a punch card for a gelato store and, in the clear photo window, a picture of Minerva glaring down the camera, a catnip mouse between her paws.

"May I see what else you've written?" I asked Laurent. He passed his notebook to me. I flipped through the pages, smiling at what I saw. There was a page labelled "Dinner Menu for Mom's Birthday" with the note "nothing too spicy!" and another page labelled "Healthy, light breakfast menu for Noelle." I flipped the notebook shut and grinned at him.

"Laurent Roche, I've discovered your true self. If I'm a secret grump, then you, Monsieur, are a secret happy person."

Laurent's eyes widened. "I've never heard anything so offensive in my life. My entire personality is built on being a grump. I'll have you know that today alone I've complained to two shops about the quality of the fish they're selling."

"That's just, like, a normal Thursday for a French person," I said with a shrug. "No true grump makes thoughtful menus for birthdays, or visits a gelato shop enough to have (I paused to pull out the card) one purchase left before he gets a free scoop, or keeps a photo of his cat in his wallet. I didn't even know people still printed out photos."

"I chose that photo of Minerva because she looks like she wants to murder the entire human race," Laurent said. "That's a very grumpy thing to do."

Even as he spoke, I was shaking my head and grinning. "Own up, Roche. I bet you even smile when it's a nice day outside or you see a little kid laughing while eating an ice cream."

"You have entirely the wrong idea of me," Laurent said archly. "I hate both children and nice weather. Ice cream is fine, though."

He moved his wallet away from a splatter of oil that I'd missed. "I will tell you one thing I do love above anything else, and that's a clean kitchen." Without waiting for me to respond, he stood and opened a cabinet, then began pulling out cleaning supplies.

"Oh, don't worry. I'll do that later."

"I insist. You made the entire meal."

I was tired enough to let him have at it. Laurent topped off my wine glass then got to work, piling dishes into the sink and scrubbing down my countertops. He really did seem to be enjoying himself. I watched his biceps strain the fabric of his shirt as he washed the dishes, his back to me.

Yasmine was right. His arms did bear more than a passing resemblance to many of those Greek god statues in the Louvre.

As Laurent tidied up, I started to get nervous again. I still had no idea if this was an actual date, or if Laurent was just being polite to a neighbor, or if it had started as a date but had then become so insane it was now no longer a date. (Or if it had started as not a date and my baking had been enough to win Laurent over? One could hope.)

But even if this wasn't a date, I could still see Laurent again. If he didn't initiate, then I would. I should wait a few days to not seem too eager, I decided. And I should suggest something simple. Coffee? Or was that still too much?

Maybe I could knock on his door, tell him I was on my way to pick up coffee, and ask if he needed anything? I think that'd be OK. The important thing was to start small. And I shouldn't say anything at all to him for at least three days so I didn't overwhelm him.

Baby steps, that was the way to do it.

I smiled at Laurent, secure in my plan.

He smiled back. "I want to take you to dinner."

"What?"

Of course this night had one more curveball to throw at me.

"I want to take you to dinner," Laurent repeated. "There's a place called La Forêt that I think would be perfect. "You made this wonderful meal for us, so for our second date, I don't want you to do any work."

As he rattled off the restaurant's selling points, I stared wonderingly at him. Not only was Laurent perfectly confident that this had been a date, he also knew he wanted to see me again.

"That sounds wonderful. My next night off is Tuesday," I said, still not quite believing this was happening. I was expecting at any moment to wake up and find myself back in the smoking, oil-soaked ruins of my kitchen.

"Perfect. And gelato afterwards? I'll get that free scoop," Laurent said, grinning.

"I expect nothing less from a man who probably keeps a gratitude journal and has an album of his favorite sunset photos saved on his phone."

Laurent raised an eyebrow. "A pretty snappy comeback for a woman who I expect has hated the human race at least once when a diner showed up to Le Jules Verne in athleisure clothes."

"Wrong again. I adore it when diners show up in nothing but a sports bra and spandex shorts. It's the perfect outfit for a fancy dinner."

My pulse raced as we grinned at each other. There was a flush of color in Laurent's face. I told myself it wasn't just due to the wine.

Laurent asked if he could take a piece of the tarte tatin home, so I wrapped half of it up for him. At the door, we said our goodbyes. I thought he might kiss me on the lips, and he seemed to consider it for a moment, leaning forward and then pulling back. But I guess no one's confidence is unshakeable all the time. In the end, we kissed on the cheek. Not that it wasn't thrilling to have his cheek pressed to mine. He smelled like pastry and woodsy-scented shampoo (and slightly of burnt oil, but that one's my fault). When we broke apart, I wondered if I looked as dazed as he did.

"I'll see you on Tuesday then," he said when we broke apart. "À bientôt, Margot."

Chapter 13

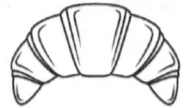

I floated through work the next day, impervious to the strenuous attempts the diners at Le Jules Verne made to bring me back down to Earth.

The wheels started coming off barely thirty minutes into the lunch shift. There must have been something in the wine Paul was pouring because nearly every table I had was anxious or unhappy.

"You know, we tried to make a dinner reservation but couldn't," one particularly aggrieved couple informed me. "We had to settle for lunch, and it's throwing our whole schedule off."

"I'm so sorry about the trouble," I told them. "Fortunately, afternoon is my favorite time to be in the Eiffel Tower. The light makes everything gorgeous." But that did nothing to placate them.

They spent the entire meal checking their watches and ordering me to bring out the courses more quickly so they could get back to their itinerary. Each time I brought out a new dish, they scarfed it down as I was still explaining it, clearing their plates in under a minute.

As I was removing dishes, I caught a glance of a sheet of paper at the man's elbow. It was their itinerary for the day, each hour filled with at least one activity.

My quick look was enough to see that they had four museums to visit, and they'd be ending their day with a ballet production of Sleeping Beauty. (I'd seen that ballet last week and knew it was a solid three hours.) They gestured for the check the moment they finished their final course (I was expecting it and had the bill ready and waiting), then left nearly at a run.

"Well, I hope they enjoy their trip," Leïla said, passing by as I cleared the table. I looked at her and grinned. She'd been steadily gaining confidence and was no longer so silent and worried-looking at work. Now she was even making quips.

During the break between the lunch and dinner shifts I made a beeline for the kitchens. There, I sat on one of the tiny stools and recounted my dinner with Laurent to Chef La Croix. He found the experience very trying.

"How, *how* can you walk through every precise step of a recipe when you bake, but when you fill a pot with oil and put it over a fire you never think to test the temperature?" he said despairingly, eyes turned heavenward. "I am certain Alain Passard's staff do not hurt him like this."

I was in such high spirits that his reaction didn't even slow me down. Plus, I didn't find Chef La Croix nearly as terrifying as I had before.

When I got to the part of the evening where I underbaked the tarte flambée crust, Chef La Croix actually dropped his ladle and covered his face with his hands.

"I would prefer to be stabbed with a steak knife than present an underdone tarte," he said, his voice slightly muffled. "I would rather be force fed a PB&J sandwich, with its flabby white bread and offensive flavor profile, every day until my death rather than pull a dish out of the oven early."

Chef La Croix regularly expounded on his hatred for peanut butter and jelly, and I let him continue for some time before interrupting.

"And we're going to La Forêt next week," I said, grinning like a maniac.

Chef La Croix dropped his hands. "You don't deserve a nice meal. You don't deserve anything more than American white bread and water for the remainder of your life."

He sighed heavily. "But I'm happy for you. Now please, let me get back to my risotto. And never, *never* let me hear about you underbaking a crust again."

Yasmine was hardly any better. Though supportive of my cooking attempts, she actually made fake retching noises when I went on too long extolling Laurent's virtues.

"Sorry," she said, not looking a bit of it. "It's just that you've been on *one* date with him."

I rolled my eyes. "It's not bad to be excited about a new date."

Yasmine smiled. "I've never met anyone who's been on so many terrible dates yet remains such a hopeless romantic. You're right. Just promise me that when he starts acting like a jerk—*if* he starts acting like a jerk," she quickly amended when I shot her a look, "You dump him. Remember that guy you dated who complained nonstop about you baking late at night?"

"I do, and I did dump him," I reminded Yasmine. "He certainly didn't deserve my midnight croissants."

Yasmine still looked serious. "Just tell him that if he ever makes my happiest friend cry, I'll scratch the hell out of every one of his nonstick pans."

I grinned. "I'm sure that'll have Laurent shaking in his patent leather shoes."

It had been unseasonably cold all week, and the skies opened just as the dinner shift began. Rain came down in buckets.

"The weather is terrible," a woman at my first table said. Her tone suggested I had purposely conspired with the weather gods to ruin her day.

"Paris certainly likes to keep us on our toes!" I said, pouring them water. "We have vin chaud on the menu if you'd like something to warm you up."

"We should get a discount because of the weather," her partner said. I simply smiled at that.

When I brought their first course—a gorgeous citrus salad with fresh crab—they appraised it with pursed lips.

"It's not very much food," the woman said.

"This first course is an apéritif," I explained. "Your meal includes seven courses, and nearly all our diners feel they've had a satisfactory amount of food by the end of it."

"It seems very basic for the price we're paying," the man told me. Despite Luc requesting all diners to leave their umbrellas in the rack up front, this man had insisted on bringing his with him. He'd even dragged a chair over to lay the umbrella on it.

For a moment I was distracted, watching the chair's fabric saturate with water. Once they left, I'd have to take the chair to the staff room and blast it with a hair dryer.

"I very much hope you enjoy the salad," I told them, smiling wide. "I'll return when you've finished to explain the next course."

The rest of the meal was just the same: they were unimpressed by the food, they complained that their sodas didn't have enough ice, they wanted to know when it would stop raining.

I should know by now that some people are just intent on being miserable, but it still bothered me to have unsatisfied guests. I kept hoping that, if I just presented this new course, just fixed this new problem they had, then they'd become happy and have a good experience after all.

But that didn't happen, and as I brought out the final course, the woman actually rolled her eyes, as though nothing could offend her more than the two cups of chocolate mousse I was now bearing toward them.

Despite their unhappiness, the couple had stayed for quite a while (and eaten every bite of their meal). It was late by the time they left, and I wasn't expecting any new diners. But there was an elderly couple at the front. I heard them explaining to Luc that they'd had a terrible time getting a taxi and were late for their reservation, but was there any way they could still have dinner?

Luc beckoned me over. "Can you take the Iliescus?" he asked in a low voice. "They were going to be Colette's, but I sent her home because all her other tables left."

"Of course." I smiled at the couple. "Welcome to Le Jules Verne."

The restaurant was nearly empty by now, so I led them to one of our best tables, right next to the floor-to-ceiling windows. It was true that the rain obscured most of the view, but, at that moment, the Eiffel Tower lit up. The Iliescus were momentarily mesmerized by the twinkling, golden lights. I caught myself watching the light show, too. It was still captivating, even after all these years.

Paul, who'd been on his way out the door, hurriedly came back, shrugged out of his jacket, and put his suit coat back on. He patiently explained the wine list to them. When I brought out their first course, their faces lit up.

After explaining the dish, I chatted with them for a few minutes. They were Elena and Vasile Iliescu, they told me, in accented but fluid English, on holiday from Bucharest. It was their first time in Paris. From the way they spoke, I sensed it would likely be the only time, and that this was a trip they'd dreamed of for years, maybe decades, planning out every detail. And after it was over, they'd reminisce about it for the rest of their lives.

They were dressed beautifully, in the way their generation always did. The dress code at Le Jules Verne was only smart casual, basically no t-shirts, shorts, or sneakers, and we had a difficult enough time enforcing that. But Monsieur Iliescu was wearing a dark gray suit, and his wife was resplendent in a red and black dress, her makeup carefully done, and a sparkling brooch holding back her hair.

I wanted every person who eats at Le Jules Verne to leave happy, but for people like this—for whom the meal meant so much—I get a sort of desperation to have the experience surpass even what they'd imagined.

Fortunately, the Iliescus were delighted with everything. Madame Iliescu admitted she didn't eat seafood much, but when she tasted the crab salad, she chewed for a moment, then her eyes went big.

"Oh! That's good salad!" she declared, and my heart leapt.

I talked to them more between courses, asking them about Bucharest and telling them about a trip to Transylvania I'd taken with a college friend years ago.

They told me about their grandchildren and the rural village they'd grown up in. This was only the first night of their stay in Paris, and Monsieur Iliescu pulled out a creased piece of paper with their itinerary carefully written out to see if it met my approval. I gave a few suggestions here and there, but, on the whole, I told them they'd planned a wonderful trip for themselves.

When they finished their meal, they asked me to take a photo of them, then a photo of the three of us, which Yasmine stepped in to take. Afterwards, Madame Iliescu took my hands between hers.

"Thank you for this evening," she said fervently, as though I'd done much more than just be a decent server for a single meal. As I watched them leave, all the annoyances from earlier in the day faded away.

"Every now and then it's worth it, isn't it?" Yasmine mused beside me. I could only nod.

After work, I walked home leisurely. It had stopped raining, and all of Paris smelled clean and verdant.

When I got to my floor, I turned down the hallway and saw the outline of a small package next to my door. I was grinning before I even picked it up. I smelled through the wrapping that it was another quiche, this one with tarragon in it, and maybe goat cheese? There was a note as well.

Attempt 2. Eagerly awaiting all your thoughts -L

I ate the quiche before bed and didn't stop smiling until I fell asleep.

Chapter 14

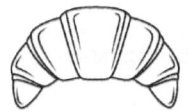

La Forêt was located in the 3rd arrondissement, on the tiny Rue des Barres, which had existed in Paris since medieval times and was still brimming with gargoyles and gothic roofs and uneven cobblestones.

I arrived early, but Laurent was already there. Through the restaurant's large windows, I saw him standing just inside. He was peering intently out a window, but in the wrong direction. This meant I was able to observe him without him noticing as I walked up to the restaurant.

He was standing a little stiffly, his briefcase resting against his feet. He was still dressed for work, but he'd taken his suit jacket off and rolled up the sleeves of his shirt. There was a little gel in his hair, as though he'd attempted to tame his curls, but whatever it was, it hadn't been enough. They flopped over his forehead like they always did. In one hand was a neatly folded newspaper.

As I got closer, I saw it was turned to the crossword puzzle. I couldn't make out his answers, but I imagined they were neatly written, and in ink, too. He was turned just away, so I only saw his profile, but that was enough for me to observe a single green and golden eye. A little thrill ran down my spine when I realized it was *me* he was looking for so intently.

I was nearly at the entrance when Laurent saw me. He broke into a lopsided grin and hurried to open the door. Again, we kissed on the cheek, and again I felt heat pulse through me when his cheek pressed mine. I was half-tempted to grab his face and kiss him right there.

Save it for dessert, I told myself as I followed our server to our table.

Laurent walked behind me, and as he did, he placed a gentle hand on the small of my back. I wasn't sure whether it was to protect me from being jostled or out of a simple desire to touch me, but, in either case, it set me tingling all over.

When we got to our table, Laurent smoothly stepped in front of our server to pull out my chair. I'd seen a thousand men attempt the same move at Le Jules Verne, but none of them had managed to do it with Laurent's finesse. Charmed, I smiled at him as I sat down.

"This place is lovely," I said.

The restaurant was small and paneled with dark wood, but the space still felt bright due to the large windows letting the light stream in. The ceiling was pressed metal, with a fleur de lis motif, and the walls were hung with watercolors of conifers.

"I hoped you'd like it. I've been here twice and had an excellent meal both times."

Laurent passed over a menu, pointing out his recommendations. I liked that he gave his opinion then left me to it. I'd had too many dinners where my date decided to order for me because he "just knew" what I'd like best.

When our server came by, we got moules-frites to start, and I ordered a brandy-based cocktail and the chicken braised in cider. The specialty of the restaurant was pork, and I looked at Laurent to see if he was dismayed that I was ordering chicken. But he only smiled.

"A smart choice."

Laurent ordered a glass of Bretagne cider and the cotriade, a seafood stew. Our drinks came, and we clinked glasses. In both my personal and professional lives, I was used to driving conversations, but Laurent beat me to it.

"How has your week been?" he asked.

I was about to give the usual platitudes, but he seemed genuinely interested—his eyes alight as he leaned forward, closer to me—so I gave the real answer. I told him about the new fall menu at Le Jules Verne, how lovely serving the Iliescus had been, how I was sad that summer produce was thinning at the markets, and the cake ideas I was considering for Colette, whose birthday was next week.

Not a bit of it was revelatory, or even particularly interesting, but he kept his golden eyes on me the whole time. His gaze was so intense I warmed under it.

"And...and you? How have things been?" I asked, feeling slightly off-kilter.

"Nothing nearly as interesting. I finally finished unpacking. Other than that, mostly working."

"How's work? You work in an office now?"

"Yes. For a shipping company. It's not particularly enjoyable." He spoke lightly, but I saw from the tightness in his face that there was some deep unhappiness there.

"Right. Of course," I said, flailing for a new conversation topic. "Where were you living before you moved into the building?"

Laurent gave a small smile, a real one this time. "Aix-en-Provence, where I'm from. Back when I was being an insufferable boor, I believe you mentioned having been there?"

"Several times. I love it there. Was it hard to leave?"

Laurent moved his fork half a centimeter so that it was perfectly parallel with the rest of his cutlery. "Not particularly. My girlfriend left me, so I needed someplace new to live anyway."

Ah, zero for two. I grimaced in embarrassment.

But, to my surprise, Laurent laughed. "You walked right into that one. Don't worry. We were a poor match." His tone was relaxed, but I noticed he took a rather large gulp of water. "My parents and sister wanted me to stay in Aix, but it had too many difficult memories."

Yes, I understood that completely.

"I knew I wanted a change in scenery," Laurent continued. "Paris was the obvious choice."

I smiled. "It always is."

Laurent took a sip of cider, and I watched him as he closed his eyes, savoring the taste as a smile crept across his mouth. I found the corners of my own mouth turning up. A grump could never appreciate a drink the way Laurent did.

Laurent opened his eyes, still looking a little dreamy. "Beautiful," he declared, setting his glass squarely back in the center of his coaster. "What about you? Your accent isn't Parisian."

"I'm from Alsace. Colmar, specifically," I said, naming a town in northeastern France, close to Germany and Switzerland.

"Ah, Colmar," Laurent said, smiling the way French people usually did when I told them my hometown. I understood why. Colmar—with its cobblestone streets and overflowing flower boxes and medieval half-timbered houses—was easy to love.

"Colmar, Paris, and you mentioned living in Martinique. Have you lived anywhere else?"

I laughed. "A few other places. Do you want to hear all of them?"

"Of course."

I settled back in my chair. "Well, I was born in Austria, but my mother and I moved back to Colmar shortly after, and we lived there until I was about five. Then we moved to Brussels. That was nice because it was close enough to home that we could still visit a lot. We stayed there for two years, then moved to Martinique when my mother was offered a pastry chef role at a new hotel there. We were in Martinique for about a year and a half, then we moved to Washington DC for about three years while she was a pastry chef at the French Embassy. After that, we were in Madrid for about a year, then back to Colmar for a few years, then my mother moved to London after I finished secondary school."

"Is she still there now?" Laurent asked, smiling.

I ducked my head. I'd had years to practice, but I was still so bad at telling people.

"She died, actually," I said quietly, looking down at the table. "About five years ago. Well, closer to six now. She was in a car accident."

I chanced a glance at Laurent. He looked crestfallen. I knew I looked miserable too, because I've never been able to talk about my mom without being on the verge of tears. It had made countless dates uncomfortable, and I was sure he'd be joining the long line of men who made their excuses (with varying degrees of believability) and quickly exit rather than deal with the woman who's still cut up over her mom's death.

Nervously, I raised my eyes. Shockingly, Laurent wasn't glancing around for an exit or mumbling about an errand he had to run. He was looking right at me.

"That's both of us stepped in it this conversation," he said, a tiny sad smile pulling at the corners of his mouth. "I'm so sorry about your mom. When my sister got sick, I couldn't even consider the possibility of her not making it. It took my breath away."

"Thanks," I mumbled, dropping my gaze again. "It was very hard. My dad was never in the picture, so after my grandparents died, she was the only family I was close to."

"And she was a pastry chef?"

I smiled. "She was an amazing pastry chef."

Laurent smiled back, the smile that lit up his entire face. "You clearly got her talent. Have you ever considered becoming a professional?"

My mood, which had been slowly inching upward, plummeted again. I shrugged uncomfortably. "I tried once. It didn't work out."

I was worried Laurent would ask me to elaborate but, perhaps noticing my discomfort, he changed the subject.

"Was it difficult moving so much growing up?"

"Sometimes," I said, my shoulders relaxing. "Sometimes it felt like my mother dragged me to every corner of the world." I smiled faintly, remembering. "But she loved going to new places, starting fresh. I'm not quite the same way. I'm happy to be back in France, and to stay here. I still visit Colmar often as well. It's the one place that's ever really felt like home."

Laurent smiled. "That's wonderful to have a home you want to return to. I've always wanted to get away from Aix. My sister, on the other hand, loves it there. Noelle went to university less than an hour away, but she still came back every weekend because she missed home. She helped me move in when I came here, and I think even that made her a little homesick," he said, laughing. Laurent's face softened as he spoke of his sister.

Our mussels and fries arrived, and we paused to try them. They looked gorgeous, the fries golden brown and shining lightly with oil, with flecks of sea salt dotted across them. The mussels had been steamed in cider and Pernod and were swimming in a pool of sautéed shallots, garlic, and parsley. I fished one free of its shell and tipped it into my mouth. It tasted perfectly of the sea, but the sea enhanced, the sea melded with aromatics and layers of flavor.

I remained still a few seconds after swallowing it, savoring the moment.

"They're wonderful," I told Laurent, and his face lit up.

"I was worried about choosing a place you wouldn't like," Laurent said, and his concern for my happiness, even though we barely knew each other, was so sweet it was almost painful.

By the time we'd finished the moules frites, I was on my second drink, having switched to the cider Laurent was enjoying. It gave me the courage to ask the question I'd been wondering about since learning of his past as a chef.

"At the gala meeting, Fatima mentioned the restaurant you owned."

Laurent froze, his drink halfway to his lips, then gave a reluctant nod. I took it as permission to continue.

"I'd love to hear about it."

Laurent took a slow sip of his cider, then put his glass down with a sigh. He looked tired all of a sudden, but when he met my eyes, he smiled.

"It was called Les Champs D'Or," he said, and I heard in his voice how much he had loved it.

"After secondary school, I went to culinary school then worked around France and Italy. The biggest, most important dream I had for myself was to open my own restaurant. I had planned on opening a restaurant in Tuscany or maybe Lyon, but when some friends of my parents offered me a head chef position with partial ownership of a new restaurant in Aix, I jumped at the chance. I had to clean out my savings to afford even just the partial ownership."

"But it was worth it," I said, not really needing to hear the answer. His feelings were clear on his face.

"More than anything I've ever done," Laurent said softly. "When Les Champs D'Or opened, it felt like I'd finally found my purpose. It made all the work, and stress, and long hours worth it. My life shifted from a jumble of jobs and fraught decisions to a path leading me right to where I needed to be."

As Laurent spoke, the tension in his shoulders eased and the lines around his eyes and mouth smoothed. He stopped fidgeting with his utensils, trying to get them perfectly parallel to one another. Instead, he let his hands drop into his lap.

Looking at him, his eyes alive with passion, I realized that the Laurent I had seen—tired and demoralized from work—was only a fraction of who he really was. Who he became when he was a chef.

"Why did it close?"

The light in Laurent's eyes went dark. "A lot of reasons. Mostly it was because I was foolish," he said, with a finality that encouraged a change in subject. I could certainly understand not wanting to discuss past career failures.

Moments later, our main courses arrived. My chicken looked glorious, the skin golden-brown and crackly, resting on a bed of sautéed leeks and apples. The intermingled scents of cider, poultry, butter, and thyme wafted over me. I cut off a piece of dark meat, and it was so tender it practically slid off the bone. I speared a sliver of apple, too, and put it in my mouth. As I chewed, I found myself smiling. It was all done so perfectly. I looked up to see Laurent watching me.

"It's wonderful," I said fervently. "This is the best chicken I've had in ages. How is the cotriade?"

Laurent's meal looked just as delicious as mine. The stew's broth was rich and golden with chunks of fish, onions, potatoes, and leeks bobbing around in it.

"Excellent," Laurent said. "They included eel, which adds a depth of flavor that I like. I would have added just a splash more of vinegar though," he added with a wink.

"Oh, I know that chef type," I said, happy to talk about something that didn't dredge up painful memories. "Your kind always finds a way for a dish to be improved. Chef La Croix is exactly the same."

"You know, he has quite a reputation in the cooking world. Beyond his cooking prowess, I mean. Is he really a terrifying old monster?"

I laughed again. "Not really, although I think he enjoys having that reputation. He probably makes up most of the rumors himself. I've realized recently that he's actually a softie," I added impishly.

"Jean-Baptiste La Croix? I'll believe that when I see it," Laurent said, laughing now, too. "How are your ideas coming along for the gala?"

"I have some. They may not be that good, though," I said, losing confidence.

Laurent frowned. "And why wouldn't they be?"

"I mean, I'm just a home baker," I said, remembering Sabine's unimpressed expression as she read over my credentials. "I don't know nearly as much as a professional pastry chef."

"I wouldn't be so certain. Personally, I'd be thrilled to have that tarte tatin you made served in any restaurant I was running."

I'd been looking at my hands, but now I glanced at Laurent, looking so earnestly at me. A heady emotion came over me–a mixture of happiness and the urge to cry.

"Thank you. That's very nice of you to say," I told him, once I was sure my voice wouldn't wobble.

It started to rain, so we decided to nix gelato and split a slice of cherry clafoutis for dessert instead. Laurent pulled his chair around to my side of the table so our elbows were nearly touching. Having him so close to me—I could see a sprinkling of freckles across his nose I'd never noticed—made me giddy.

"How appetizing," Laurent said, eyes locked on mine. "Ladies first."

I thought he'd wait for me to cut off a piece, but instead he cut into the clafoutis himself. Plump cherries were nestled in the creamy base, their juices spilling into the pale custard and turning it pink. A few drops dripped off the piece he'd speared with his fork.

"Open wide." My whole body tingled at the sound of his voice.

Obeying, I parted my lips; Laurent slipped the forkful into my mouth. It was still warm. The flavor of tart cherries and sweet custard exploded in my mouth. I chewed slowly, my eyes never leaving Laurent's. After I'd swallowed, I insisted that he try the clafoutis himself, but he fed most of it to me, bite by bite. I was nearly panting by the time the plate was cleared.

Outside, rain was coming down heavily, so Laurent hailed a taxi. As soon as we were seated inside, he took my hand. We were quiet on the ride back. All my thoughts were focused on every part of my body that touched Laurent's. I ran the pads of my fingers over the scars and burns his hands had accumulated from years of working in kitchens.

When we arrived at our building, we had to break apart to leave the car, but after Laurent paid, he opened my door and helped me onto the sidewalk. It was still raining, and I watched a raindrop slide down the bridge of his nose and drip to the ground.

"Should we go insi—"

Laurent's lips were suddenly on mine, and everything else fell away.

His mouth was warm and eager, and he tasted slightly of cherries. His arms came around my back to grip me firmly. I stepped closer so that our bodies pressed together: chest to chest, hip to hip, thighs to thighs. We were getting soaked to the skin, but I was only dimly aware of the rain. A blazing heat ran through me. I felt as warm as if I was sitting next to a fire.

The top button of Laurent's shirt had come undone, exposing a triangle of smooth, wet skin at his throat. One of Laurent's hands came up to my hair, and he stroked it gently, then moved to the base of my neck. He ran his fingers gently across the tender skin there. I gasped a little, and Laurent pressed his mouth more firmly to mine.

My thin linen dress was plastered to my skin, and Laurent's clothes weren't much better. We were so soaked it felt as though there was nothing between us.

Laurent cupped my face, and his fingers traced the line of my jaw as the rain fell around us. Several raindrops slid into my mouth, and their coolness was a startling contrast to Laurent's hot, probing warmth.

When I ran out of breath, I pulled away reluctantly, gulping air. Laurent was staring unashamedly at my chest. I realized that my bra showed clearly through my soaked dress. At least I'd worn one of my expensive bras, all lace and silk. My nipples stood out clearly under the thin fabric.

Through Laurent's wet shirt, I took in every hard line of his chest. I'd never seen him so mussed. His hair, little wet squiggles now, dripped onto his forehead. His tie was thrown over one shoulder, and his shirt clung tightly to his abs. I looked again at his bare throat, glistening in the rain, and wondered hotly what the rest of him looked like under all those wet clothes. Then he pulled me back in, and every thought fled my mind as our mouths met hungrily.

Just then Laurent's phone buzzed. Our thighs were still pressed tightly together, and I felt its vibration through my clothes.

With a groan, Laurent pulled back and fished his phone out of his pocket. As he read the text message, his shoulders slumped.

"Work. Of course. They always need something." He looked at me and attempted a smile. "I'm sorry, Margot. They're going to keep bothering me until I do this."

Disappointment coursed through me, but Laurent's sadness bothered me more. I hated to see him so upset.

"Don't worry. Your work's just keeping us respectable. I was close to pulling your clothes off in the street."

Laurent smiled, and some of the sadness lifted from his face.

"I guess we should go inside," he said.

We held hands up the stairs and to my apartment door. There Laurent kissed me again, sweetly and softly.

"You know," he said, his face still close to mine. "I forgot to ask what you thought of my second attempt at the quiche."

Oh no.

I squeezed my eyes shut. Even though this gorgeous man had me trembling all over, I still couldn't lie.

I swallowed hard. When I spoke, my voice was barely above a whisper. "The crust still tasted store-bought."

Silence. I opened my eyes a sliver. Laurent was staring at me, nonplussed. I could only imagine what he thought of me, a woman he'd just wined and dined, then nearly ravished in the street, who couldn't even bother to tell a white lie about his baking skills.

Laurent's mouth opened, and I thought he'd make a sharp retort. But then he began to laugh.

That got me going, and we fell against each other in a fit of hysteria. I might have even started crying, but we were both so soaking wet I really had no idea.

Through my laughter, I dimly heard footsteps approaching, but it wasn't until I heard Madame Blanchet's voice that I jerked up and tried to get a hold of myself.

"Margot? Laurent? Are you alright?" she asked, her tone as unruffled as always.

"Yes, Madame Blanchet," I assured her, hiccupping a little. I didn't dare look at Laurent. I was barely holding my laughter back as it was.

"Well, that's good. I was afraid someone was doing amphetamines in the hallway." Madame Blanchet looked my rain-drenched self up and down. "I'm glad you chose a black brassiere, Margot. Too many young people are wearing this newfangled colorful lingerie. It's tasteless."

"Yes, thank you, enjoy your evening, Madame Blanchet!" Laurent said as I crossed my arms over my chest and died a thousand deaths.

After Madame Blanchet had retreated back down the stairs, I let out a strangled giggle.

"She's going to tell all her friends about us."

Laurent kissed me again. "I relish the thought."

"But, how does she know what young people are wearing for lingerie?"

"Some questions are better left unanswered, ma chérie."

Laurent kissed me a final time. "Now I really have to return this call. Thank you for understanding. Let me know when your next day off is, and I'll start thinking of plans. Until then, I need to keep working on that quiche." He smirked, his eyes soft and bright.

Inside my apartment, I took a hot shower and scoured my body with my eucalyptus body scrub until I was pink and shining. I ran cocoa butter all over my skin, then made myself a cup of tea. Sitting in the windowsill, I sipped my tea slowly, replaying the entire date in my mind.

Despite the cozy warmth of my apartment, I shivered. It was almost a little frightening to be this into someone. For all the dating I've done, I didn't remember ever before having this overwhelming passion, of feeling so full of emotions they seemed close to spilling over.

I huddled closer against the window, and my movement knocked a small bundle of papers to the ground. I bent to see what they were. Of course. It was an application for pastry school, halfway finished. I tossed it back on the ground. Nothing was going to ruin the rest of this evening.

Chapter 15

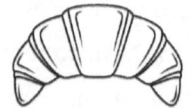

"Well, I'm glad you at least kissed," Yasmine said as she struggled with her dough. "I wish you two had been able to seal the deal, though."

I stood in Yasmine's kitchen, trying to follow the recipe her mother had written out for Makroud el Louse cookies. There was another gala meeting in a few hours, and I was trying my hand at some North African desserts as I refined menu ideas.

"I'm so happy for you, Margot," Yasmine's mother said, coming in to appraise our progress. "Maybe this will be the relationship that sticks."

"Mom, *oh my god,*" Yasmine said, switching briefly to English. "You don't need to remind her of all the losers she's dated."

I reached for the orange blossom water. "Don't worry, Madame Saidi. I understood what you meant." And there was certainly a part of me that hoped, too, that this relationship with Laurent would be more than a fling.

"Don't mind her," Yasmine said to me. "She's just thrilled that somebody she knows is in a relationship."

"It certainly isn't you," Madame Saidi said pointedly to her daughter.

"I tried that once, and it went disastrously, remember?" Yasmine said, meeting her mother's gaze without blinking.

I busied myself with rolling out my dough. Yasmine had gotten married—and divorced—before I'd met her. As she'd described it, she'd been young, caught up in a new relationship, and heavily pressured by her parents—especially her father—to get married quickly.

"It was a nightmare from start to finish," Yasmine had said the first time she'd recounted her marriage. "I can't even describe what it feels like, Margot, to dread going home because the person you share that home with is hellbent on making your life miserable. I started feeling nauseous every time I walked through the front door. I never want that for you."

Yasmine's father had vehemently opposed his daughter getting a divorce, but Madame Saidi had gone to bat for her daughter, and Yasmine and her mother make a formidable pair. Eventually, the divorce went through, and, by the time I met her, Yasmine had sworn off any sort of serious dating.

Right now she was grinning at her mother. "Why should I get into a relationship when I do so well on Tinder? Margot, did I tell you about the guy I hooked up with on Sunday? An Athenian descended directly from the Greek gods themselves, I swear. And the body oil he had..."

Yasmine winked. "Well, let's just say he had a dozen scents and we gave them each a test drive."

I laughed. Yasmine was goading her mother, but I knew Yasmine's dating habits still caused tension between her and her parents. Madame Saidi just wanted to see her daughter happy, but Yasmine's father was much more traditional. He made it clear he detested Yasmine's proclivity for casual dating and thought it lessened any chance she had for another marriage. ("That's just an added bonus," Yasmine always said.)

"Why do yours look so much better?" Yasmine complained, looking between our cookies. While my dough was smooth and shiny, hers was lumpy, and there were streaks of sugar where it hadn't been mixed completely.

"Because you never cook," her mother said. "I tried and tried, but you only wanted to go dancing or waste your life lounging in cafés." Yasmine rolled her eyes, then mother and daughter smiled fondly at each other.

My chest tightened, and I turned my attention back to the cookies.

When they came out of the oven, Madame Saidi tasted one of mine and declared it excellent. "You're so talented, Margot. The gala is lucky to have your skills." She took the four best cookies and wrapped them in a checkered cloth. "Now go bring these to your boyfriend."

I blushed to hear Laurent referred to as my boyfriend, although it was true. I'd dated a few American men and seen plenty of American movies, and dating there always seemed so fraught. Just endless discussions of when to become exclusive, what officially counted as "dating," when to give each other labels...

In France, it was much simpler. If you went on a date, kissed, and wanted to keep seeing each other, then you were in a relationship. Easy as that. So I *would* go bring these cookies to my boyfriend.

"Margot," Yasmine said as soon as we'd stepped out of her apartment. "Don't listen to my mom when it comes to relationships. Seriously, listen to her advice on literally anything else, but not relationships."

I frowned. "What do you mean?"

"Just that she wants everyone to be in a relationship. She wants everyone to get married. And I'm not opposed to that," Yasmine said, her eyes wide and animated. "It's just...It's just that I know how much you sometimes idolize marriages. But they're not always wonderful. They don't always make a relationship wonderful."

I rolled my eyes. "Of course they don't *always*. But sometimes they do. My mother always said her own parents never really treated each other well until they got married when she was young."

I glanced at Yasmine. She looked worried and unhappy. "I know your mother said that," she said finally. "You've told me that a lot."

Color rose in my cheeks. So what if I did? People retold family stories all the time. But I knew what Yasmine was carefully not saying: that I'd also told her many times about my mother's bitterness over my father never marrying her. My mother had been convinced that if they'd been married when she'd gotten pregnant, my father would have devoted himself to his wife and child, instead of walking out of our lives without a glance back.

"If he had *chosen* me, Margot, things would have been different," my mother had said over and over again.

Yasmine was still frowning at me. "Margot, every time there's another proposal at the restaurant, I see you going starry-eyed. I don't want you to get carried away with Laurent."

I rolled my eyes, trying to lighten the mood. "Yasmine, I've been on like two dates with Laurent. I've barely even started sewing my wedding trousseau. You can like someone without getting carried away."

"I know," Yasmine said, her face softening. "Just don't try to force a relationship because you have some end goal. I learned that the hard way."

I was annoyed at Yasmine's implication that I was losing my head over Laurent, but when I looked at my friend, I saw her face pinched with concern. I knew she only wanted to save me from the unhappiness she'd experienced.

I smiled. "I know I can trust you to always keep my head on straight. Now let's get to the meeting. You know how it kills me to be late."

This gala meeting was to show us the kitchens we'd be using for the event. When I arrived, Laurent was already there. Naturally, he was scrubbing down the tables.

I walked up and watched as he obliterated whatever miniscule smudge had caught his ire.

"I'm glad you're spending time doing what you love."

Laurent kept his eyes on the table, but I saw him smirk. "We curmudgeons need to find happiness where we can. This is a nice break from shouting at people on scooters and complaining about tourists." He turned to me. "And I can see you've ramped the sunshine up to eleven. As usual."

I grinned even wider. "I made you Algerian cookies."

Laurent took the little bundle in his hands, placed it on the shining countertop, then kissed me thoroughly. When we broke apart, I noticed several people had filed into the room.

Laurent blushed, but I had no regrets. Yasmine hadn't said anything against indulging in too much kissing.

"Good afternoon!" Fatima sang out as she came into the room, several sous chefs and an irritated-looking Sabine trailing in her wake. "Welcome to the kitchens you'll be using for the gala. I want you all to get acquainted with them early on so that you can develop your menus with their equipment and limitations in mind. Let me walk you through the highlights, then I'll let you explore on your own."

The kitchens, like the building itself, were worn but functional. They didn't have Le Jules Verne's gleaming row of stovetops or massive walk-in refrigerators, but they were certainly a step up from my tiny, rusted kitchen.

"Margot, there's the area that'll be yours," Fatima said, pointing me to one end of the room. I walked over and appraised the two ovens, a range with four burners, and ample counterspace. Pulling open the cabinets, I saw they were full of equipment like stand mixers and baking sheets.

"What do you think?" Laurent asked, sidling up alongside me.

"It has everything I need."

Laurent rolled his eyes teasingly. "Of course it does."

"And what does the resident grouch think of the kitchens?"

Laurent grinned. "I'll make it work."

"See, there's a tiny optimist inside you begging to be let out. One day, you're going to catch yourself humming your favorite song while you cook, and eventually you'll move up to greeting strangers on the street."

Laurent shuddered.

"Monsieur Roche, how is everything?" Fatima asked, appearing beside us.

"It fits my needs," Laurent said diplomatically, "But I was wondering where the freezers were."

"Right next door. I'll show you," Fatima said.

As she and Laurent left, I turned back to the cabinets to take a thorough inventory of what they contained. Maybe some random piece of equipment would provide the inspiration to help me finalize my menu. I was pulling out baking sheets when someone spoke behind me.

"How is everything coming along?"

I turned to see Sabine watching me.

"Oh. Very well, thank you. It's actually better than I was expecting."

She was standing so close we were nearly nose-to-nose. I could smell her Coco Mademoiselle perfume. She still looked irritated at whatever had been bothering her when she walked in.

"It must be overwhelming for you to try to manage all the baking on your own," she said.

I shrugged, choosing to ignore whatever passive aggressive message she was hoping to relay. "I'm looking at it as a challenge."

"What do you have for the menu?"

"I haven't finalized it yet, but one of the ideas I had was to make croissants with a baklava filling. You know, honey, nuts, maybe pieces of dried fruit."

I was actually extremely excited about this idea. It seemed like the perfect combination of two iconic recipes.

But Sabine was shaking her head. "I don't think so," she said, lips pursed. "It's too obvious."

"Too obvious?"

What was this, a magic show? Was there supposed to be some sort of surprise reveal?

"Yes." Sabine nodded. "Much too basic. If you were a professional, you'd understand what I meant."

It was like she knew just how much I was struggling to feel confident. The one idea I was really happy with, she went and poked a hole in.

Internally, I was a mess of anxiety, but I chose to only shrug and smile, knowing it'd rankle her. "I've served a lot of people, and what I've found is people generally love to see a dish they're expecting. It's comforting, and it makes them feel smart for having predicted it'd be there. In any case, we can ask Fatima what she thinks."

Sabine was looking more irritated than ever. I'd have to tell Laurent that he was no longer the resident crank. This woman had run off with the prize.

"What else have you come up with?" she asked, a disdainful eyebrow raised.

I hesitated to make sure my voice wouldn't come out shaky. I certainly wasn't going to let this woman see she had me flustered. "I have an idea to make mille feuilles with a Middle Eastern filling—there are a lot of options there. Also, my mother had her own recipe for palmiers. Every time she baked them, people loved—"

"No."

Sabine spoke quietly, but the distaste in her voice was so strong I took an involuntary step back and bumped into the countertop.

"Sorry?"

"No, you're not baking palmiers for my gala," Sabine said, irritation clear in her voice now. "This is a high-level, professional event, not your family Christmas party. Find something more sophisticated. I'm not sure why Fatima ever pushed for you to take this role. You're clearly out of your depth."

The level of her anger disturbed me. This could not just be about the dessert menu for a charity event. "It's weeks before we need to have the menus set," I said, carefully keeping my voice steady. "If you don't like any of the ideas I have, that's fine, but it's far too early to be calling me a bad choice."

Sabine seemed about to say something more, but, at that moment, Fatima and Laurent came back into the room, animatedly discussing refrigeration techniques. With a final glance at me, Sabine turned on her heel and stalked out of the room.

Laurent hurried over, frowning. "Is everything alright?"

I considered telling him about the interaction, but decided it wasn't worth it. Sabine's doubts in my abilities were too close to my own, and voicing them would only make me feel worse. Instead, I smiled. "Absolutely. Are you ready to leave? I'm starving."

After a week of steady rain, the sun had returned in full force. Laurent and I had just enough time for a picnic lunch before I headed off to work the dinner shift.

We walked to Parc Monceau, with its soaring archways and worn, regal grandeur. Once there, Laurent spent roughly five thousand hours walking up and down the grass until he found the right spot to have our picnic.

We settled onto the large blanket Laurent spread out, our shoulders touching and our heads tipped back so that the sun shone on our faces.

Laurent had several of his shirt buttons opened, and I spied a peek of blond chest hair. It seemed like such an intimate part of his body that I almost felt as though I was seeing him in his underwear.

That'll be next, I hoped.

"These cookies you made are sublime," Laurent said, taking a bite of one. "I can taste the orange water. They remind me of the final course I had at a Moroccan restaurant in London. It was one of the best meals I'd ever had." He lay back in the grass and closed his eyes. The sun highlighted the gold strands in his hair. "You've been everywhere; what's your favorite meal you've eaten?"

I laughed. "Do you want the real answer, or the answer I give to keep people happy?"

Laurent opened his eyes and smiled lazily. "The real answer, always, but now you've made me curious so I want the fake answer, too."

"Well, the fake answer is the best meal I've ever eaten was at *La Perle d'Ivoire* in Lyon.

"Oh yes," Laurent said, sitting up in his excitement. "An excellent choice. I ate there a few years back. The quenelles were on another level. A top five lifetime meal for me, for sure."

I nodded. "Yes, the meal was perfect. But, for me, the *best* meal I've ever had means the meal I enjoyed the most, and that depends on more than just the food, you know? The circumstances matter, too."

"I agree," Laurent said slowly. "But you've suddenly terrified me." He laughed. "Let's hear it. I can take it."

"Well..." The memory still made me smile. "I was seventeen or so. It was summer, and I was visiting a friend in Marseille. It was burning hot, and we'd spent all day at the beach. We lost track of time, and by the time we got back to town, we were half-starved and dying of thirst. We stopped at the first place that seemed like it could remotely have food."

I paused, unsure of how much this would pain Laurent. "It was a petrol station."

His eyes went wide. "Margot Delcour, do not tell me—"

"It was," I said, plowing through. "I bought a bag of vinegar chips and an orange Fanta, and nothing in my life has ever tasted as wonderful as that meal."

I was half-laughing, but I hadn't looked away from Laurent. The French do not mess around with their fine dining. I've had dates walk out of the restaurant after I'd told that story.

Laurent had dropped his head into his hands. His shoulders shook, and I was worried that I'd hurt this man so much with my love of crappy food that I'd actually brought him to tears. But then a giggle escaped him, and when he raised his head, I saw that he was laughing so hard he could barely breathe.

"Oh, that's perfect," Laurent said, gasping for breath. "I love it. And it makes me want an orange Fanta. Have you told La Croix that story?"

"Of course not. I'm still alive, aren't I? It's my life's goal that my boss never find out about my love of fast food."

"What's your favorite fast food meal?"

"A quesarito from Taco Bell with extra nacho cheese sauce."

Laurent's brow furrowed. "The most troubling part about that statement is that you did not need a single second to come up with that answer."

I shrugged. "I know what I like."

"Yes, and apparently that's seven times the daily recommended sodium intake and a healthy risk of salmonella." He grinned. "You're absolutely right. You should take that information to the grave."

Still laughing, Laurent uncorked the wine, and I began spreading out our food.

"How's your menu for the gala coming along?" I asked.

Laurent pulled out his notebook and flipped it to a page that was uncharacteristically messy. It was full of cramped margin notes and penciled-out lines.

"I think I'm finally making some progress. Now that I have all my cooking equipment unpacked, I can actually start trying out some of my ideas. I've been writing up a recipe for coq au vin marinated in harissa that I'm going to have you try once I do an initial test run."

"That sounds delicious," I said, looking at his notes for recipes like kebbeh stuffed with a pâté filling and shakshuka ratatouille.

I hesitated, then decided to plow forward with my question. "Do you think if I made croissants with a baklava filling, that'd be too obvious?"

"Too obvious?" Laurent said blankly. "What does that even mean?"

"I don't know," I said, tugging at a hangnail. "I thought it was a good idea, but then it seemed like maybe it was too basic, and I know I don't have professional knowledge to fall back on—"

"Hey." Laurent spoke softly, but his eyes were locked on mine. "I don't want to hear you doubting yourself. You're an outstanding baker, and you don't need any certificate to prove it."

His confidence made me blush. Maybe I could actually pull this off. In any case, I should be focusing more on Laurent's opinion than Sabine's. I tucked my head against his shoulder, and he pulled me close.

"I'm nervous about the gala myself," Laurent admitted. "I haven't cooked in any sort of professional capacity for well over a year. This is my opportunity to see if I still have what it takes." He smiled at me. "We'll survive it together."

I leaned back on the grass so that I had a clear view of the sky. "Does your family cook a lot?"

Laurent arranged himself next to me. "My mother's parents managed a brasserie for decades, until they retired. My mother and her siblings worked there when she was young. They all made sure I caught the cooking bug."

I smiled. "That's lovely. I was always envious of people with close families."

"You say that, but you've never experienced Christmas dinner with my family. It's absolute mayhem," Laurent said, but he was grinning. "Now, tell me what you're thinking of for your gala menu, and I'll tell you how brilliant it is."

I looked at Laurent sprawled out on the blanket, long strands of grass caught up in his hair. We'd been sharing a bottle of Pinot Noir, and the wine had turned his lips a dark red, so that they looked even more sensual than usual. He must have gotten some sun recently as well, because his nose was slightly burnt.

Yasmine's warning was in the back of my mind, but I barely paid it attention. Whenever I spent time with this grouchy, cat-loving, neatness-obsessed chef I always came away happier. We barely knew each other, but I already could feel myself on the brink of falling for him.

I grinned, and Laurent pulled me in for a kiss. (That was one of the many wonderful things about Paris. No one cared if you were affectionate in public. Hell, chances are they're probably making out themselves.)

As Laurent cupped my face and our breaths intermingled, I felt such a surge of happiness and confidence that I was certain I could conquer any problem set before me.

I should learn how to bottle that feeling. I knew I'd be needing it again, sooner or later.

Chapter 16

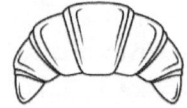

The next day, I heard a soft knock as I was drinking my morning tea. When I opened the door, I found a familiar-looking package resting on the ground.

Attempt 3 was all the attached note said.

I hurriedly brought it inside and unwrapped the paper to reveal a slice of perfectly golden quiche. It had caramelized onions and—I sniffed—maybe Gruyère? Whatever it was, it smelled beautiful. I flipped it over. The crust was nicely browned, but Laurent's always were. The proof would be in the tasting.

The first bite I didn't get enough crust, so it got lost in the flavor of the quiche (which was superb). For the next bite, I cut away some of the crust to taste it on its own. I chewed it slowly.

Oh. Damn.

Instead of the shoe-leather-inspired crusts of Laurent's first two quiches, this was shockingly close to perfection. It was crisp. It was buttery. It was flaky. It was flavorful.

Laurent had added thyme to the dough, which I'd always thought too fussy a step, but here it worked, adding another layer of flavor to the quiche, something green and fresh to cut through the heaviness of the eggs and cheese and onions.

I savored every last buttery crumb before getting my phone.

You've finally listened to my advice, I texted, adding a winking face. *Don't let work drag you down.*

Laurent wasn't the only one working long hours lately. Le Jules Verne had been especially harried this week. The Prime Minister of Spain and her boyfriend would be dining at Le Jules Verne tomorrow. Not only that, her boyfriend was planning to propose at dinner.

We weren't unused to VIPs at work, but they normally didn't require so much security and preparation. As the server with the best Spanish skills, I'd be waiting on them. I'd served famous people before, and it didn't particularly faze me. But I certainly wanted to do a good job with Prime Minister Abascal and her soon-to-be fiancé.

When I got into work that afternoon, Chef La Croix was near the point of apoplexy.

"WHAT IS IT THIS TIME?" he roared, sending everyone in the kitchen scrambling. "These people ask for changes to the menu as though I am a lowly restaurant that serves fast food. Even at McDonald's they would be offended by this."

"What's the matter?" I whispered to Yasmine.

"The Prime Minister's boyfriend has a somewhat...limited diet," she said in a low tone, looking out to make sure Chef La Croix wasn't barreling our way.

"He's asking for all sorts of modifications to the menu, and he wants the final course changed entirely. Said he and the Prime Minister had wine and cheese on their first date, so that's what he wants to end the meal with. Chef refused, but the owners told them he had to make the changes."

"A complete change to the final course?" I repeated, watching Chef La Croix rage around the kitchen. "He's taking it better than I expected."

"I know," Yasmine agreed. "He only swore in two languages during the phone call, when you know he usually swears in three when he's really angry. Luc mentioned meditation classes to him last month."

Yasmine paused as Chef La Croix bellowed for a new cutting board. Three were immediately thrust at him.

"I thought Chef was going to skewer Luc at the time, but maybe he took the suggestion to heart."

Le Jules Verne could make changes for dietary reasons if given enough lead time, but to change an entire course based just on habit was an affront to Le Jules Verne and to Chef La Croix.

Diners tried to do this occasionally ("Oh I love macarons; do you think I could have some of those for dessert instead?"). We always explained that it wasn't possible, and it bothered me that we were being forced to go along with these changes now, just because of the guest's political rank.

"He's making other demands, too," Yasmine continued. "They want to be in Le Comptoir now," she said, naming Le Jules Verne's private dining area for small groups.

"And they want the material of the napkins changed. Apparently, synthetic fibers irritate Señor Costa's skin. He wants the napkins to be only pure cotton or linen."

I glanced at Chef La Croix. His jaw appeared permanently clenched, but he was no longer shouting.

I looked at Yasmine. "I need to get the name of his meditation guru."

"I'm so glad I'm not the one serving them. Oh, these look delicious," Yasmine said as one of the souf chefs handed us each a chocolate mousse.

"I think I'll be OK," I said, taking a bite of mousse. It was creamy and velvety, the bittersweet taste of dark chocolate offset by a drizzle of salted caramel that dripped down the edges of the ramekin.

"You always say things will be OK," Yasmine said with a grin. "How's Laurent?"

"Being worked to the bone. I've barely seen him this past week."

"Poor Margot," Yasmine said. "You finally find someone decent, and he's a workaholic, just like you."

I took another bite of mousse. "Don't worry about my troubles; we need to end your dating drought. Have you seen the photos of the Prime Minister's security team that were sent over? There's one who's just your type. You should flirt with him while I'm hustling out the courses. Here, look."

***

The next day I woke up early even though I wasn't working until the dinner shift. I was feeling my nerves and decided some baking would settle my mind.

A loaf of brioche–the buttery, airy bread with its cloudlike texture–would do nicely. I'd work out my anxious energy with all the kneading.

I was fist-deep in sticky dough when there was a soft but insistent knock at the door. I knew that knock. As expected, when I opened the door, I saw Madame Blanchet's diminutive form, Bijou squirming in her arms.

"Good morning, Madame," I said as I wiped dough from my hands with a towel.

"Margot, there is a towering man here for you," she said, stroking Bijou. "He looks like one of those mercenaries with the Foreign Legion."

"A mercenary?" I repeated blankly.

"He said his name was Jean-Baptiste." Bijou gave a little bark.

"Wait, Chef La Croix?"

What on earth was he doing here? How did he even know where I lived?

"Did he say anything else?" I asked.

"Only that it was urgent and nothing you could be doing with your life was more important than speaking to him," Madame Blanchet said calmly.

Baffled, I ran back into my apartment, scrubbed my hands under the faucet, then hurried down the stairs, dodging Madame Blanchet as I went.

Chef La Croix looming on my doorstep was one of the odder sights I've seen in my life. For one thing, I'd never seen him without his chef's coat, and certainly not in the jeans and striped sweater he was wearing now.

He was smoking a cigarette with one hand and using the other to smooth down his hair, which was blowing all over in the wind. On his face was a look of absolute murderous rage.

"Margot!" he barked as soon as I stepped out. "Another crisis."

I was still reeling from seeing my boss at my home, but I managed to nod.

"The Prime Minister's boyfriend now wants—*non*, he is demanding—a particular type of cheese served for the dessert course. Tetilla cheese. It's from his hometown in Galicia. You'd think he'd be able to eat enough there," Chef La Croix growled. "Even though this is France, and we are a French restaurant, I've been ordered to include it in the meal."

Chef La Croix took a final drag from his cigarette, then dropped it and stomped on it with such force I thought he might crack the pavement. He lit another cigarette and looked at me.

"I need to get to the restaurant and begin cooking, and your apartment is the only one on my way, so I'm giving this task to you. Before your shift, I need you to find tetilla cheese. It must be from Galicia. I'm told Señor Costa has a habit of voicing his thoughts on social media when places don't meet his standards."

I started to roll my eyes, then stopped because it would be unprofessional, then remembered my boss was chain smoking on my doorstep while complaining about a political VIP and an eye roll probably wouldn't do any harm. So I eye rolled.

This was one of the most stressful aspects of working in the service industry: you could do everything perfectly for a thousand diners, but if the 1001st didn't like something, even if what they wanted was objectively unreasonable or even impossible, they could thrash you all over the internet and ruin your reputation.

I'd known restaurants that had shuttered over a single disgruntled guest. Le Jules Verne was too established for that, but if the Prime Minister's boyfriend voiced his displeasure publicly, it could certainly take time for us to recover from the effects.

"I'll do it," I said firmly. "I promise." Chef La Croix appraised me for a moment, then nodded.

"We beat them in the war, you know," he said, taking a long drag on his cigarette.

"That would be the, uh, Franco-Spanish War? From the 1600s?"

Chef La Croix began walking away. "And don't let them forget it."

***

Thus commenced the most frantic afternoon of my life.

My first step was my local fromagerie, which I'd shopped at for years. I didn't remember them selling tetilla, but I hoped I'd only overlooked it. It would be just the break I needed, to simply go down the block, purchase the cheese Le Jules Verne desperately needed, then walk into work like a hero.

But the owner shook his head. "I'm sorry, Mademoiselle Delcour, but we don't sell tetilla. Would you be interested in something similar?"

I explained the situation, and he pulled out his contact list of other fromageries in the city. While I waited, simultaneously grateful and anxious, he called a handful of the closest, but none of them sold tetilla. One of them suggested a shop that was known for selling Spanish goods, but when I tried calling them, they didn't pick up.

"It's not too far," I said looking at the location on my phone. "I'll take the métro there. Thank you!" I called as I ran out the door.

Two stops on the métro later, I found myself in a new shop, again with the owner shaking his head. "We only get occasional shipments of tetilla, and we've been out for weeks. But I may have another place for you."

This shop was across the city, so I ran back down the steps to the métro, squeezed myself into a hot, crowded train, and tried not to look at the time too often. That journey ended in defeat as well, as did the next one, and the one after that.

"Why would I sell Spanish cheese here?" one owner asked, and that seemed to be the general sentiment.

I was starting to get as wrathful as Chef La Croix. Who goes to France and demands they be served a food you could eat every day in Spain?

By now I was out of breath, overheated, and had to get ready for work very soon. Standing outside the most recent shop, I scrolled through my phone. Maybe I should try a supermarket? Some of them had a pretty decent cheese selection. There was one sort of on my way home.

One final, sweaty métro ride later, I found myself standing in the cheese section of a grocery store, pawing at each bundle to see if it was tetilla. I searched through the entire selection twice, then found a worker and asked him.

"We don't have that here," he said, shaking his head. He turned away to continue his restocking. I was left alone in the aisle, having an internal meltdown as shoppers parted around me.

I'd promised Chef La Croix I would do this, and I'd failed. We weren't going to have the cheese, and the Prime Minister's boyfriend would throw a fit.

I pictured Chef La Croix, perfecting each course of a meal that'd be forgotten as soon as this one shortcoming came to light. Maybe they'd cut the staff, then Yasmine wouldn't be able to save up enough to move to Switzerland, Colette would have to drop out of her costume design course, Paul's wife would have to go back to work and leave their twins...

I looked at my watch. I had to get back home now and shower; I was already cutting it close. There wasn't time for anything else.

Unless...

No. We'd barely started dating and, besides, his work was keeping him shackled to his desk. Even if he wanted to help me, he wouldn't be able to. It was the middle of the work day. There was absolutely no way I was going to bother him.

I pictured my coworkers' crushed expressions again.

Ughhhh.

I pulled out my phone and dialed a number, half-hoping he wouldn't pick up.

"Margot?" Laurent sounded startled. Which, of course he was.

Chapter 17

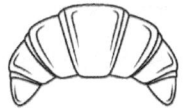

"**M**argot?" Laurent said again, louder this time.

I hurriedly cleared my throat. "Hi, sorry, I don't have a lot of time to explain, but can you do me a favor? I'm desperate." My words flowed into each other I was speaking so quickly.

"Of course," Laurent said immediately. My heart leapt at his lack of hesitation.

"I know you're busy, and you have so many other more important things to do, but there's this cheese…"

I explained the situation, trying to keep a note of hysteria from creeping into my voice. "Do you know anyone who might sell it?"

"I'll try every contact I have." Laurent sounded completely unfazed, as though being asked to procure a specialty cheese for a new girlfriend was a regular occurrence. My heart banged painfully in my chest, whether from stress or my feelings for Laurent, I wasn't sure.

"Thank you, thank you so much. If you can, bring it to Le Jules Verne. We don't need it until the final course, so you have a few hours," I said breathlessly, trying to give Laurent all the information he needed as I hurried back to the métro. "And remember, it has to be from Galicia!"

I raced home, made myself presentable in record time, and arrived at work just in time to assess the situation before diners began arriving.

It wasn't great. Security was crawling all over the restaurant, everyone looked on edge, and if the clangings and strings of expletives (in three languages) coming from the kitchens were any indication, Chef La Croix was not in a particularly cheery mood.

And I wasn't going to make things any better.

I crept into the kitchen, hoping to catch one of the sous chefs and deliver my news quietly, or maybe I could just write a note? But as soon as I stepped through the doorway, knives paused and every head swiveled to look at me.

There was complete silence.

It was Chef La Croix who finally spoke. "Well?"

I wished he wasn't holding a literal cleaver in his hands.

"I couldn't get it," I began, and everyone's face turned to pure terror. "But I asked a friend!" I said hurriedly. "He knows a lot of people, and he's going to do everything he can to get it. He's a chef!" I added, as though that would make a difference.

Something very interesting was going on with Chef La Croix's complexion. He was going redder and redder, and his face now looked distinctly fuchsia. I really did wish he'd put down that cleaver.

I was braced for an explosion of rage, but Chef La Croix only nodded, his head moving jerkily. "Alright. Let's hope he comes through."

Deadly silence followed. I took it as an excellent time to exit the kitchen.

I fled back to the dining rooms to find Leïla and Luc panting as they moved tables around at the direction of the security team.

"Leïla had to take over for me," Yasmine said, coming to stand beside me. "I was ready to tell them to drag the tables themselves if it bothered them so much. All this trouble for two people."

"There are some paparazzi outside!" Colette said excitedly, using perfect *pointe* technique as she stood on her toes to look out the window.

Once every table had been moved to the precise centimeter of floor space specified by the security team, Yasmine, Colette, Leïla, Luc, Paul, and I stood in an anxious line, waiting for the first guests to arrive. The Prime Minister and her boyfriend were supposed to arrive early, to be seated before anyone else.

A member of the security team walked over. "I have just been informed the Prime Minister and Señor Costa are running late. At least thirty minutes."

"Of course," Yasmine growled. We all looked anxiously at one another.

"I guess...someone needs to let Chef La Croix know," Luc said, looking like a man heading to the guillotine.

"La Croix?" The security member who'd just spoken to us grinned. "Like the sparklin—"

"*Por favor,* I beg you," Luc said, cutting across him. He clasped his hands together in supplication. "*Never* make that joke. It will cause the end times."

The grin slowly slid from the man's face. Luc turned to the kitchens. A minute later I heard a muffled oath, a loud clanging, then silence.

"I'm glad I'm not you," Colette whispered to me. My sole job for the evening was to attend to Prime Minister Abascal and Señor Costa and ensure their evening was as close to perfection as possible. Which, of course, couldn't happen unless Laurent found that damn cheese. I'd checked my phone just before heading onto the floor, but there was nothing from him. After being calm for weeks, this visit was finally making me nervous.

I looked around the clean, minimalistic lines of Le Jules Verne, all decorated in shades of pale green and ecru, and tried to soak in some of the soothing ambience.

It failed. Miserably.

Diners began arriving, and I made my way to the staff room, cooling my heels and checking my phone compulsively as I waited for the VIPs to show up. Still no update from Laurent. Hopefully this delay would buy him enough time to come through.

A full seventy minutes after their scheduled time, a security guard announced that the Abascals had arrived. I smoothed my clothes, then went to stand by the elevator doors. When they opened, the first to step out were two new security guards. Behind them was the couple.

They resembled each other: tall, thin, dark-haired. The Prime Minister was smiling widely and shaking hands all around; clearly, she was used to the political game. Her boyfriend, standing behind her, looked annoyed. I hoped it was just nerves before a proposal and not anything deeper.

I stepped forward to greet them. "Good evening, and welcome to Le Jules Verne. I'm Margot Delcour," I said in Spanish.

"You have an accent," Señor Costa said, as the Prime Minister warmly shook my hand.

"That's very perceptive of you," I said, careful to keep any note of sarcasm out of my voice. "I'm originally from Alsace. Allow me to show you to your table."

As I led the couple and their trailing security team across the dining rooms, I took the time to shrug off my irritation. I knew I had an accent in Spanish, but I also knew that it was slight. Again, I wondered why Señor Costa had come here if all he really wanted was to eat Spanish food and be served by Spaniards.

He's proposing tonight, I reminded myself. *This has to be one of the best nights of his life.* I'd fake a Spanish accent and dance a flamenco if that's what he needed.

Like many people, Señor Costa had informed us he'd be proposing during the final course. I suppose people felt it added some element of surprise, but I always thought it only extended the anxiety. Why not propose right away and spend the rest of the evening exulting in the glow of being newly engaged?

But my job was to pull off the logistics, not offer feedback. That meant I really had to rustle up the cheese that would apparently play a starring role in the proposal.

"Here's your table. It's one of the best in the restaurant," I said cheerfully, once we'd reached Le Comptoir.

"There's no view of the city," Señor Costa pouted. He sounded like a child.

"Ah, Le Comptoir's view is of the inner mechanics of the Tower," I said. "Look, you can see the pulleys and wheels working as the elevators go up and down. No one else in all of Paris has this view."

Allowing Señor Costa to continue staring out the window, I pulled out a chair for the Prime Minister. The table had been carefully set with 100% linen napkins and covered by a 100% linen tablecloth. Paul came over just then to explain the wine options and make recommendations. They chose a Spanish wine, of course.

"Here is your first course," I said several minutes later. "It's a citrus and crab salad featuring—"

"There's no fennel, correct?" the Prime Minister asked. "We saw it on the menu, but we don't like the taste."

"No fennel at all, Prime Minister," I said with a smile.

Between the two of them and their special requests, I got enough steps in to meet my exercise goal for the entire week. He wanted a different type of pepper, she wanted her salad dressing on the side, he wanted the temperature turned up, she wanted the music turned down, they both wanted new napkins after every second course. I wondered how two such picky people could ever have found a partner they were content with.

But they had. These two difficult, fussy, demanding people had each found a person who had chosen them, who had picked them alone from among the billions of people on the planet.

And here I was, standing on the periphery, imagining what that could feel like.

No use moping about that now, I told myself as I hurried back to the kitchens to get a knife that was "less sharp" for Señor Costa. I wasn't going to let any hint of my negative feelings show. Every question they asked, I knew the answer to. Every request they had was cheerfully carried out.

As I brought their empty plates from the fourth course back to the kitchens, I decided the evening was actually going pretty well.

Except for the damn cheese. I'd been running into the staff room to check my phone every chance I could, but there'd been just one text from Laurent: *still trying.*

Pushing down my panic, I brought out the fifth course. It was roast duck, beautifully glossy, with a raspberry reduction sauce and caramelized vegetables.

"My grandparents had a poultry farm," Señor Costa mentioned, and I pressed him for details, doing anything I could to stretch out the time. There was just one more dish before the final course, when they expected to see tetilla.

But dinner had been going so well, maybe they wouldn't care? I allowed myself to hope, but when I brought out the sixth course, a trio of profiteroles, Señor Costa frowned.

His frowning made *me* frown. Who could have a problem with profiteroles? They were notoriously tricky to make, but these looked gorgeous. The pastry balls were crispy, the custard in the middle was creamy and perfectly set, and they were topped with a drizzle of chocolate ganache. I could have devoured the entire plate right there.

"I prefer not to eat chocolate," Señor Costa said, looking disdainful again. "I thought that had been understood."

Frantically, I thought back to the notes I'd seen on the couple. The chocolate mousses had been eliminated in favor of the dessert cheeses, but there hadn't been any mention of it being because Señor Costa didn't like chocolate. I thought he'd just wanted the cheese.

"My apologies," I said, hoping my smile didn't come off more like a grimace. "I'll be right back with profiteroles without chocolate."

Both of them remained unsmiling. "I expected more from a restaurant that charges these prices," the Prime Minister said.

"I'll return in just a moment with the correct dish," I assured them again. I felt their eyes on me as I walked across the restaurant.

Another server must have heard what had happened and passed it along to the kitchen. I saw they were already hustling to plate new sets of profiteroles.

"I prefer not to eat chocolate," Colette mimicked, her voice pouty. "Who is this manchild?"

"Keep your voice down," Leïla pleaded. "And we still don't have the tetilla."

"Still nothing?" I asked. Leïla shook her head.

"What if we put every cheese we have on the plate and not even mention the tetilla? Maybe he won't notice?" I suggested halfheartedly.

Colette shook her head. "A member of their team gave the kitchens the engagement ring. Apparently Señor Costa wants the final course brought out with the ring on *top* of the tetilla."

I sagged against the counter. Señor Costa wouldn't be getting the meal or proposal experience he wanted. All this work, and the night was going to end in failure. I'd really thought that Laurent would come through.

I looked past Leïla into the kitchens. Chef La Croix was hanging his head, and he looked as tired as I felt. One of the sous chefs actually reached out to pat his shoulder.

In the hallway, there came a soft chime: the indication of an elevator arriving. As one, we turned toward the sound. It was too late for new diners to arrive.

In the moment before the elevator appeared, everything was completely still. The hum of the pulleys working was the only sound to pierce the silence. Dimly, I imagined Señor Costa watching the mechanisms move, his lips pursed with displeasure. I was holding my breath as the doors slid open.

The first thing I saw was the toe of a very shiny shoe.

My breath caught.

There was a moment when nothing moved, and I could hear the blood pounding in my ears. I took a ragged breath, the shoe lifted, and there suddenly was Laurent, looking tired and unsure and elated all at the same time. He stepped out of the elevator. In his hand was a small round of cheese.

I could have kissed him. More than that, I could have tackled him to the ground in a fit of passion previously unseen at Le Jules Verne. I restrained myself, slightly, but still ran to him and grabbed his hands in mine.

"You found it?" I breathed.

"I told you I would," Laurent said, his eyes shining.

"How did you leave work?"

"Oh, don't worry. There's a provision in the company manual that allows time off for cheese-related emergencies." Laurent grinned.

I looked down at the cheese, so hard won, and almost laughed. *Tetilla* meant 'nipple' in Spanish, and the cheese's shape made it *quite* obvious how it got its name. It looked so sexual, sitting there in Laurent's hand. My face flushed, and I was half-relieved when Chef La Croix came over and whisked the cheese away.

"You saved us tonight," I told Laurent. His hair was mussed, and he smelled like rosemary and citrus. There was only a handspan between our faces. I leaned forward to kiss him and—

"Margot, the Prime Minister and Señor Costa are waiting for their prof-iteroles," Leïla said apologetically.

Her voice knocked me out of the bubble I'd been in. Reluctantly, I took a step back.

"I have to go, but thank you," I told Laurent again. Somehow, I was still holding onto his hands. I couldn't seem to let them go.

Laurent wasn't letting go of me, either. "Knock on my door when you get back. Whatever time it is, I'll be up."

"Of course. I have to go now," I said again, finally wrenching myself away. "But thank you! Thank you so much!"

All smiles this time, I returned to the couple bearing profiteroles untainted by chocolate. I stood there, glowing with happiness as I agreed that, yes, they did look much better now, and, yes, it was tiresome when restaurants didn't listen to their customers. Señor Costa's heart didn't seem to be in the complaints, though. I suspected he was only thinking about the proposal now.

Chef La Croix himself put the platter for the final course in my hands. Arrayed on it were a variety of cheeses and fruits. In the center was the tetilla with a large diamond ring over its tip. It looked mildly obscene to me, but that's what Señor Costa had asked for.

"Almost done," Yasmine whispered as I made to step back onto the floor.

I beamed as I brought out the platter. Señor Costa followed me with wide-open eyes as I made my way to their table. When I was a few steps away, he took Prime Minister Abascal's hand between his own.

"Emilia," he began, his voice catching.

I gently placed the platter in the center of the table, turning it so the large rose-cut diamond faced the Prime Minister. I already could tell that she was a woman able to hide her emotions, but even she couldn't keep her eyebrows from arching high on her forehead.

"Emilia," Señor Costa said again softly, and such a look passed between the two of them that it almost took my breath away. I stepped back so they could have their moment.

From the doorway, I watched as Señor Costa spoke a little longer. He reached for the ring and slipped it on the Prime Minister's finger. She admired her hand with shining eyes, then looked at her new fiancé. They both smiled at each other, and again I felt my chest pinch.

The couple lingered over their final course, ordering more glasses of wine as they sampled the cheeses. I stood just outside the doorway, waiting for any sign that they needed me. All the other diners were gone, and in the back, the rest of the staff were already popping champagne bottles. I could hear the hushed, ecstatic hum of their voices.

When both the Prime Minister and her fiancé had drained their glasses and eaten every last bite of cheese, I went back over. The bill had already been taken care of by the Prime Minister's assistant, so there was nothing left for me to do other than congratulate them.

"We're all thrilled for you both," I said as I pulled the Prime Minister's chair out for her. "And we wish you a lifetime of happiness together."

"It was a wonderful meal," the Prime Minister assured me, all smiles now. Señor Costa barely glanced my way. He only had eyes for his fiancée.

When the couple and their entourage finally, finally, finally, got in the elevator, I made sure I remained attentive and smiling until the doors were fully shut. Then I rushed to the kitchens and joined the party.

A cheer greeted my arrival. Paul immediately pressed a glass of champagne into my hands, and Leïla pointed me toward the platters of food being passed around.

"You were absolutely wonderful," Yasmine said as she hugged me, a fistful of profiteroles clenched in each hand.

"I would have spilled wine on their laps two courses in," Luc said.

"Maybe someone took a picture of you serving them, Margot, and it'll end up in the news!" Colette squealed.

Everyone was congratulating me, and congratulating each other, and passing around food and bottles of wine. Suddenly, the crowds parted. Chef La Croix stood before me, his face inscrutable. No one moved. I wasn't even breathing.

Chef La Croix appraised me, his eyes dark and foreboding. Then, silently, he bent down, grasped my shoulders, and kissed me loudly on each cheek.

He pulled back so that we were looking directly at each other. For a moment, the only sound I heard was the champagne bubbling in my glass. Then Chef La Croix spoke.

"What a bunch of pissers, eh?"

He began to laugh, his whole face crinkling in mirth, and I started to laugh, and that set everyone else off until I could barely breathe, and all I could think about was how perfect this moment was.

Chapter 18

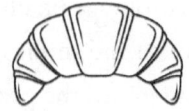

It was late when the party finally wound down, and it was a brisk night, so I sprang for a taxi. Through the window, Paris glowed gold against the sharp darkness of the night. I barely noticed, though. All I was thinking about was Laurent.

He opened the door immediately after I knocked. He was still wearing a suit, probably because he'd had to work late after spending half the day on a wild goose chase for me. On his face was the widest smile I'd seen from him. I could hardly picture the grumpy man I'd served weeks ago.

"How did it go?" he asked as he pulled me into his arms.

I breathed in the citrus scent of his hair. "Perfectly. I mean, they were terrible, but the meal went wonderfully. All thanks to you."

Laurent's golden eyes crinkled with happiness. "Are you hungry? I know how easy it is to forget to eat while working in a restaurant."

"I'm famished," I admitted.

Putting an arm around me, Laurent led me to his kitchen and pulled out a chair. "How does a croque-monsieur sound? I know it's not fancy, but I can make a good one."

"That'd be wonderful," I said as I sank into the chair.

Laurent tied his apron around his waist and poured me a glass of Beaujolais. As he whisked together a bechamel sauce, I told him about the meal, recounted the demands, the returned profiteroles, the triumphant presentation of the tetilla... I felt as light as air as I spoke.

Laurent assembled the sandwiches, brushed them with melted butter, and set them in a griddle. As they toasted, he gave me his undivided attention. Then, at some unseen sign, he turned around and took the croque-monsieurs out of the griddle. They were cooked to perfection.

He tried to shoo Minerva out of his chair, but she only sniffed and curled tighter into a donut. Laurent decided to accept defeat gracefully and eat his croque-monsieur standing. He garnished our plates with a sprinkling of minced chives, then set my croque-monsieur in front of me.

It took me about five seconds to devour it.

"That was delicious," I said once my plate was cleared. "Ten out of ten, no notes."

Laurent had only taken a few bites of his, but he must have realized I was still hungry because he stood up and went to the fridge.

"I was saving these for the grand finale," he said as he set down a ceramic platter between us. "It's no quesarito, but I think they'll do." On the platter were a dozen oysters gleaming in their half-shells. He reached for a shallot, finely mincing it with practiced precision, then added it to a bowl of white wine vinegar and cracked pepper. The sharp, tangy scent of the mignonette sauce mingled with the scent of our wine. I couldn't take my eyes off Laurent.

He turned toward me, a single oyster in his hand.

I didn't speak; I barely moved. All I did was part my lips just enough for Laurent to bring the oyster shell to my mouth. He tipped it in, and I swallowed slowly, savoring the cold brine, the slick curve of the oyster, and the sudden brightness of vinegar and shallot.

A drop of mignonette clung to my lower lip. I licked it off.

"Mon dieu," I breathed. "That's indecently good."

Laurent smiled his crooked smile as he tipped another oyster into my mouth. It had barely slipped down my throat before Laurent caught me up in his arms and pressed his mouth to mine. I returned the kiss eagerly. All I wanted was Laurent. Every centimeter of me that wasn't touching him was screaming out to be pressed against his body.

Without a word, Laurent pulled me out of my seat and brought me to the couch. He cupped my face in his hands. I could feel the scars he'd earned from his years of cooking. He kissed me on the forehead, his lips warm and soft, then trailed kisses down my face. He kissed my nose, then each cheekbone, then came a line of feathery-soft kisses on my chin and along my jawline before he again pressed his mouth to mine. I was nearly giddy with desire.

Laurent sank backward, stretching out on the couch and pulling me on top of him. His hands sank into my hair, and he reached his mouth hungrily to me, kissing and nipping his way from my jaw down my neck. When he reached my clavicle, he sucked gently. A moan escaped my lips.

Remembering something, I sat up abruptly.

"The quiche you made." I could barely remember my name at the moment, but I wanted Laurent to know this one thing. "The third one. The crust was amazing."

Laurent looked surprised, then he started laughing. He pulled me down for another kiss.

"I'm delighted to hear that," he said, once he'd finished kissing me. "But that wasn't the third quiche I made. It was only the third quiche I sent to you."

Well, now I was curious. "How many quiches did you make?"

Laurent was already flushed, but his cheeks went a shade darker. "Thirty-seven."

I couldn't help it; I started laughing.

"What exactly is so funny?" Laurent growled, trying to sound stern, but only managing to sound sexy.

"It's just that," I said, gasping as I tried to catch my breath, "I once made eclairs ten times in a week to get the choux pastry perfect. I thought *that* was messed up. You broke three dozen." A final hiccup escaped me. "Do you measure your garnishes with a ruler to make sure they're all angled to the same degree? That's what Chef La Croix does."

"You don't even want to *know* the things I've done to make a dish perfect," Laurent said, eyes sparking.

"I do want to know," I said, resting my chin on Laurent's chest.

"You don't. You'd be horrified and run screaming from this apartment." I felt his chest vibrate under me as he laughed. Laurent tugged me up so that his face was just centimeters from mine. "And I can't be scaring you away," he murmured.

His hands slipped from my neck down my back. I was still wearing the black silk dress I'd gone to work in, although it must have an unholy number of wrinkles by now from being bunched around my hips as Laurent and I romped on the couch.

Laurent was making gentle circles at the small of my back. I shifted until I was fully on top of him, my heart hammering. His body was solid beneath me, heat pressed against heat. I skimmed my hands down the firm smoothness of his chest, pausing to swirl my fingers in the patch of blond hair at his neckline. A soft groan escaped him.

It made me smugly satisfied to know I had that effect on this man, but then Laurent's hands trailed to the backs of my thighs, and my own composure slipped. My vision went black as I arched against his touch. His fingers were cool against my skin.

He lifted us both to our feet, still kissing me. For a moment I drank in the sight of him: untamed curls, golden eyes, the dimple just forming to the right of his half-smile. He was still wearing his apron. Suppressing a laugh, I tugged on its strings. It fluttered to the ground.

With maddening patience, Laurent folded it neatly and set it on the coffee table.

"It'd bother me if I left it like that," he admitted sheepishly.

Somehow, that grin made me want him even more.

I reached for his shirt, but Laurent had already started unbuttoning it. Impatiently, he peeled it and his tight gray undershirt off. His bare stomach was taut, a faint trail of blond hair leading lower.

Lightheaded with desire, I closed the gap between us, my palms flattening over Laurent's chest. Goosebumps broke out on his skin, and before I could savor it, he was kissing me while his fingers found my zipper. In a breath, my dress was sliding down my arms.

"Margot," Laurent groaned, his voice turning my name into something urgent and desired.

Suddenly, Laurent scooped me up, holding me close as I rested my head against his chest, safe in the circle of his arms. He had chef arms, hard and muscled, and he balanced my weight easily as he carried me to his bedroom.

I'd glimpsed the space before, but never entered. Even now, flushed and tangled with him, I smirked: not a hair out of place. I bet he ironed his sheets.

But Laurent didn't seem concerned about the sheets getting wrinkled now as he tossed me onto the bed. I suppressed a laugh as I imagined him folding our discarded clothes, but he seemed happy enough to let them pile messily on the ground.

As he looked at me, a quiet sound escaped Laurent's lips, something halfway between a sigh and groan. He swung a leg across my hips, straddling me. Held in place by his thighs, the only thing I could do was try not to drown in his touch. Only the thin lace of my panties separated us.

Laurent kissed me again, more urgently now, sucking my bottom lip and tracing me with his tongue. Before my dizzy, loved-up mind could catch up, Laurent had slid off the bed and knelt on the ground. I felt him slide my panties down my legs. Lifting my head, I saw his mouth curve into a crooked grin. And then all I saw was stars.

I clutched at him, at the sheets, at anything that would hold me together. Laurent paused, smug, grinning up at me, before I dragged at his shoulders in desperation. Obliging, he climbed onto the bed and pressed the full length of his body against mine. He moved against me, and every nerve in my body ignited.

I raked my hands through his hair, along the hard lines of his back.

"Margot," he groaned into my mouth. The sound alone nearly finished me.

All of Laurent's smooth self-assurance that had been so prominently on display the first time we'd met was gone. In its place was this sweating, tousled man, undone and entirely mine.

"Margot."

I will never get tired of hearing that voice speak my name.

"I need to kiss you."

Laurent looked so desperate I nearly laughed.

"Then kiss me, mon chérie." I tipped my legs back so that my ankles were roughly in line with my head (Thank you, Yasmine, for suggesting we take that yoga class, which was objectively terrible and full of sweaty, grunting people, but got me into the habit of stretching).

Laurent followed me down, pressing me into the mattress as he pressed his mouth to mine.

I tangled a hand in his damp curls. His low, animal moan rolled through me, carrying me over the edge until I broke apart beneath him.

When at last he shuddered to stillness, I held him close, both of us gasping.

"Laurent," I whispered.

He cracked one golden eye.

"Next time," I murmured, "keep the apron on."

***

As our breathing quieted, we lay on the bed, Laurent curled around me. Between the Prime Minister's meal being over (already that dinner seemed so long ago) and finally consummating things with Laurent, I was giddy with happiness. A laugh bubbled out of me, and I buried my head in Laurent's shoulder, shaking with giggles.

"What's so funny?" he murmured.

"Nothing," I whispered as I snuggled closer to him. "You saved me, by finding that cheese."

He opened an eye and smiled. "There was no way I was going to let you down. I would have bought a small herd of cows and made the cheese myself if that's what it took." His voice was still low and hoarse. It brought me back to how he'd sounded in the throes of passion, and I shivered.

I turned so that we lay side-by-side, facing each other. Laurent looked rumpled and sleepy and deeply happy.

But wait. There was one thing I had to check.

"Laurent?" I whispered. He turned a sleepy face toward me.

"If I wanted to bake croissants at three in the morning, would that bother you?"

Laurent blinked. "You want to make croissants now?"

"No, just hypothetically. If, one night, I want to get up at a random hour and do some baking, would that bother you?" I was completely still as I watched him drowsily contemplate the question.

"Why would that bother me?" he said finally. "I cook at odd hours all the time. I'd just hope you'd save a croissant for me." In the warm dark, I grinned like an idiot, some nameless fear having dissolved away.

We fell asleep like that, entwined in each other. Sometime later, I awoke to see the first streaks of dawn filtering through the windows. Laurent must have awoken in the middle of the night and spread a blanket over us. I snuggled deeper in it, moving closer to Laurent so that we were touching again.

My last thought, as I drifted back off to sleep, was this: For the first time in a very long time, I wasn't lonely.

Chapter 19

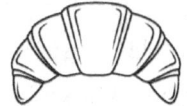

Weeks passed, and Paris slipped further into autumn. The tourist crowds thinned out, and Parisians returned from their summer holidays. Street stalls selling roasted chestnuts began popping up along the Seine, and although diners still crowded the outdoor cafes, they did so with checkered blankets spread across their laps, shawls around their shoulders, and clusters of burnished leaves at their feet.

I used the bounty of apples that now crowded the markets to make batches of desserts: apple cakes, apple galettes with vanilla ice cream, delicate crêpes with caramelized spiced apples, apple jams and jellies, thick apple pies with cheddar cheese mixed into the crust...

Mixed into all of that, into each of my days, was Laurent. He'd stop by my apartment in the mornings, and we'd share coffee and croissants. We both worked late, but in the evenings we'd cook together in his apartment. The windows would fog up with steam from the oven as we sipped wine and prepared our meal. We'd fall asleep in his bed, smelling like the ingredients we'd worked with that day: butter and sugar for me, rosemary and black pepper for him.

I don't know when it happened exactly, but one day, in the middle of a dinner shift, I realized that I was no longer wistfully watching happy couples. I'd *become* part of a happy couple. I had someone who had chosen me.

Still, underneath it all, a current of anxiety pulsed through me. The gala loomed closer each day. I ricocheted between being confident in my skills and feeling that I was out of my depth. What if no one liked what I baked? What if I baked something too long or seasoned it wrong or forgot an ingredient? It's not like Paris was a city forgiving of mediocrity in food.

Laurent tried to shore up my self-esteem, but, some nights, after he'd fallen asleep beside me, I lay awake replaying recipes in my head, calculating sugar ratios, obsessing over garnishes. Baking for the gala had awakened something in me that had long lay dormant. I'd always loved baking, but I'd gotten safe with it. Now, I was drawing on all my skills, and I could only hope they'd be enough.

One evening, I sat in Laurent's kitchen as he plated dinner. He'd gone all out tonight. On the wooden cutting board he set before me was a series of miniature tarts, each a different flavor.

They made a row of crisp, golden crusts and bubbling fillings. There was an heirloom tomato and caramelized onion tart with brown butter dripping off its edges, a blueberry and lavender tart with a mini pitcher of sweet cream beside it, a wild ramp and morel mushroom tart bubbling with Gruyère, and, finally, a salted pork and leek tart, the velvety pieces of pork looking like they would melt like cream in my mouth.

Laurent watched me anxiously as I took a bite of the tomato and onion tart.

"How's the puff pastry?" he asked, his face so wracked with concern I nearly laughed. "I made seven different versions, and this was my favorite, but I still think it's too heavy."

"It's really good," I assured him, licking a speck of onion from my finger. "The flavors are perfect. You just need to work on making the pastry a little flakier."

Laurent sighed. "That's always my problem. I'll need to watch you make it again."

"Don't go morose on me," I said smiling. "Here, come sit down and enjoy this feast you made."

While Laurent tidied up (he always insisted on doing the dishes), I pulled out my phone and checked my email. There was a new message with the subject line "GALA EXPECTATIONS."

It was from Sabine.

Probably just the dress code and such, I told myself as I clicked it open.

Margot,

I've reviewed the sample dessert menu that you sent Fatima. Frankly, I'm not convinced your ideas align with the level of sophistication we're looking for. Many of your recipe suggestions felt amateur, and your execution photos don't inspire much confidence. I strongly suggest stepping back and allowing an experienced pastry chef to take over. This is one of the foundation's most high-profile evenings, and we simply cannot afford mediocrity.

Regards,

Sabine Berlioz

The email blurred. I blinked and read it again. And again.

Laurent was talking about something as he soaped up the dishes, but I couldn't hear him.

My greatest fear had been found out and put into writing by this woman: I wasn't good enough.

How could I have forgotten? I should never have let Yasmine convince me to volunteer for the gala, never have let any competitive streak with Laurent make me lose my head. Sabine was right; I wasn't cut out for this.

Unbidden, a memory floated to the surface: My mother sitting beside my ten-year-old self in front of the oven as we watched my very first batch of macarons bake. Macarons were a serious undertaking, my mother had told me gravely. I remember wanting to make her proud so badly I'd given myself a stomachache.

When my mother judged it to be the right time, we'd pulled the macarons from the oven, and appraised their glossy shells.

"They look very good," my mother had said. "But how do they taste?"

She'd lifted two from the silicone mat and passed one to me. I'd let it dangle in my hand, my attention wholly on her. My mother flipped the macaron shell over, split it in half, inhaled its scent, then popped the entire thing in her mouth.

I remember how it felt like the world had gone still. I remember every detail: the smudge of almond flour on my mother's cheek, a few stray curls falling out of her chignon, how just the corner of her mouth had quirked up to give me that first rush of hope, her mouth splitting open, and finally, her laughing in pure delight as she opened her arms and I ran into them.

"Margot, they're wonderful," she said as I held her tightly, enveloped in her scent of vanilla and spices. "Absolutely outstanding, mon amour. And just think, if your first batch of macarons is this good, you'll be doing laps around me soon enough."

But she was wrong.

Laurent noticed I wasn't responding. He came around and put a hand on my shoulder.

"Everything alright?"

I responded by bursting into tears.

Laurent's arms came around me. "What happened?" he asked urgently. "Margot, what's wrong?"

I couldn't speak, so I just passed over my phone with Sabine's email still glowing on the screen.

Beside me, Laurent went tense. He held me and stroked my hair, murmuring soft things, as I cried myself out.

When I petered out to just a few sniffles, he offered me a tissue and directed me to his couch. Then he dragged over a chair and sat on it so that we faced each other, knees touching.

"Margot, forget about that email," he said firmly. "It doesn't matter."

"Doesn't matter?" I cried. "Sabine basically fired me!"

As a new rush of tears came, something soft gently pushed against my knee. I opened my eyes and saw Minerva staring at me, her own yellow eyes unblinking. Insistently, she pushed against my knee again. When I reached a trembling hand out to pet her, she jumped into my lap and curled herself into a donut.

I took a gulp of air. "She doesn't think I'm good enough. She and Fatima thought my ideas were amateur," I said, and the final word was half a sob.

I glanced at Laurent. He looked just as he did the night I'd met him, full of glowering anger.

"Margot, you are an outstanding baker. Truly you are. Fatima knows how lucky she is to have you. As for Sabine…That might be slightly my fault."

His words were so unexpected that I paused in wiping snot from my face (I've always been a messy crier) to stare at him.

Laurent looked distinctly uncomfortable. "Sabine and I know each other. For most of our lives, in fact. We went to school together, and Sabine is the sister of my former girlfriend. She's hated me ever since her sister and I broke up."

I shook my head, as though to help this startling piece of information sink in. "You know Sabine? You dated her sister? Is that how you got the gala position?"

"No! A mutual friend suggested me to Fatima because he knew I wanted to get back into cooking. I thought Sabine and I would hardly see each other."

I frowned. "But I thought your girlfriend cheated on you with a coworker?" I clapped my hand over my mouth as soon as the words were out.

Laurent flushed scarlet. "How do you know that?"

Now I was blushing, too. "Some women were gossiping about it at the first gala meeting."

Laurent dropped his head. "Yes. They're correct."

"But why would Sabine hate you when her sister cheated on you?"

Laurent sighed. "I'll explain, but let me warn you that this period was me at my absolute lowest. I don't expect you to be impressed."

I stayed silent as he gathered himself.

"You know how hard it can be to run a restaurant?" Laurent finally said. "When I was running Les Champs D'Or, I couldn't handle the thought of it failing. Whenever anything went wrong, I'd throw all my energy into fixing it so I wouldn't lose this dream I'd fought so hard for."

Laurent's mouth twisted. "It meant giving up a lot of things. I stopped seeing friends. I couldn't be bothered to have Sunday dinner with my parents. My girlfriend and I had recently moved in together, but we barely saw each other. She begged me to spend time with her, but the restaurant always came first. I was so consumed with work I can hardly blame her for cheating on me. I'm sure she told Sabine just how thoroughly I'd abandoned her. When she left me, I thought that was my rock bottom."

Laurent glanced at me, then suddenly away. It was such a guilty gesture, like something a child would do.

"It gets worse. Things started to fall apart at the restaurant. Profits were slipping, one of my sous chefs spiraled and had to go to rehab, the owners were on me to try this new trend, then that one. At the same time, Noelle was diagnosed with cancer. Ewing sarcoma, cancer in her bones." Laurent looked exhausted. He looked a hundred years old.

"That should have been my sign to pull back and spend time with my sister. But I couldn't. The thought of losing my restaurant was unbearable. It would mean everything I'd worked so hard for had failed. That *I* was a failure.

"So I just dove in deeper. It got so bad I cut myself off from everyone and spent most nights sleeping on a cot in the kitchens. And all the while my sister was wasting away, bent double in pain, spending her days in hospitals."

Laurent looked at me, and his eyes were full of tears. "I'm so ashamed of that time in my life. I blocked everything out and focused only on the tiny aspects of life that I could control."

My heart hurt for him. The quirks I'd noticed: his spotless apartment, the need for everything to be neat and organized, his perfectly-pressed clothes...They were all an attempt to find order in a life that had spun into chaos.

"I hate myself for it," Laurent said quietly, a tear rolling down his face. "My sister gets cancer, and I reorganize my spice rack."

"People react to grief in strange ways," I said gently. "The afternoon after my mother's funeral, I went to a department store and spent five hundred euros on a vase. For some reason, I thought it would ease the overwhelming sadness I was feeling."

Laurent wiped his eyes. "I know. And I lost the restaurant anyway. It wasn't turning the profit the owners wanted, so they closed it down. I wrecked all those relationships for nothing."

"The morning that I went home and apologized to my family for everything, Noelle had been stuck inside for days and was desperate to get out of the house. I offered to drive her anywhere she wanted. Do you know what we did?"

"What?" I whispered.

Laurent's face softened. "We went to an ice cream shop. She ordered chocolate in a waffle cone, and I got pistachio. Her immune system was still weak, and it made me nervous for her to be around people, so I drove us out into the middle of nowhere, where there were only farms nearby. All the canola fields were in bloom. Watching Noelle lick her ice cream and laugh as it dripped down her hands, I realized that even when your life has an enormous hole ripped through it, it's still beautiful. It's still so full of beauty. When you dropped into my life and gave me those delicious, squashed macarons, I knew you would only add to that beauty."

Laurent's face was glazed with tears, but he still smiled. "Don't worry about Sabine. She has it in for me, and I'm sure she recognized from the start how captivated I was by you. So now she has it in for you, too. She's just blowing hot air.

"I've talked to Fatima; I know she's impressed by your baking skills. As she should be," Laurent added, grinning. "I'm not exaggerating when I say that, if you ever went to pastry school, you'd amaze them."

I'd just managed to regain a tiny bit of composure, but that comment sent me spiraling.

"Wait, what did I say?" Laurent asked as my face crumpled.

I slumped back into my seat. Minerva, still in my lap, raised her head in disapproval.

"I did go to pastry school," I sighed. "I wasn't good enough for it. I was so bad they kicked me out."

There. The biggest shame of my life, out in the open. I had no idea this random Thursday evening would result in Laurent and I sharing our deepest failures.

"They kicked you out?" Laurent sounded completely nonplussed. "Margot, you're incredible at baking, though. How long ago was this?"

I took a few slow breaths, trying to steady myself. "I guess it's been six years now." I wiped a hand across my eyes. "All I ever wanted to do was become a pastry chef, like my mother. She'd saved up money for so long so I could go. She was so proud when I got into the same pastry school she'd gone to."

Keep going, I told myself.

"It was hard, harder than I expected, honestly. I was in the kitchens for ten or twelve hours a day, just baking, baking, baking. Normally that'd be fine, but this school was just a bad fit." I sighed.

"Or maybe any pastry school would be a bad fit for me. I don't know. The pastry school was in Vienna, and I worried it wasn't what I wanted. It's fully steeped in the classics, with no room for innovation. That's not how I usually bake, but my mother so badly wanted me to go to her same pastry school, and I was so happy to make her happy.

"Everything I made was just a little wrong to my instructors. They hated any changes I made to the recipes. I was miserable, and I even started to hate baking, but I never breathed a word to my mother. I figured I'd just push through, get my certificate, make my mom thrilled, then go off and bake how I wanted.

My voice caught. "But then my mother died a few months in." I sighed. "It was just like the wheels came off. Everything I made was burnt, or soggy, or tasteless, or...it was all just terrible."

My voice wobbled and, impatiently, I cleared my throat. "The instructors already weren't impressed with me, and by then I was so bad it was pulling everyone else down. One day, after I absolutely ruined a batch of canelés, the head instructor asked to speak with me after class. She was quite kind about it, but it was clear the decision was final."

I cleared my throat again. "All that money my mother had saved, all the pride she'd had in me, was for nothing. She was so convinced I was a good baker. At least she never got to see how I ended up." I pressed my lips tight together. I could feel my face burning. It was amazing, really, that the shame hadn't lessened one bit over the years. It still threatened to eat me up.

I chanced a look at Laurent. His eyes were filled with tears. As I watched, one slipped down his cheek.

"Margot," he said softly. "I don't know what happened then, but I can tell you today that you're an utterly amazing baker. You've made things I would be proud to have in any restaurant I worked at. I'm being completely honest when I say that your talent is incredible. You're going to be amazing at the gala. Have you..." He hesitated. "Have you ever considered going back to pastry school?"

I laughed miserably. "I've filled out applications about fifty times. I always lose my nerve, though. What if the first pastry school wasn't actually a bad fit, and I'm just really not good enough? I'd hate to let my mom down like that."

Minerva stood up and resettled herself on my lap. Laurent watched her, smiling, then looked up at me. "Well, I won't tell you what to do, but I can promise you something. I know your mother would be proud of you. That I can tell you without any doubt. You don't need to be perfect to make someone proud."

That, of course, made me cry again. Laurent's arms came around me, and he pulled me close to his warm chest.

"I'm so sorry about your mother," he said, his voice rough. "I'm so sorry you've had to live all these years feeling like you weren't good enough."

Laurent held me as I cried myself out. When I finally shuddered to a stop, I was trembling and there was snot all over my face. Laurent thoughtfully passed over the box of tissues. I gave him a watery smile.

"I do think you should consider pastry school again," he said gently. "You shouldn't let one bad experience stop you from the career you've always wanted. And you certainly shouldn't worry one moment about Sabine's opinion."

I looked down at my hands. There was a smudge of blueberry on my thumb. I wanted to believe Laurent. I wanted to be the type of person who was brave enough to try again.

I sighed. "Let's just enjoy dessert. I want to know what you think of this new pear turnover recipe." I smiled until Laurent smiled back at me.

Chapter 20

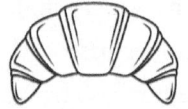

"Do you think they'll like me?" I asked for perhaps the thousandth time.

Laurent was peering at the timetable in the Gare de Lyon station, trying to figure out what platform our train was leaving from, but he paused to wrap an arm around my waist.

"They'll adore you. And if not...well, my family are gluttons and you're bringing half a bakery with you." He grinned. "You'll win them over, one way or another." He turned back to the timetable. "There we are. Platform eight."

When Laurent had originally asked me to spend the holidays with his family, Christmas had seemed ages away. But now that the time had come, I was jittery with nerves. Celebrities and heads of state I could deal with any day, but Laurent's family? That was another prospect altogether.

The days leading up to Christmas were some of the busiest of the year at work. As my anxiety over this visit grew, I'd half-hoped I'd be able to use work as an excuse to wiggle out of going. But Yasmine had squashed that idea by immediately picking up all my shifts that she could, and Leïla had quietly, but firmly, insisted on covering the rest.

Laurent adjusted my bag on his shoulder and gave an exaggerated groan. "I amend my statement. There is a full-scale bakery in here."

He wasn't wrong. I baked when I was stressed, and I baked when I was meeting new people. This visit had created such a perfect storm that I'd stopped buying flour from the store and instead called the supplier to send boxes of ingredients to me directly.

"Margot, what is all this?" Madame Blanchet had asked when the shipment arrived, carried into the building by two burly workers. "Are you stocking up for the apocalypse? It's good you realize that it's coming, but oats are the better option, ma chérie. They last longer."

I wasn't sure what Laurent's family would like, and he'd been extremely unhelpful in telling me that they liked "everything." So, I'd baked everything.

In my bursting suitcase were three types of croissants: plain, pain au chocolat, and ham and cheese. There were also macarons, carefully packaged to avoid them getting damaged, chocolate and vanilla eclairs, toasted cardamom bars, sticky caramel gingerbread, tomato and cheddar cheese scones (a gorgeous recipe I'd picked up while living in America), a glossy fruit tart, and finally, because I'd rather die than meet anyone new without having these to gift, half a dozen baguettes, still warm from the oven.

"Should I have baked a cake too?" I asked.

"Margot, you're going to cause a flour shortage," Laurent said, laughing again. "You've done plenty. They'll all love you."

I bit a nail worriedly. The amount of baked goods I was bringing wasn't as crazy as it first appeared. Laurent himself admitted that his family was large. There were his parents and, of course, his sister Noelle. Then there was the army of cousins, aunts, uncles, and grandparents who would assemble at the house over Christmas.

Although, to be honest, even a small family gathering would have overwhelmed me. I hadn't really celebrated any holiday since my mother had died. The first Christmas after, my grandmother had still been alive, so I'd gone through the motions of the day, even though I was still numb to everything. She'd passed away a few months later, and even though there were some aunts and uncles who I'm sure would have let me join them for the holidays, I'd moved so much growing up I wasn't close to any of them. It became easier to just stay home and pick up extra shifts so others could spend time with their own families.

But now I was being forced to remember what it was like to be part of a family unit again, and I was terrified. Hence all the baking.

The train from Paris to Aix-en-Provence was over three hours, but it passed easily. Laurent insisted I take the window seat, so I watched as nearly the whole of France flew by, all the cities and villages and farms where people were getting ready to celebrate Christmas—or, as I did, grit their way through the holiday season until it passed.

I was feeling cozy right now, though, warm in my cashmere sweater and with my baked goods safely tucked away in the rack above us. Next to me, Laurent was flipping through a cookbook and making neat notes in the margins.

I leaned over his shoulder to see what he was writing. In a list of ingredients for soup au pistou, he'd crossed out "two celery stalks" and replaced it with "two-and-a-quarter celery stalks."

"You can't possibly think that quarter of a celery stalk makes a difference," I said teasingly.

"It makes all the difference," Laurent said gravely, brow furrowed as he continued reading the recipe. "I made this soup once with only the two stalks, and it was unbalanced." He glanced up. "You always carefully measure ingredients when you bake."

"Of course. But I've also never spent an hour at the market trying to choose three carrots. What was your excuse for that?"

"That was *very* important work," Laurent said huffily. "The carrots needed to be the same width, otherwise they'd finish cooking at different times. It would have completely ruined the dish."

I grinned. No matter how many times I teased Laurent, it still riled him up. I leaned my head against his shoulder. After a second or two of pretending to be deeply offended, he enveloped me in his arms.

See? I can conquer anything with this man. His family will be a piece of cake.

My phone buzzed, indicating an email. It was from Fatima, wishing me a good holiday and signing her approval on my proposed pastry menu for the gala. Laurent had offered to straighten things out with the gala team, but I'd declined his offer. If Sabine wasn't just stirring up trouble and Fatima really *was* disappointed with me, I wanted to know so I could exit gracefully. When I'd spoken to her, though, she'd been baffled.

"We're delighted you're here, Margot," she'd assured me. "I did mention to Sabine I wanted to taste each of your ideas before approving the menu, but that's all. Sabine must have misunderstood."

Quite the misunderstanding, I'd thought to myself, although I certainly hadn't said that to Fatima. In any case, gala plans had gone ahead, and Sabine hadn't tried to stir up any more trouble.

I was jolted back to the present as we pulled into the Aix train station.

"Good lord," I murmured, looking at the crowd assembled on the platform. "Half the town's here."

"That's just the Roche family welcoming party," Laurent said, peering out the window. "Look, they're all waving." He waved back cheerily.

I suddenly had an idea of what it must feel like to be an animal in a zoo. There had to be at least two dozen people there, all (like Laurent) smartly-dressed, good-looking, and grinning widely. They were all talking over each other and laughing as the train eased to a stop.

When we disembarked, we were swarmed like celebrities.

"You must be Margot, welcome to Provence!" a woman with thick glasses said.

"How was the train ride?" an elderly man asked.

"Are you hungry?"

"Did you bring us presents?" a redheaded boy asked me hopefully.

"I'm glad you forgave my dumb big brother for that night at the restaurant. He really was such an ass." That came from Noelle, the petite blonde woman I recognized from Le Jules Verne, although she looked hugely happier than she had that evening. Laurent caught his sister up in a hug.

I gave up trying to answer any of them. Instead, I just smiled and kissed any cheek that presented itself.

There was a caravan of cars parked outside the station, and Laurent and I were hustled into Noelle's green Peugeot. Up close, Noelle looked the way I imagined fairies would when I was a child: pale and delicate, but pulsing with life. She had the same gold-flecked eyes as her brother.

"I have no idea why you gave Laurent another chance, Margot, but I'm glad you did," Noelle said. "I could tell you were a nice person even when you were telling Laurent off. Which, again, he completely deserved." She flashed a grin.

"Mom and Dad are at the house," Noelle said to her brother as she checked her mirrors. "They've been going insane getting everything perfect. The gardeners are on holiday so Mom had Dad trimming the hedges with her kitchen shears."

"Ah," I said, turning to Laurent with a grin. "So the perfectionism trait is inherited?"

"Did Laurent ever tell you about the time he skipped school?" Noelle asked, smirking. I shook my head.

"Noelle, I don't think this is the best way to—" Laurent began, but his sister spoke over him.

"He paid me ten euros to pretend to be our mother calling him out sick, hid in the garden until our parents left for work, then spent the day reorganizing the entire kitchen." Noelle had the same laugh as Laurent.

"Apparently, the way our mother had it organized had been driving him crazy. When my parents got home and saw everything moved, Laurent tried to claim a vagrant must have broken in, not stolen anything, and taken the time to divide the rice into eight perfectly equal containers."

"Only eight? These days he's up to ten rice containers," I said. Noelle and I both laughed as Laurent crossed his arms and grumbled about the challenges of living with the slovenly.

It was a fifteen-minute drive to Bouc-Bel-Air, the little village Laurent had grown up in. As Noelle expertly navigated the narrow streets, I peered out the window at the caramel-colored stone buildings. There was a clocktower, rows of pretty shops, and the crumbling remains of the town's medieval castle perched on a hill. Surrounding the town were low, wild mountains, and I knew the sea must not be too far.

"What a beautiful place," I said, half to myself.

"Isn't it?" Noelle agreed, tucking a strand of her bob behind her ear. "Laurent's been dying to leave his whole life." She pulled up to a stone house surrounded by a sprawling garden. Laurent's parents were waiting for us out front. As soon as I got out of the car, his mother embraced me and kissed me on each cheek.

"I'm so happy to meet you, Margot," she said warmly. "I hope the train ride wasn't too long."

Laurent got his good looks from his mother: she had the same blond curls, although hers were long, and the same golden eyes and chiseled nose. She was casually yet elegantly dressed in a bronze-colored dress and cerulean shawl. She somehow looked both homey and ready for a night at the opera. Laurent's father was stockier and had dark hair, but when he smiled, his whole face crinkled in delight, the same way Laurent's did.

They led me inside, past the foyer and into the kitchen. Just seeing it made me smile. It was full of shelves, which were themselves full of various crockery and copper pots. There were red amaryllis in a ceramic vase and several bottles of wine on the table. The floor was stone, smooth and almost shiny from decades of wear, and the walls were brick. That should have made the room freezing, but there was a large fireplace with a roaring fire. I immediately wanted to settle into a chair with a pastry and glass of wine.

"Where's Grand-mère?" Laurent asked his father.

"Your uncle is still picking her up; she had to finish packing. But they'll be along for dinner," Laurent's father told him. Laurent relaxed a bit.

"It's better to ease Margot in slowly. Meeting Grand-mère right away might terrify her," Noelle said.

I smiled, assuming a joke, but everyone looked serious.

"What's wrong with your grandmother?" I asked Laurent quietly.

"Oh, nothing's the matter with Grand-mère," Laurent's mother said, her tone deliberately light. "She just takes a while to warm up to people."

I looked at Laurent, wanting more information, but all he did was squeeze my shoulder reassuringly.

Just then, the door banged open and in flooded the rest of the family. They filled the kitchen to the brim, but in a way that made it seem full, not overwhelming. I was introduced to Laurent's cousin Celine, who had the same smile as Laurent. Her two daughters launched themselves at Laurent, squealing with happiness at seeing their uncle and begging him to bake cookies with them.

"I will," Laurent promised, trying to keep his balance while holding them both. "But do you know who's going to help us? The best cookie maker I know." He pointed in my direction, and both girls turned toward me, their eyes wide.

Immediately, they clambered down and began peppering me with questions about what cookies we were going to make, would they have chocolate, and could we start right now?

Other family members began pouring glasses of wine. Laurent put the bag filled with my baked goods on the table, where it was promptly attacked.

"Oh Margot, these are fabulous," his mother said, holding a pain au chocolat in one hand and using the other to give my hand a gentle squeeze. "And what a beautiful ring. I've always loved emeralds."

"Thank you," I said, turning the ring so it caught the light. "It was my mother's." To avoid any awkward questions, Laurent had told his parents about my mother before we'd arrived. Laurent's mother clearly remembered, for she pressed her hands to mine. It was just for a moment, but it was enough for me to feel the warmth in them.

"Laurent said you were a good baker, but he didn't say you put half of France's bakeries to shame," Celine said, a bit of frosting from the éclair she'd just bitten into on the tip of her nose.

"Do you know Père Noël? Are these from him?" Celine's younger daughter asked imperiously, a macaron in each hand.

Being with Laurent's family was warm and easy, but still, after so much family togetherness, I was glad when Laurent and I finally escaped for a little time on our own.

"This was my bedroom when I was growing up," he said, leading me across the garden.

"Your parents made you sleep outside?"

"No, silly. Here." He stopped in front of a stone shed. "See?" he said, looking at the tiny building proudly. "Ah, they haven't been weeding properly." Laurent bent down to pluck a weed that was perhaps two centimeters tall. Then he opened the door and ushered me in.

Any thoughts I might have had about the Roches banishing their son to the shed disappeared as soon as I walked inside. It was like a treehouse, or a fort. A very, very tidy fort. There was a double bed spread with a patchwork quilt, a shelf with rows of cookbooks (carefully organized by descending size), a desk in the corner with a bronze lamp, and, in the other corner, a clothes rack with every item perfectly pressed, naturally.

Near the door, an orange tabby raised its head from the basket of blankets it had been sleeping in and blinked at us.

"That's Beau," Laurent told me. "He comes and goes as he pleases. Minerva kept trying to murder him whenever I brought her here. That's why she now stays at home with a sitter." I bent down to scratch Beau between the ears.

"And look here," Laurent said, opening another door. I peered inside and saw a toilet, shower, and sink. "It's a real bathroom. My father set up the plumbing."

"A flushing toilet? My goodness, we really are in the lap of luxury."

Laurent quirked an eyebrow. "Oh, I see. Are you making fun of my childhood abode?"

"Not at all," I replied, equally serious. "And I'm not thinking at all that your parents must have banished you here, like a barnyard animal, because you're clearly their least favorite child. That thought never crossed my mind."

"A barnyard animal?" Laurent repeated. "I'll show you a barnyard animal." He tossed me on the bed and straddled me, his mouth hot on mine. His hands were busy at the buttons of my sweater as he kissed me urgently, his tongue running over my swollen lips. I pulled his hips close, feeling him hard beneath his jeans.

The final button of my sweater came undone, and cold air wafted over my skin. Laurent quickly remedied the situation by pulling me close as he unhooked my bra. It slid off as I fumbled with his jeans, my anxiety over meeting his family replaced with urgent desire.

Laurent raised himself a few centimeters so I was able to slide his jeans off over his hips. I peeled Laurent's shirt off as he pulled my jeans down to my ankles, then off my feet. Clad only in our underwear, I maneuvered so I was fully beneath Laurent's shuddery, warm body. He grazed my neck with his teeth.

I had my legs wrapped around Laurent's waist when his phone buzzed. He groaned.

"Let me just check that. They'll come knocking at the door if I don't respond."

I sighed, sinking back into the pillows. "Well, it's nice to know we still get cell phone reception in this hinterland."

Laurent rolled his eyes theatrically as he got up. He crossed the room, which gave me the opportunity to admire his taut muscles and just how nicely tanned he was.

Laurent looked at his phone, then came back over and gave me a kiss on the tip of my nose. "My mother can't find the braiser since I last reorganized the kitchen. I have to dig it out so we can have dinner."

I sighed. "I suppose I won't make your family go hungry just to satisfy my lust. I'll shower so I'm presentable," I said, pulling him down to kiss him again. Laurent trailed a string of kisses from my chest to my belly button before pulling on his clothes. Before he left, he kissed me a final time, groaning low in his throat before he finally pulled away.

Laurent's father must have some serious plumbing skills because the water in the shower was hot and strong. I took my time lathering up and combing conditioner through my hair, wanting to look my best for the family dinner. As I was rinsing off, I heard Beau knock something off the end table. A loud crack reverberated across the shed.

Oh no, I thought, quickly stepping out of the shower. *Little beast better not knock my phone off next.*

"Cut it out, Beau!" I shouted as I ran out of the bathroom.

Beau, from the nest he'd made in the bedcovers, raised his head and looked at me disdainfully. He turned to the other person in the room. It wasn't Laurent.

Chapter 21

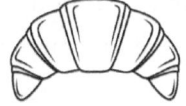

S tanding not a meter from where I stood naked and dripping wet was an elderly woman. An elderly woman I had just shouted at. She was wearing low heels, a maroon dress, a string of pearls around her neck, and a look of disdain that blew Beau's out of the water.

This was it. This was the moment of my death. It must be because I don't know how someone could keep living when their only wish was to be swallowed immediately by the earth.

Goodbye Laurent, it was fun, but your grandmother thinks I'm a naked, screaming banshee, and now I must leave this world.

Laurent's grandmother didn't look shocked, although it'd be much better if she did. Instead, she simply looked imposing and mildly disapproving, as though jumping out of the shower to scream naked at strangers was a peculiar hobby she hoped I'd soon grow out of. Looking as though it pained her, she extended a hand.

"I am Madame Roche." Every word was like ice.

I hadn't moved a centimeter since I'd seen her, still waiting desperately for the whole swallowed-by-the-earth moment to happen already. Mechanically, I extended a wet hand and grasped her fingers. I dimly wondered if I should kiss her hand, she seemed so much like a queen.

Just then, Beau gave a yowl, and it shook me out of my horrified stupor. "PleaseexcusemeI'llberightbackIjustneedtogetdressed."

I fled back to the bathroom.

Once inside, with the door firmly locked, I contemplated the possibility of just staying here forever. It'd be tough, but I could make it work. It certainly beat the idea of venturing back into the outside world.

Why was Laurent's grandmother even in this cursed shed? And where the hell was Laurent?

I took as long as humanly possible to get dressed and do my hair, but, eventually, I had to open the bathroom door. Madame Roche was standing right where I'd left her. If anything, she looked even more terrifying now.

I switched into work mode, telling myself she was just another stranger to chat to; I did that every day. No need to recall that I'd been stark naked when we'd met, although the puddle of water where I'd been standing was an unhelpful reminder.

"Enchantée, Madame Roche," I said, all smiles. "My name is Margot Delcour. I'm visiting from Paris with Laurent. How was your journey here?"

Madame Roche regarded me stonily. "How did you meet Laurent?" From her tone, it was clear she was thinking a brothel or worse.

"Laurent moved into the apartment next to mine. We hit it off right away. I could smell him cooking—"

"What do you do for work?" she interrupted, still looking imperious.

"I'm a server at Le Jules Verne in Paris." I smiled again. My cheeks were beginning to hurt.

Madame Roche sniffed. "Laurent's last girlfriend was a lawyer. A very successful one."

Ah. OK then, she's that type of person.

"That's wonderful," I said, forcing another smile. "Both my grandfathers were lawyers, and they loved their work."

Madame Roche had opened her mouth to ask what I'm sure would be another blunt and borderline-offensive question when the door banged open and Laurent rushed in, looking harried.

"Grand-mère! Now, come on, I know Uncle told you that you'd be staying in the house for this visit. I wanted to be back in my old room." He looked between us, his face still somewhat frantic. "You've already met Margot?"

"Yes," his grandmother replied icily. "It was illuminating."

I could tell Laurent was looking at me, but I was too embarrassed to meet his eyes.

As Laurent hustled his grandmother out, she stared at me over her shoulder the entire time, until he firmly shut the door behind her. That done, he leaned against the door and heaved a sigh of relief.

"That's not the way I wanted you to meet Grand-mère, but at least now it's out of the way." He went to hug me, then paused, noticing my expression. "What's the matter?"

It all came out: Beau, the shouting, the nakedness, the handshake during the nakedness...I'd sunk to the ground with my head in my hands as I told most of the story, and every time I looked at Laurent his expression of concern slipped more and more as he struggled to hold back his laughter.

"This isn't funny!" I exclaimed. *That* was what sent Laurent over the edge. I glared at him as he collapsed to the floor, shaking with laughter. I can't believe I'd let this man half undress me less than an hour ago.

When Laurent finally got ahold of himself, he wiped his eyes, a stray giggle escaping here and there. "*Au contraire*, that story is objectively hilarious."

"You don't think she'll tell anyone?" I asked worriedly.

"Oh, I'm sure she's already told everyone," Laurent said, and he laughed again at my reaction. "Don't worry; you were never going to win her over. *I* still haven't won her over, and I'm her grandson. Grand-mère is just a tough nut to crack. I should have warned you earlier, but I thought we'd have more time before she arrived."

"She appears to be a fan of your ex-girlfriend." I knew I was treading potentially dangerous ground, but something about being full-frontal with Laurent's grandmother had turned me reckless.

Laurent rolled his eyes. "Yes, my ex is the granddaughter of one of her old friends. Grand-mère is the one who set us up, actually, and she was the only family member who approved of our relationship. I should have taken it as a sign to run screaming in the opposite direction. Now come on, we don't want dinner to get cold."

There were roughly ten thousand things I'd rather do than face Laurent's family, but I allowed him to guide me back to the house.

When we stepped inside, I briefly hoped that Laurent's grandmother hadn't mentioned anything about The Incident. But then I realized that everyone was being just a little *too* friendly. And it didn't help that Noelle was over in the corner, nearly crimson from choking back laughter.

I fled to the kitchen, where Laurent's mother was finishing up the meal. When she saw me, she didn't say a word. Instead, she hugged me, holding tight for a moment. It was a small gesture, but so unexpected that tears sprung into my eyes.

"Can I help with plating the food?" I offered, hurriedly blinking my tears away. "I like to keep busy."

The big dinner would be tomorrow, on Christmas Eve, so today the menu was fairly simple, although everything looked delicious. There was roast chicken, cod braised with tomatoes and olives, endive salad, and a cheeseboard piled so high I was terrified it'd collapse on me as I brought it to the table.

Laurent's parents had one of those grandiose dining rooms common in older homes. Several tables had been pulled together to make a massive table, and chairs seemed to have been brought in from all corners of the house. That should have meant plenty of opportunities for me not to sit near Grand-mère, but as soon as I took my seat, she chose the seat directly across from mine. Every time I glanced her way, I found her eyes boring into me.

But dinner was pleasant, overall. I had Laurent on one side, and Michel, one of Laurent's cousins on the other.

"Who is the craziest diner you've ever served?" Michel asked.

That story (which involved a suitcase full of wigs, fake paparazzi, and an attempt at smuggling a Dutch oven full of beef stew out of the restaurant) was enough to get us nearly to dessert.

When I'd finished speaking, I took a sip of wine. "Do you make it up to Paris often?"

Michel shook his head. "I live in Corsica and don't leave much. The holidays are the only time I can convince myself to get off the island."

"Oh, I love Corsica. I haven't been in years, but I remember it being so beautiful. Do you enjoy living there?"

"Yes, very much. Good food, good beaches. We have a beautiful one, Plage de Tahiti. It's very relaxed. No clothing requirements." Michel smiled anxiously, and I knew he was trying his best to relate to me. But a nude beach?

Out of the corner of my eye, I saw Laurent's grandmother. For the first time, she was grinning.

Excellent. Now the entire Roche family thinks I'm an out-of-control nudist.

"Why does your grandmother hate me?" I asked Laurent later. The meal had ended and we were hand-in-hand, making the trek across the yard to his shed.

Laurent tucked me under his arm. "That's just how she treats everyone. It's not personal. You should have heard the things she said when Noelle dyed her hair blue back at university." Laurent opened the door to his shed-home. "Come on, let's focus on the twenty-odd family members who adored you. Tomorrow, I'll take you around town, and you won't need to see Grand-mère until dinner," Laurent said, closing the door behind us.

"But for now, let's get back to what we were doing earlier before we were so rudely interrupted." He pulled me to him, hands slipping under the back of my sweater.

He didn't need to tell me twice. "Alright. But make double sure you lock the front door."

Chapter 22

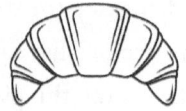

The next morning, we woke early and had coffee and hot rolls with Laurent's parents before anyone else (and one person in particular) was awake. I tried to help his parents prepare for dinner, but they declined all assistance and told us to enjoy ourselves.

We could have taken the Peugeot, but it was a beautiful day, one of those crisp-cold ones with a brilliant blue sky, and Laurent and I both wanted some fresh air.

We strolled along the country road into town, passing farms and little clusters of houses. Every time a car drove past us (which wasn't often), the driver inevitably rolled to a stop. Recognizing Laurent, they got out and greeted him effusively, explaining that they were an old classmate/neighbor/librarian who was thrilled to see their prodigal son back home for Christmas.

Bouc-Bel-Air was full of Christmas cheer when we reached it: fairy lights strung across the trees, window decorations in every storefront, and a towering fir tree, bedecked with ornaments, in the currently-dry village fountain.

As we walked, Laurent pointed out key places from his youth: the tiny cinema, the street where the monthly antique market that his mother never missed was held, the primary school with cheery drawings hanging in the windows, the sprawling formal gardens, which were closed for winter but were apparently gorgeous the rest of the year.

Despite it being Christmas Eve, plenty of people were out, walking with their families or shopping for last-minute gifts. Plenty of them stopped Laurent here too, and although I could see how life in such a small town might be suffocating, I found it heartwarming that Laurent came from such a tight knit community. It was worlds away from how I grew up, just me and my mother, moving every time she got bored of a place.

As we continued our stroll, I glanced at Laurent. He looked gorgeous in Provence's golden light, and I was overwhelmed with the desire to kiss him. So I did. We were still caught up in each other when a car honked very close by. The sound startled us apart.

"*Merde*, Noelle, what are you scaring people for?" Laurent said, frowning as his sister rolled down the window of the Peugeot. She beamed at us, not looking a bit remorseful.

"I've been sent to Aix to pick up missing ingredients, and I thought you two might like to join."

We hopped in the back seat and sped to Aix as Christmas songs poured out of the radio. Noelle dropped us off close to the center of town, promising she'd meet up with us once she'd finished her shopping. I'd be happy to spend the entire day wandering Aix, admiring the honey-colored buildings, verdant town square, and understated elegance of it all. But Laurent had a place to show me.

"This way," he said, pulling me along. We walked along the sidewalks, passing shops selling lavender and olive oil and stepping into the street to let carolers, children looking longingly into store windows, doe-eyed couples, and everyone else pass by. Laurent finally turned down a narrow stone street and stopped in front of...

"An Applebee's?" I said, looking between him and the restaurant. Was this some sort of joke? Did Laurent really think my love of American chain restaurants was so strong that I wanted to eat at one on Christmas Eve? (I mean, he wasn't wrong.)

"Oh," I said, as the pieces fell into place. "This was your restaurant. This was Les Champs D'Or."

Laurent didn't hear me. He was looking at the building. He had the deep scowl he always wore when he tried to hide his feelings, but I saw the anguish breaking through beneath it.

"There isn't much sidewalk here, but the town would let us shut down the street and put tables outside in the summer," he said softly, looking through the windows. "My Aunt Lisle stitched all the tablecloths. We had a bouillabaisse special every weekend, and every Friday I'd drive to Marseille's fish market and pick out the seafood." He paused and cleared his throat. "We had an Easter lunch every year, and the place would be full of families, people I'd known my entire life, spending their holiday enjoying food I'd made."

Laurent's jaw went rigid, and I knew he was trying hard not to cry.

"Isn't it awful," he continued, his voice strained, "To reach a point in life where you think you've figured it all out and the hard parts are over, and then it all falls apart on you?" He leaned his head against my shoulder, still unable to wrench his eyes from his former restaurant.

I took his hand. "Hard luck that they turned it into an Applebee's, of all things. Although, have you tried their boneless buffalo wings with the lemon pepper sauce? I hate myself for saying it, but one time at university we ordered them—again, don't hate me—and they weren't half bad. Want to get an order to go?"

I was doing my best to make Laurent smile, and he rewarded me with a tiny upturn of his mouth.

"You're always cheering me up," he said, planting a kiss on my hair.

"That's the duty of a sunshiny person."

He turned back to the restaurant. "It had a terrible kitchen setup," he said, trying and failing miserably to sound blasé. "And it echoed like crazy." He put an arm around my shoulders. "It's hard to go home again."

"Don't I know it."

Laurent pulled me closer, so that I was cocooned in his arms. "I'm being too morose, even for a grump. I can't be dragging you down with me. Come on, we'll look at Aix's Christmas tree."

When we returned in the afternoon, Celine's daughters ran up to me, begging to make cookies. I took over a corner of the kitchen and taught the two girls, and Laurent, how to make mantecados, an anise-flavored shortbread recipe I'd learned in Madrid. The cookies came out of the oven just as it was time to sit down for dinner.

Laurent's family followed the traditional Provençal menu for Christmas Eve. There were seven dishes of vegetables and seafood local to the region and thirteen accompanying desserts, mostly small things like figs, candied fruit, and walnuts.

I'd contributed nougat, made from one of the very first recipes my mother had taught me.

The next day, Christmas dawned cold and bright. There was no shortage of cheer in the Roche household. Happiness pulsed from every corner of the home, but I couldn't get myself to take up the feeling. Every time I tried, it was as though it slipped past me.

Laurent's family suddenly felt like too much: too big, too loud, too happy. While Laurent prepared the Christmas dinner duck, I slunk back to the shed and lay in bed, Beau purring in my arms.

Nestled in the blankets, I stared dully at the ceiling. I'd really hoped this would be the year I enjoyed the holidays again. I had everything I should have needed: loving boyfriend, his welcoming family, a beautiful setting. But it all fell flat.

They annoyed me suddenly, the Roche family. They did Christmas all wrong with their Provençal food and suffocating village and so many people and so much noise and so many chairs crammed around the table that you hit someone with your elbow whenever you moved a centimeter.

Of course I wouldn't enjoy Christmas here. Christmas meant Coq au Riesling simmering away on the stove, and gingerbread baking in the oven. It meant board games with my mother and carols playing quietly on the radio and my grandparents arguing good-naturedly about whether we needed to throw another log on the fire...

Squeezing my eyes shut, I pictured my mother in a dress and pearls, looking elegant as she tested the top of the kugelhopf to be sure it sprung back perfectly.

"Here, Margot, feel it for yourself," she'd tell me, watching as I touched the top of the cake with a fingertip. "It's important to get it right. Good baking can brighten any day of the year, but on Christmas...that's when you really can make food people think is magic."

You need to get on with your life, I told myself. *It's either that or you spend every holiday crying with—at best—an indifferent cat for company.*

I looked at Beau. "No offense," I assured him. "I'm tired of me, too."

Beau twitched his tail and turned so that his fluffy cat backside faced me.

I sighed, then got up and scrubbed my face in the bathroom. After brushing my hair and applying some makeup to cover the blotchiness crying always left me with, I felt well enough that the wave of cheerful noise didn't make me want to flee back to the shed when I re-entered the Roche home.

Laurent was in the kitchen, finishing up the duck.

"Are you alright?" he asked, looking concerned as he chopped a pile of olives.

"I'm fine," I said brightly. "I just took a nap to make sure I had enough energy to devour all this food you made."

"Speaking of food, how's it coming along?" Noelle called from the other room. "We're all starving, Laurent."

"Just another few minutes," Laurent said, then grumbled under his breath as his knife worked back and forth across the olives.

"It's OK if they aren't chopped perfectly evenly," I told him. "Your family would probably much rather eat uneven olives than wait until midnight for dinner." Which was when things would be ready if his pace continued, although I didn't mention that part.

I could tell Laurent was about to make a grumpy remark, then he turned and saw me holding back laughter. He grinned, his shoulders relaxing.

"You're right. Let the barbarians eat their uneven olives. It's all they deserve, anyway."

As Laurent plated the food, Noelle laid out the dishes, and I lit candles so that the entire dining room flickered with their light. Then I heaped my plate with everything and sat between Laurent and Noelle, laughing as their parents argued over whether they should take up beekeeping.

Even Laurent's grandmother seemed to have toned down her acidity. A little. She did make one comment about how I should be the one dishing food from the platters, "since I was so good at serving people," but I ignored her and no similar comments followed.

After dinner we gathered in the living room to exchange gifts.

"Oh, Laurent. It's beautiful," I breathed as I lifted a silver necklace out of its box. The emerald pendant sparkled in the candlelight.

"It's to match your mother's ring."

I reached out to kiss him, then noticed my bare hand with a start.

"Oh! I lost it. Laurent, I lost my mother's ring." My voice trembled. I'd always cherished my possessions, and this one, a piece of jewelry I remembered seeing on my mother's own hand so often, was particularly precious. My eyes suddenly filled with tears.

"It's OK," Laurent said, his arm going protectively around my shoulders. "We'll find it. It's in the house. It must be. I'll set my parents to look for it. Nothing escapes my mother when she does her weekly deep clean. She'll find it; I promise."

"Alright," I whispered, forcing myself to steady my breathing. Laurent was right. It would be OK. But it still felt like yet another reason to add to this day's unhappiness.

At that moment, there was a knock at the front door. It was a jarring sound, and everyone's head swiveled toward the noise. Laurent looked just as confused as I felt, but his grandmother had already sprung up and was heading to the door. I heard it creak open.

"Merry Christmas! I know you asked me to come, but I hope I'm not intruding," an unseen voice said. There was something familiar about it. Laurent's head shot up.

"Not at all. Merry Christmas, dear. Come inside," Laurent's grandmother replied (speaking far kinder than she ever had to me).

"We have a visitor," his grandmother announced as she led the newcomer into the room. "You all remember Sabine."

I was so startled my new necklace nearly slid through my fingers; I had to clutch it in a fist to keep it from falling to the floor. There she stood on the Roches' scarred stone floor—my apparent arch-nemesis. She had a camel scarf covering her hair, and her cheeks were rosy from the cold. Laurent's parents were frozen for a moment, then they lurched to their feet, greeting Sabine with kisses on her cheek.

Laurent's grandmother was speaking again. "Excuse the intrusion, but I had a gift I wanted to give the Berlioz family. I heard Sabine knew Laurent's new friend, so I decided to invite her over." She turned directly to me and grinned triumphantly.

"You and Sabine know each other?" Laurent's mother asked me, smiling uncertainly.

"Oh, yes," Sabine said. "Margot is actually our little baker for the gala I'm running. Our professional pastry chef dropped out, and Fatima asked if a friend could take her place. It was very kind of Margot to accept, even if it is a lot for her."

I wondered if anyone else could hear the venom in Sabine's voice.

"How lovely you're working together," Laurent's mother said politely.

"We've been enjoying Margot's baking all weekend," his father said. "The gala is lucky to have her."

"Yes, well." Sabine's smile slipped somewhat.

"Your sister couldn't join you?" Laurent's grandmother asked.

Sabine smiled sweetly. "Oh, no. Camille is with her husband's family today. Did you hear she and Adrien eloped last week? It was terribly romantic."

Laurent stiffened beside me as his grandmother clapped her hands together in delight.

"How marvelous," his grandmother said.

"It is," Sabine agreed. "I've never seen her so happy." She shot Laurent a glare. "But I have to get back to my own Christmas dinner now. Thank you for the gift," she said, taking the small package Laurent's grandmother offered. "Merry Christmas," she said, and her gaze lingered on me as Laurent's parents walked her to the door.

The door shut, and I heard Laurent's father furiously whispering to Grand-mère. Laurent's mother hurried back into the room.

"Who wants vin chaud?" Laurent's mother asked, her voice a little higher-pitched than normal.

"I certainly need a drink," Noelle said, glaring toward the front door.

I took a mug of vin chaud, but the drink did little to warm me. I was still feeling down when Laurent and I escaped to the shed. Laurent, who was normally so attentive, seemed wrapped in his own unhappiness.

"Laurent?"

He lifted his head and met my eyes.

"Was Adrien, you know, was he the guy Sabine's sister...got with when you were still together?"

"Yes. That's him." He sighed. "They deserve each other, I suppose." Laurent attempted a smile but couldn't quite complete it.

What a depressing Christmas this had been. And I'd had such high hopes.

Laurent opened his door and took my hand. "I know today's been hard for you."

Normally I would have denied it, insisted I was full of the Christmas spirit, but I just leaned closer to Laurent. He led me to the bed and sat down next to me.

"Do you want to know something that'll make the day better?"

I half shrugged. I could hardly imagine how Christmas could be salvaged.

Laurent waited until I looked up at him. Then he smiled, this time for real. "My parents think you're great," he said, still grinning. "They've been telling me so all day. My father wanted to know if I was serious about you."

"Oh," I said listlessly. I looked around to see if Beau was lounging somewhere.

"I told him I wanted to marry you."

I was so surprised that I leapt to my feet. "Are you joking?"

He laughed. "Of course I'm not. This isn't a proposal because I want to do things right, but I wanted you to know how I felt about you.

"And the truth is, you're it for me, Margot."

I stared at him wonderingly. "You're serious?"

He nodded, his eyes gleaming.

I threw my arms around Laurent, and we fell onto the bed, caught up in our mutual joy.

Hours later, I lay away in the warm dark, wrapped in quilts with Laurent sleeping beside me. I felt as happy as a child on Christmas morning. No matter that Christmas was nearly over and my childhood very much so. For years, I'd watched other people find this kind of happiness at work.

Now, incredibly, it was my turn.

Chapter 23

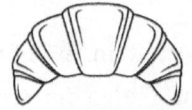

"You'll astound them," Laurent assured me as we walked into the building for another gala meeting.

It was the week after New Year's, and this meeting was especially important because we'd be making test batches of our recipes in the kitchens. I was nervous to see Sabine again, and on top of that, there'd be taste testers judging our food.

Fatima had told us they were just volunteer chefs who'd give us tips to make sure our recipes were the best they could be, but I still felt like I was about to take an exam.

Our judging panel, as it were, was already seated in the kitchens. There were half a dozen of them, including Fatima and, of course, Sabine.

Sabine was wearing a full-length gown with a plunging neckline, which one might say was too ostentatious to taste test recipes. I was tempted to point out that her bra strap was showing, but I demurred. My plan for dealing with Sabine was to simply ignore her as much as possible.

I was anxious starting off, but once I turned my back to everyone and concentrated on the recipes, my nerves eased. This was just baking. I did it nearly every day. Plus, I already had a head start. Many of my recipes required extended time for proofing or setting, so I'd come to the kitchens the day before to get them started.

That made things easier for me today, since most of the recipes only needed to be baked or get their finishing touches. As I completed each recipe, I passed out samples for the taste testers to review.

First done were the baklava croissants. Fatima had loved the idea, despite Sabine's complaints, but I was nervous to see what the panel thought of it. As each person tasted their croissant, I watched their faces closely.

"Magnificent filling," one of the chefs declared. "Was it difficult to get the honey from making the pastry layers stick together?"

"Oh, it was so hard to figure out," I admitted. "The filling in my first try was too runny and melted during baking. Those croissants were basically soggy, sticky bricks," I said, grinning. "The second time, the texture was right, but I added too much filling, and it overwhelmed the pastry. It took a lot of trial and error."

"These are very well balanced," another chef said.

Sabine spoke up. "You don't think they're too obvious? They seem very obvious to me."

Blank faces regarded her down the length of the table.

"Too obvious?" the first chef repeated.

"Sabine, dear, what do you mean?" Fatima asked.

"Oh, never mind," Sabine said, pushing her untouched croissant away. I allowed myself the tiniest smile before getting back to work.

Everything I made got compliments, even the fussy mille feuilles, which took me forever to assemble with their layers of pastry cream and puff pastry. I wasn't very well-versed in food styling, and the chefs gave me excellent tips for decorating them.

If I'd thought Sabine randomly popping up at Laurent's on Christmas would somehow soften her feelings toward me, I quickly learned that was untrue. She had barbs for each of my recipes: they were too plain or too heavy or some other thing.

But everyone ignored her, and I barely paid her attention myself. I was too happy talking shop with people who knew the intricacies of baking and what it took to create pastries that delighted a crowd. I scribbled down everything they said, my confidence swelling little by little.

Laurent's first dishes were finishing up by the time I served my final dessert: the macarons. Not a single one of the judges could think of a way they could be improved.

Buzzing from their compliments, I took a seat at my work station to observe their comments on Laurent's food. Sabine would probably be vicious, but I'd tried each of these recipes Laurent had created, and I knew they'd send the judges into raptures.

But Sabine was strangely enthusiastic about Laurent's food. She declared his couscous sauteed in duck fat "sublime" and told the chef next to her that Laurent's chicken fricassée with sumac and mint was the best thing she'd ever eaten in her life. Laurent frowned at her compliments, but otherwise his attention was on the chefs. As they spoke, I saw his eyes glowing the way they did whenever he was deeply interested in a subject.

When things finally wrapped up, Fatima congratulated us on our menus.

"I'm certain that, whatever else happens, this gala will have food that is second to none!" she said proudly.

A man from the judging panel, the one sitting next to Sabine, stood. "Monsieur Roche, may I have a moment of your time?"

Laurent turned to me, his eyes still bright. "I'll be right out."

I waited for Laurent in the hall, wondering what the man was saying to him. Probably just complimenting him more on his dishes. Laurent certainly deserved it.

Just then, Laurent stepped out of the room looking like he'd just won the lottery. Surprise and nervousness and pure happiness passed across his face as he walked over to me.

"What is it?"

"That man, the man who spoke to me, he owns restaurants. He has one in Berlin that needs a new head chef. He asked if I wanted the position."

I barely stopped my mouth from dropping open. "What did you say?"

"I told him I couldn't make any decision right then, but that I'd think about it." Laurent's gaze slipped from mine; he was focusing on something I couldn't see. "Margot, do you realize what this means?" he asked excitedly. "This is the chance I've been waiting for. That's why I wanted to do this gala in the first place, to see if I still have what it takes to be a chef."

"So, you're going to take the job?" I asked quietly.

Laurent took my hands in his. "I'm not doing anything without your full agreement. But," he continued, "We could make this work. You could come to Berlin with me—"

I was already shaking my head. "I have a life here, Laurent. I can't just pack it up."

"Well, then we'll visit each other. All the time. And this wouldn't be forever. Just enough for me to get some experience. Then I can find another job in Paris or wherever you want to live."

Laurent looked so excited and happy, but I was wary. "What if things go the same way you said they did last time? Where you get consumed with work and forget about everything else? Forget about me," I added, very quietly.

Laurent's hands were warm on mine. "That won't happen," he said, all his intensity focused solely on me now. Those golden eyes were enough to drown in. "I know myself better now, and you're too important to me. You come before anything else. Absolutely anything else. You say the word, and I'll turn the job down without another thought."

I believed Laurent, believed that I could tell him I wasn't comfortable with the distance or the pressure of a chef position and he'd walk away. But I looked at the excitement stark on his face and remembered all the nights he'd come home exhausted and demoralized from his office work.

There was no possibility of me telling him to throw away this opportunity.

"I think you should go for it," I told Laurent, concentrating hard on looking happy. If there was ever a moment I needed to call on the sunniest parts of my personality, this was it.

Laurent burst into a smile and caught me up in an embrace. As I breathed in his scent of rosemary and citrus, only one thought was running through my mind: *Please don't let this be what breaks us.*

Chapter 24

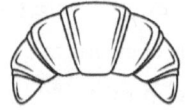

Laurent left three weeks later. All his things, so recently unpacked, were packed up again and shipped to the Berlin flat his new employer had helped set up. He'd quit his hated office job, ended his lease with Madame Blanchet, regretfully informed Fatima that he could no longer work the gala, and suggested the sous chef he thought most prepared to take his place.

Now he and I stood inside his apartment. It was bare except for one suitcase, one extremely expensive cat carrier with an extremely expensive cashmere blanket lining the bottom, and one extremely spoiled gray cat ignoring us as she tore apart a catnip mouse.

"So," Laurent said.

We were doing our best to make this separation as painless as possible. Laurent already had his train booked to visit me in four weeks, and I'd be going to see him two weeks after that. We had scheduled times to call each other every day. It wouldn't last forever. But I still was miserable.

"It's only right that you take this job," I said. "Everyone knows that Germany's culinary scene needs all the help it can get."

My delivery was weak, but Laurent smiled all the same. "That's my sunshine girl," he said, and he pulled me into an embrace. "Thank you for supporting me."

"I'm in the business of making dreams come true," I said, my voice muffled against his shirt collar. "Just promise me you won't get grumpy if a diner asks for curry sauce on their coq au vin. Remember, they don't know any better."

Laurent laughed, his chest rumbling against mine.

"And you won't turn into terrible, workaholic Laurent?" A desperate note crept into my voice.

Laurent hugged me tighter. "I promise. If I start sleeping in the kitchens and skipping showers, I'll reel myself back in."

"You skipped showers? Wow, no wonder you got dumped." We smiled at each other, both of us trying our hardest to keep things light. If we could laugh, then nothing was so bad. Right?

"Here," I said, "I brought you something." I pulled a small box out of my purse and pressed it into his hands. Laurent opened it to reveal six perfect macarons.

"I thought you deserved some that weren't broken." I said softly.

Laurent smiled at the memory. He gently lifted a macaron and bit into it, chewing slowly.

"Pistachio," he said, grinning wider. "You got the flavor just right."

His phone buzzed in his pocket. "That'll be my taxi."

Laurent looked sad but excited. I couldn't imagine how I looked; I had about twenty emotions pulsing through me.

Laurent kissed me again, then bent down to pick up his suitcase and cat carrier. I walked him to the door and held it open for him.

"À bientôt," I said. It was a deliberate choice of words. It meant, not goodbye, but closer to "bye for now." You only used it when you knew you'd be seeing the person again soon, when being reunited was a sure thing.

"À bientôt, Margot," Laurent said. His golden eyes held mine for a moment. Then he slipped into the taxi and was gone.

***

As winter trundled on, frost congealed on the windowpanes, snow turned to slush, and we passed around mug after mug of vin chaud and hot toddies at Le Jules Verne.

At the start of the year, I'd excitedly told Yasmine what Laurent had promised on Christmas. If she had any lingering doubts over our relationship, she hid them well, shrieking in surprise and promising to take me to look at rings so I could get an idea of what I'd like. Every time I thought back to that conversation it was as though I had a little flame inside me, banishing the gloominess.

Preparations for the gala continued. I worked as hard on my recipes as ever, trying not to let the fact that Laurent was no longer part of it dent my enthusiasm. He'd be at the gala, he'd promised, so he could see what I'd worked so hard on.

A frozen February morning found the culinary team doing test runs of our recipes in the kitchens again.

"I want every recipe to be a well-oiled machine by the day of the gala. You should be able to make this food in your sleep," Fatima declared, looking surprisingly stern in a ruffled apron.

I was making the macarons today, three colors to match my three fillings: lemon, pistachio, and fig. I had the recipes finalized down to the exact gram of almond flour I needed, so this meeting was mostly to assuage Fatima's concerns and butter up (as it were) a group of visiting high-roller donors with food.

Things were already bustling when I entered the kitchens. The newly-promoted head chef was just as capable as Laurent had told Fatima she'd be. From the scent wafting across the room, I could tell they were making the eggplant gratin. My heart twisted knowing they were working on the recipes Laurent had so carefully crafted.

Even if Fatima had (hopefully) been exaggerating, I'd made macarons so many times in my life that I *could* practically bake them in my sleep. As I worked through the steps, I chatted with Fatima and the culinary team. Sabine didn't seem to be here today. Maybe she'd lost interest in haunting me now that Laurent was gone. Now there's a silver lining.

I was sitting on a stool, taste-testing different flavors of harissa with the sous chefs, when my timer went off. Wandering over to my side of the kitchens, I opened the oven. And nearly cried at what I saw.

The macarons were overbaked. More than that, they were burnt, scorch marks marring their colorful tops. I pulled them out in horror.

What had happened? The oven temperature was correct, the baking time had been correct. I couldn't remember the last time I'd messed up macarons so badly. They were close to my signature dish; I'd been making them perfectly since I was a teenager. These were worse than my very first attempt, when I'd still been in grammar school.

The scent of charred almond flour began wafting across the kitchen. Several chefs turned and looked at me pityingly.

"Oh, Margot, what's this?" Fatima was suddenly beside me.

"I'm sorry," I stammered, my cheeks hot. "I think maybe this oven runs hot." It happened, quite often, in fact, and I knew I wasn't solely to blame. But I should have checked the macarons more often, should have seen they were cooking too fast. I'd gotten overconfident, and now Fatima was looking at me and my ruined creations with a deep furrow between her eyes.

"These things happen," she said, not unkindly. "But I can't have these served to our guests."

"I'm so sorry," I said again, my voice barely more than a whisper.

"It's alright," Fatima said, patting my back. "I'll see if the cooking team can whip up a dessert quickly."

My embarrassment only deepened when I realized Fatima didn't even trust me—their only baker—to come up with a replacement dessert for the donors. I guess she didn't want to take another risk on me today.

Shamefaced, I started packing my things when a voice spoke behind me.

"Oh dear. What's wrong with those macarons?"

Merde.

I turned to see—of course—Sabine standing behind me, an exaggerated look of concern on her face. Immediately, I turned away. I didn't have the energy to come up with a single thing to say to her.

It didn't matter. Sabine apparently didn't seem to need me to participate in the conversation. Out of the corner of my eye, I saw her slender finger slide across the macarons, pause at one of the blackest, and push it. It crumbled into charred crumbs.

"Oh goodness. It's such a terrible feeling to let people down," Sabine continued quietly, seemingly to herself. She lifted her head and gave me a ferocious grin. "At least Laurent isn't here to see it. Get used to that feeling."

As I reeled, she turned to Fatima. "Should we do something about this?" Sabine asked, twitching her head in my direction. "We can't have this happening the day of the gala."

"It won't," I said, looking desperately at Fatima. "It was one mistake. I know the oven now; it won't happen again."

"Fatima, this is why I was concerned about taking on a non-professional. There are just skills we can't expect them to have." Sabine shook her head sadly. If she could have managed it, I'm sure she would have had a single tear roll down her cheek, just to complete the image of her despondency.

How on Earth had I ended up arguing with Laurent's ex-girlfriend's sister to keep my role at a gala I never wanted to work at in the first place? My commitment had gone beyond doing a favor for Yasmine or even making Laurent proud. I wanted to go through with the gala for myself now. To know that I had it in me.

"Please," I said to Fatima. "I'll make the macarons again as many times as you want. You can trust me. I promise they'll be perfect for the gala."

Fatima hesitated, then smiled at me. "Of course we trust you, Margot. Come back next week and try again. I'm sure it'll go much better."

Sabine made a noise that, in a less elegant woman, would be called a snort, but I ignored it, too grateful for a chance to redeem myself.

I did Fatima one better. Over the next several days, I got permission to go back to the kitchens as often as I needed. I cooked the macarons three times, carefully watching their baking progress and adjusting the oven temperature. The following weekend, I sat in front of the oven and watched them the entire time they baked. When they came out, they were absolutely perfect.

"I knew you could do it!" Fatima exclaimed. "You're doing yourself credit, Margot." That helped my cracked self-esteem, but Sabine's words about Laurent remained floating around my head.

But Laurent had been different then, I told myself. He knew better now.

Two weeks after my disaster in the kitchens, I stood at the Gare de l'Est station, eagerly awaiting Laurent's train. It'd been a full month since we'd seen each other. I was so excited to be reunited that I was going to need to restrain myself from tackling him on the platform.

When his train pulled into the station, I moved to the front of the crowd. I was there in time to see Laurent be one of the first people to step off the train. In his hands was a bouquet of calla lilies, which he barely saved from annihilation as I flung myself into his arms.

He caught me up and swung me around, heedless of the people surrounding us.

"I've missed you horrifically," he said, after we'd kissed. "Everything's so dreary without you. There's no sunshine to counter my grumpiness."

Laurent was only here for two days, and we spent the entirety of them together, not wanting to lose a single moment with each other. At meals, during walks across the city, as we lay curled together in bed, Laurent regaled me with tales from his new job. Taking over a restaurant was always daunting, but Laurent was confident things were going well.

"All the sous chefs and line cooks and servers work together well. It's really encouraging," Laurent said.

We were sprawled out on my couch, enjoying our final evening together. Laurent looked tired but elated, and he couldn't keep the excitement out of his voice whenever he spoke about his new job. I didn't want to bring the mood down, so I didn't mention anything about my latest encounter with Sabine.

I *did* tell him about the burnt macarons, and his laughter and stories of his own kitchen disasters raised my spirits.

Laurent was happy at his new job, he and I spoke every day, we'd just spent a wonderful few days together, and we already had our next two visits planned.

We're doing it, I thought. *We're making this work.*

"Tell me what you think of this idea," Laurent said, his eyes bright.

"I thought of it because of your fusion suggestion for the gala. I want to do a plated meal that mixes Provencal and German recipes. I was thinking we'd start with rosemary and thyme pretzels with a lavender honey mustard dipping sauce. Now, do you think if I also included lavender in the breading for the schnitzel that'd be too much?"

"Lavender schnitzel? I think that sounds ghastly," I told him, and we both erupted into laughter. "But Fatima did love your lavender-honey glazed lamb for the gala. The culinary team got really creative with the presentation; you'll love it when you see it."

Laurent stiffened.

"What? What's wrong?"

"I can't come to the gala," he said. My stomach tightened. "It's during Berlin's restaurant week. I offered the owners anything they wanted to let me come back to see you at the gala, but they wouldn't budge. The restaurant is already booked solid that week; there's going to be swarms of food critics and diners who want to see what I cook. It's critical to start off on the right foot."

Laurent's eyes were wide and pleading. "I got permission to visit the week after. I know it's not the same, but we can go over every moment of the gala and how amazing your food was. You understand, right? You know I tried everything I could to be there?"

For a few moments, I couldn't even manage a smile. I understood Laurent's situation, but it was still a gut punch that he couldn't attend an event that he knew was so important to me and that was causing me so much anxiety. Now I'd have to go through it all without him.

Laurent looked so miserable, though.

"It's OK," I sighed, resting my head against his chest. "I know you'd be there if you could. When you come the next week, I'll bake you samples of everything I made, and you can give me your unfiltered opinion on whether I poisoned the gala guests or not."

"I'm sure everything you make will be delicious," Laurent said, his arms tight around me. "Thank you for being so understanding."

I hugged Laurent back, but that didn't stop my thoughts from racing. For once, even I couldn't pull something positive out of a situation.

Chapter 25

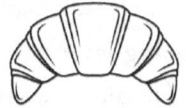

It started with a missed phone call.

I got home from work one evening and dialed Laurent at 9pm, our designated time to talk on the phone. When he didn't answer, I wasn't concerned; it wasn't unusual for work to run a little late for either of us. I poured myself a glass of wine and changed into my silk pajamas while I waited for Laurent to call me back. Except that he didn't. Not at 9:30, not at 10:00. It was almost 11:00 when my phone finally rang.

"I am so sorry," Laurent said as soon as I picked up. He sounded frazzled. I listened sympathetically as he recounted the disagreement he'd had with the owners over changes to the menu.

"Don't worry. I know you've been so busy," I reassured him.

The next week he was over an hour late for two of our calls. Another he completely cancelled because he was so busy.

We'll talk extra long tomorrow, he texted.

And we did, although it was only about work. His work. Before Laurent had moved to Berlin, he and I had made lists of places for him to visit in the city: parks, museums, coffee shops...

"This is your home now, and you should explore it," I'd told him.

But Laurent had time for nothing beyond the restaurant.

It was the owners. They were being impossible, he told me. They were grinding the staff to the bone, always wanting more with less. Laurent's best sous chef quit abruptly one day from the stress. Laurent redoubled his efforts to make up for the loss.

Now, when I talked to him, Laurent sounded joyless and half dead. He had no time to think up innovative recipes, not to mention that every idea he suggested was shot down. His hours were spent making the same fussy, uninspired dishes that had been on the restaurant's menu for decades.

"They're trying to get me to replicate the exact cooking style of chefs I've ever met," Laurent said during one phone call. "Any change I make, down to the garnish, gets criticized. I think I've already made schnitzel a thousand times."

"As long as you're not mixing lavender with it. This might be divine schnitzel intervention," I said. He didn't even bother faking laughter at the joke.

All our conversations had become like this: me listening while Laurent miserably recounted his workplace slights, day, after day, after day.

"Can I tell you about the passion fruit tart I made for Luc's birthday? The filling was tricky but—"

"Margot, can it wait until tomorrow?" Laurent sounded utterly spent.

"Oh. Of course."

But the next day Laurent pleaded exhaustion and again cancelled our call.

Just as long as you aren't sleeping in the restaurant, I texted back. I added a winking emoji, but really I was terrified.

Don't forget about me, I wanted to text him. *Don't forget what you promised. You said you wouldn't go back down that path. You chose me. You can't leave me alone.*

I felt Laurent slipping away from me, bit by bit. Our calls were reduced to every other day, and even then, Laurent missed plenty of them. When we did talk, it was always about the restaurant. How the restaurant was doing, Laurent's plans for it, how Laurent's plans were being thwarted, why he was certain a breakthrough was going to happen any day now.

"Just hang in there," he told me. I did my best. But then he had to cancel his next visit back to Paris. I'd coordinated my schedule around his and ended up spending the three days he was supposed to visit alone and depressed. Sabine's voice kept creeping into my thoughts: *Get used to this feeling.*

I hated her for the growing truth of those words. Even worse, I was afraid I was starting to hate Laurent, too.

Exactly one month before the gala, I visited Laurent in Berlin. It'd taken a fair amount of finagling and begging to again get several days off, but it was worth it.

As soon as Laurent and I reunited, everything would be alright. We'd talk through our problems, get back on the right track.

That morning, we spoke on the phone.

"I can't pick you up at the station," he told me, sounding exhausted. "I have to go into work now to confirm orders from our suppliers."

"That's OK," I said, keeping my voice cheerful. "I'll just meet you at your apartment."

Laurent had pan bagnat sandwiches wrapped and waiting for me in the fridge when I arrived, but they did little to improve the several hours I spent alone in his apartment, contemplating the empty walls and shelves.

"At least you're living your best life," I told Minerva as I read through Laurent's minute instructions for how to prepare her lunch of chicken livers and sweet potatoes. She stared fiercely at me until I set the completed meal in front of her, then set to work devouring it.

As soon as he got home, Laurent rushed to take me in his arms. "Mon amour, I'm so happy to see you," he breathed into my hair. "Thank you for being patient with me."

Seeing him again, touching him again, was enough to dispel most of my bad mood. We tumbled into bed, and I drank in the sight of Laurent's taut, tanned body. He'd lost a bit of weight in the weeks since we'd last seen each other. He was still as attractive and eager as he'd always been, but there were differences in our lovemaking now: His hipbones were sharper when they pressed against mine as he moved in and out of me. His breath came in ragged gasps from the start, and I worried it was genuine tiredness that made him sound that way, and not just a building orgasm. When he ran a hand down the soft, sensitive skin of my inner thigh, I could feel new calluses on his fingertips. In the moment, they only increased the pleasurable sensation, but later I wondered how hard he'd been working to tear up his hands so much.

Afterward, we lay together in a tangle of sheets, cool spring air wafting over us through the open window.

"It's still early," I said, glancing at my phone. "Want to get an aperitif then walk around Viktoriapark? I read it has great views."

Laurent tensed. "We can grab a drink," he said slowly, "but then I have to head to the restaurant. They need me for the dinner shift tonight."

"Laurent." My voice broke over his name. "You were supposed to have today off. I made my schedule work with yours, I came here on the train, I sat alone in your apartment for hours, I fed your cat. Now you're telling me you're leaving to go to work?"

Laurent scrubbed a hand over his face. For the first time since I'd met him, he had several days of stubble growing across his cheeks. "I know. I'm sorry, but I only just found out this morning that one of Berlin's biggest papers is sending a journalist over tonight to review the restaurant. I have to be there."

He reached for my hand beneath the sheets. "You know I wouldn't do this if I could possibly avoid it."

I teetered on the brink of saying it: assuring Laurent that everything was fine, that of course this was beyond his control, and I'd find some way to occupy myself until he had time for me. But my anger was growing stronger than my patience.

"What about the rest of the time I'm here?" I asked. "Will you have to be at work then, too?" He looked away, and something hardened inside me.

"Laurent, I didn't get into a relationship to keep feeling lonely. You've had this job for, what? Two months? And you're already breaking your promise. You're already falling back into the habits you swore you had given up."

"No—" I said, speaking over him when he tried to interrupt. "I don't want to hear another excuse. I don't want to hear another apology. They've stopped meaning anything to me. Every week, sometimes every day, there's another reason you can't make time for me. You're already missing the gala. Tell me Laurent, where do I fall on your list of priorities? Because for me, you're at the top. The absolute top. Can you say the same?"

"Margot." I recoiled at the irritation in his voice. "You're being unfair. We both knew this would be hard. We both knew I'd be busy. I'm doing my absolute best here, stretching myself in every direction, and you're not giving me any credit."

"No," I said furiously. "You're not turning this back on me. This isn't because I'm not understanding enough. I'm not going to grin and bear it like I've always done or...or try to look for a silver lining or focus on the positive. This is not fair to me. You made a *promise*. We set boundaries, and you're blowing right past them."

I suddenly couldn't stand another moment of being in bed with this man. Tearing back the sheets, I reached for my shirt and jeans. Once dressed, I looked at Laurent again. He looked absolutely exhausted.

"What do you want me to do, Margot?"

"Choose me!" I cried. "Show me I matter." Tears streaked down my face. "Don't leave me alone."

Laurent crossed his arms and looked away. "You know you matter more to me than anything. But that doesn't mean I can give up everything else." His voice was tight and clipped, exactly the way it had been the night we'd met. "I know the timing is bad, but this is *one* evening. Just let me work this dinner, then we'll be back to spending time together."

"Until the next time."

Laurent looked at me, then glanced at his bed stand. His phone was there, and I knew he was checking the time, checking to make sure that he wouldn't be late for work. The knowledge that even now—in the middle of our worst fight—he still couldn't stop thinking about work, sent anger coursing through me.

Laurent looked away, his gaze focused on some empty corner of his apartment.

He wasn't reacting enough. I wanted him to hurt as much as he'd hurt me. "If Noelle was still sick, would you abandon her now? Leave her alone all over again?" The words spilled out before I could decide if I'd regret them.

Laurent flinched, his face flushing, then going pale with barely suppressed anger. Finally, I was getting somewhere. He turned away and spoke through a tightly clenched jaw. "Of course not."

"So it's just me you're abandoning?"

Laurent whipped back around. "At least I'm going after my dream! You have one setback and you give yours up forever."

The force of his words, and the ugliness of them, hit me like a blow.

"I'm sorry you see my mother's death as just a 'setback.'" I was trying to sound wronged and angry, someone to be feared, but my voice was too choked with tears to sound anything other than pathetic.

Laurent's hard expression wavered. "I didn't mean it like that."

I felt empty inside, like a dried-out husk. I glanced at the clock. "You don't want to be late for work."

Laurent turned, then turned back to me. For a second, something flickered across his face, and I thought I'd gotten through to him, chiseled my way through his icy walls and cruel words to get to the real Laurent. This was just an argument; this wasn't the end for us. This was the man I wanted to be with forever, who proved that I was good enough. But then the hardness came back into Laurent's face, and he again turned away from me.

Without another word he got dressed, grabbed his bag, and was out the door. I made no move to stop him.

Alone in Laurent's miserable, stark apartment, I crawled back into bed and dissolved into tears.

After some time, I felt something soft brush against me. Opening my puffy eyes, I saw Minerva sitting on the edge of the bed. She regarded me as coolly as ever, but when I hesitatingly took her in my arms, she didn't protest. She only lay a fuzzy paw against my face.

I lay in Laurent's bed, cuddling his scruffy cat, until I cried myself out. This couldn't be happening. The one good thing in my life couldn't be falling apart.

But it was. I lay in bed for another miserable hour, working through what I needed to do.

When Laurent returned, well after midnight, we regarded each other for several long moments. I broke the silence.

"I'm sorry for what I said earlier about Noelle."

Laurent looked so miserable. "I'm sorry for what I said, too. It wasn't fair for me to compare our situations."

"Laurent," I began, and I saw him tense against my words. "I can't do this." It hurt so badly to say it out loud. "You know I love you, but I can't be in a relationship where I'm continually being let down."

Laurent was staring at the ground. "I'm sorry you feel that I'm letting you down." His voice contained absolutely no emotion. He looked like a man defeated.

"What if you..." my voice failed. I cleared my throat and tried again. "What if you cut back your time at the restaurant? Like you planned originally."

Laurent shook his head, his gaze still on the ground. "I can't pull back now," he whispered. "It'll ruin my career. They'll fire me straight off, and I need a good recommendation from them if I ever want to get another chef position. I'd be dooming myself to a lifetime of office jobs."

"And being with me isn't enough to convince you to quit?"

For just a moment, he raised his eyes to mine, then he was back to staring at the ground. "It isn't like that. You and I could make it work. It's just hard right now. You're the one making me choose."

I spoke softly. "You once chose me. Before all this."

Laurent didn't even bother looking at me.

So that was it then. I had no ideas left, nothing to pull out of my back pocket that would turn things around and save this relationship.

"I booked the overnight train back to Paris," I said, my voice as flat as his. "I should probably leave now."

Finally, Laurent lifted his head. His eyes were nearly as red as I'm sure mine were.

"I'm sorry I failed you."

I was still overwhelmed with hurt and anger, but Laurent looked so sad standing in his doorway. I crossed the distance between us, wrapped my arms around him, and breathed in the scent of the kitchens he'd brought home. Then I deliberately stepped away and grabbed my bags.

"I'm going to call a taxi."

We stood together in his doorway, not speaking or touching, for the few minutes it took for the taxi to arrive. When it did, I looked at Laurent a final time.

What do you say when your world is crashing down around you?

"Bonne chance, Laurent," I whispered.

He took a step closer and placed a gentle hand on my waist. For a wild moment, I thought he would kiss me, and we'd be caught up in a passionate embrace and throw away all our worries about the future, and his job, and managing this relationship, just to keep this happiness we'd found.

But all he did was lean close and place a soft kiss on my cheekbone.

Then he opened the door, and I stepped out into the night.

Chapter 26

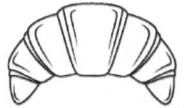

For the next several days I simply went through the motions of my life: get up, shower, get dressed, walk aimlessly around the city until I exhausted myself, then crawl back into bed and wait for night to pass. Of course I had ended up back where I always did. Of course I'd ended up alone again. It was a relief to return to work, just to feel like I had some sort of purpose again.

And there was going to be a proposal tonight.

Austin Winters had been emailing Le Jules Verne extensively for the past two months, wanting to get every detail just right. Everything was set: the ring had been dropped off yesterday, and I'd be the one to slip it in his girlfriend's champagne glass before serving the drinks. As I stepped into the restaurant, I blocked out every thought of Laurent. The only thing I wanted to focus on was having this engagement go as perfectly as possible.

Luc called me over when Austin and his girlfriend, Jackie, arrived. Jackie was thrilled with the restaurant, but Austin looked distinctively queasy. I gave him a reassuring smile while Jackie was admiring the wallpaper.

Jackie and Austin were both young, in their early twenties. They'd met in a French class at university they told me in slow, careful French.

"Your accents are very good," I told them, smiling. "Our sommelier will be over shortly, but, until then, can I start you off with something to drink?"

"I'll have champagne," Austin said immediately. It would have been slightly more natural if he'd at least looked at the menu, but I could work with what he was giving me.

"Very good, Monsieur. And you, Mademoiselle?"

"Oh, I have a bit of a headache. Just water for me," Jackie said with a smile.

Austin looked terrified, but I knew there were plenty of ways out of this.

"Excellent, Mademoiselle. Sparkling or still?"

"Still, please."

If she'd said sparkling, that would have solved the problem, but I still had other options. I smiled at Austin, trying to convey that everything would be fine. He looked faintly green.

I brought out their drinks, and as the courses began rolling out, Austin started to relax. He and Jackie giggled over inside jokes together, discussed the food, pulled out a map of the city and marked the places they wanted to visit tomorrow.

The talk of tomorrow—when the proposal would be over and they'd be happily engaged—seemed to breathe new confidence into Austin.

He'd asked for photos of the proposal, which Yasmine would be taking care of, but after I brought their fourth course out, I ran to the staff room to get my phone and snap a few surreptitious photos of them. They looked so young and happy sitting there, heads bent together as the sun set over Paris behind them.

Before I brought out the final course, I asked if either of them wanted something else to drink. Austin returned to looking like a deer in headlights and requested another glass of champagne. He looked desperately at Jackie, willing her to follow his decision. But she just smiled sweetly and ordered an Orangina.

I almost winced myself at that. I certainly wouldn't be dropping a diamond ring in a glass of that cloudy orange juice so the poor girl might swallow it before realizing anything was amiss.

But it was fine; I knew exactly how I was going to handle this. A glass of champagne, on the house, and as she went to clink glasses with Austin, she'd notice something sparkling amidst the bubbles in her glass and then...Well, after that, Austin would probably be happy to buy his new fiancée all the Orangina she could ever drink.

I again smiled reassuringly at Austin. He grimaced in return. In the staff room, I took the ring box from where it was being kept in the safe, poured two glasses of champagne, and dropped the ring in one of them. It looked lovely, the diamond sparkling amidst the champagne.

They probably will want a photo of that, too, I thought, snapping a few.

"Ready?" I asked Yasmine, who was coming in with a stack of empty plates. She patted her pocket, and I saw the outline of her phone.

The two glasses in hand, I paused for a second, savoring the anticipation. With a jolt of surprise, I realized I hadn't thought about Laurent for nearly an hour. I was actually even a tiny bit happy right now. I straightened my skirt, then walked out to the dining room. Poor Austin looked at me like I was the Grim Reaper himself, but he'd be alright soon. Better than alright, in fact.

"Perrier Jouët Grand Brut," I said smoothly, setting a glass before Austin. "And one on the house for you, Mademoiselle," I said, putting the other glass—the key glass—in front of Jackie.

She looked confused for a moment, then smiled politely, clearly not wanting the champagne but not wanting to appear rude. That was fine; she'd understand what was happening in just a moment. I took a discreet step to the side, so Yasmine had a clear shot of the couple.

"Cheers to us, Jackie," Austin said, his voice shaky.

Jackie lifted her glass to his, then frowned, peering at it. My heart quickened.

"There's something in it..." she said, turning the glass around to try to get a better look.

Austin shot up like his chair was on fire. "Here! Let me get that for you." In his nervousness, he practically ripped the glass from Jackie's hands. But once he was holding the still-full glass of champagne, he suddenly looked lost.

Our eyes met. I saw him start to reach his hand inside the full glass—a terrible idea—and shook my head. I indicated the empty water glass (which I had purposely not refilled) at his place. Austin caught on quickly enough and dumped nearly all the champagne into the cup, until just the ring was left, sitting in a tiny pool of bubbles. He fished it out, and kneeled beside Jackie.

"Jackie Rees, you make me the happiest man on the face of this Earth..."

It happened slowly. Jackie had looked shocked when Austin began his speech, but as he kept going, pouring out the reasons he loved her, her expression didn't change to delight. Her eyes remained wide, her body tense.

Austin hadn't noticed. He plowed through the whole of his speech and was now kneeling in silence. The ring he clutched in his fingers had begun dripping onto the carpet. He was still beaming.

I turned toward Yasmine. She was watching the scene with growing horror. Her phone dangled from her hand, forgotten.

Austin reached for Jackie's limp hand. She didn't resist. He went to place the ring on her finger, and I let out a sigh of relief. She was just surprised, that's all. Everything was fine.

Jackie seemed to suddenly realize what was happening. In a quick, jerky motion, she pulled her hand back. Someone at another table gasped quietly. From the corner of my vision, I saw that the entire restaurant had turned to see what was happening: a slow-motion trainwreck.

Austin's face was partially obscured from my view, but I still witnessed the range of emotions he went through: confusion, surprise, a hint of a smile (perhaps she was just joking?), then dawning horror as he caught up with the rest of us. He looked at Jackie.

"No?"

He barely made a sound.

The only person in Le Jules Verne who looked more miserable than him was Jackie. Silent tears ran down her face, and I could feel her reluctance to hurt this man in front of her.

She shook her head. Two tears splashed down onto the hand Austin still held, ready to slide the ring on.

The air went out of the building. Even the kitchens were silent. I saw one of the sous chefs poke her head out to see what the lack of commotion was.

I—who had been trained for every contingency, who knew what to do if a guest flipped a table in a rage, if lightning struck the Eiffel Tower, if a kitchen fire destroyed all the food, if a guest sat down and calmly informed me that they had a bomb in their bag—could not think of what to do now.

Abruptly, Jackie stood up and fled toward the exit. That was enough to bring me to my senses. I jumped into action. I turned to Yasmine and jerked my head in Jackie's direction. In a flash, Yasmine was at the table, grabbing Jackie's forgotten purse and coat. She caught up with the girl at the elevators.

In the oppressive silence, I heard her whispering to Jackie as she offered her tissues and hit the elevator button.

That was one half of the doomed lovers taken care of. But Austin was still kneeling on the ground, looking like he'd just been sucker punched. I went to him.

"Here, come this way," I said, pulling him up gently. The ring fell from his numb fingers, but Austin didn't even notice. I grabbed it before leading Austin to the staff room.

Once there, I sat Austin in a chair and closed the door. Technically, no guests were allowed back here, but that was the last thing on my mind right now. I grabbed a carafe and a clean glass, and poured Austin some water.

"Drink this," I told him, pushing the glass into his hands. Austin took it blindly. He seemed barely aware of where he was. Suddenly, he jerked his head up.

"The ring?" His voice was hoarse.

I dunked the ring in a new glass of water so it wouldn't be sticky, dried it, then returned it to its box and passed it over to Austin.

For several long moments he stared at it.

"It's a lovely ring," I said, to fill the silence.

"Has this ever happened before?" he asked, still looking at the ring as though this bezel set diamond held the answers to the universe.

"Oh, all the time," I lied.

"Everyone is probably talking about me out there," he said miserably.

"No, not at all. They're back to thinking about their meal." That was true. It was amazing how quickly people put an unusual incident out of their mind when a new plate of food was set in front of them. And I knew the entire staff would be working double time to make sure the next courses went out as quickly as possible.

Austin sniffed, and I nudged a box of tissues toward him. "Why do you think she said no?" His voice cracked on the word "no," and my heart cracked a little more for him.

I sank to the ground across from Austin, suddenly exhausted. Work had let me forget my own misery temporarily, but now it hit me full-force.

"I don't know," I sighed. "Sometimes things that have every reason to work out just don't."

"I probably should have talked about us getting married before proposing," Austin said in a small, sad voice.

I wholeheartedly agreed, although I certainly wasn't going to compound his sadness by saying so.

Austin pulled out a tissue and blew his nose. "She's the only girlfriend I've ever had. I didn't really have anything to compare us to, but I thought we were doing well."

I wanted to tell him that excuses were unnecessary. I was too deep in my own relationship implosion to judge anyone.

A tear trickled down Austin's face. "Do you—" he paused as his voice wavered. "Do you think I can get her back?"

I sighed. That was the million-euro question. How many people had asked it throughout history, I wondered? How many miserable people, feeling that there was nothing left in this world if one particular person wasn't in it with them, had repeated that hopeless, useless question? Millions, probably. Millions of miserable people.

And two of them sat in Le Jules Verne's staff room right at this very moment, utterly defeated.

I had no answer for Austin, but he didn't seem to expect one. We sat in silence for a while, Austin fiddling with the ring box and me wondering what Laurent was doing.

"Um, Miss?" Austin's voice yanked me back to the present. I looked at him. "What do I do now?"

"I'll take you out through the kitchens; none of the other guests will see you leaving."

"But..." Austin's voice trailed off, and my heart went out to him again. I knew what he wanted. He wanted a game plan, a surefire way to win Jackie back so that, a year from now, they would look at each other across the altar and see this evening as an amusing misunderstanding, a minor blip in a loving and lifelong relationship.

"I can pack up the final course; if you're still hungry."

"I still need to pay," Austin began, but I waved him to silence.

"On the house." Le Jules Verne would probably comp the meal themselves, and if they didn't, I'd cover it. There was no way I was going to make this man pay for the worst dinner of his life.

Austin stood up, then faltered again. "We're staying in the same hotel room. We still have two days left of the trip," he said helplessly.

Alright, time for a plan.

"The first thing is to get another room," I told Austin, "Even just a bed in a hostel. Text Jackie that you want to give her space, and she can have the hotel room to herself. Then ask if there's a time tonight you can get your things from the room without bothering her. Who knows, maybe she'll want to talk things out. But if not, get your seat on the plane moved before check-in. A transatlantic flight is not the time to try to repair a relationship."

Austin nodded, looking overwhelmed. "What if she doesn't want to see me at all? I mean...she ran out of the restaurant. How am I going to spend two days alone in Paris?"

I smiled, despite everything. "That I can help with." I pulled my notebook from my pocket. "Now, what do you like to do?"

Several minutes later, I sent Austin off, a written itinerary in his pocket, and a box containing two chocolate mousses in his hands. He'd taken the food, although I couldn't imagine he'd actually want to eat the mousses, given the memory associated with them. But who knows? Maybe Jackie was waiting back in the hotel room for him, appalled by her mistake, and the ring would be on her finger at the end of the night. I didn't feel optimistic about it, though. But, to be fair, I wasn't feeling optimistic about anything these days.

***

That evening, I sat in my window seat and stared dully outside. I'd loved this view since the first time I'd walked into this apartment. To me, it captured the very essence of Paris: the ornate buildings, the allées of graceful plane trees, the beautiful people walking to and fro, and the Eiffel Tower, unmistakable in the distance. For five years I'd lived here, this place I'd fled to after my mother's death and my failure at pastry school. That was thousands of sunrises, thousands of dusks, thousands of evenings spent looking out the window.

For the first time, its view didn't enchant me.

I sighed, the sound cutting through my silent apartment. "I can't keep going on like this."

Chapter 27

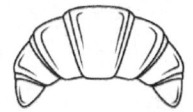

When things are falling apart (which they certainly were for me, and in quite a spectacular fashion), when everything appears hopeless, a true child of France knows that there is only one thing to bake: the croissant. There is nothing that demands such attention and patience, and reveals such a sublime reward, as whorls of buttery, flaky dough baked to golden perfection.

A few hours before dawn, I decided that sleep was going to remain elusive. I got up, put the dough hook on my stand mixer, and measured out flour, salt, sugar, and yeast into the bowl. Then I made a little well in the middle and poured in water and milk.

I made myself a cup of tea while the yeast did its thing. When I was done, I added in the butter and turned the mixer on again. Not having the inclination to do anything else, I stared at the dough as it mixed, watching it become smooth and glossy. After ten minutes, I pulled on a piece of it to make sure it was the proper consistency: stretchy and not sticky.

I wrapped the dough in plastic wrap, stared blankly at a magazine while I waited for the requisite hour to pass, then moved the bowl to the fridge and tried to get a few hours of sleep.

It worked, a little. I awoke, not refreshed, but at least not as exhausted as I had been. I wondered what Austin and Jackie were doing, if there was any hope for them, or if Austin had passed the night in a bunk at a hostel, wondering how his life had so suddenly come apart.

Speaking of lives coming apart, what was Laurent doing right now? Working, of course, or catching a few hours of sleep before he returned to working. I wonder if he even thought of me.

But enough of that. Back to baking.

I worked my way through the steps, forcing myself to make everything neat and perfect. The harder I concentrated on baking, the fewer unsolicited thoughts that could creep in. I took the dough from the fridge, then rolled it into a rectangle, each side and corner perfectly formed. Then I stretched the dough over the cold butter I'd similarly rolled into a rectangle, making sure there was not a single crack in the seams. I put it in the fridge to rest.

Once it had, I took the dough out and cut it into thin rectangles. Then I cut each of those in two to form triangles. Next—my favorite part—I rolled each triangle into the classic croissant shape, starting at the wide end, and taking care to keep the point centered and the shape gently curved. I gave them each an egg wash, then put the croissants in the oven to proof.

It was nearly dawn by the time the croissants were done proofing, but time was meaningless. I pulled them out of the oven just as the sun peeped over the horizon and began soaking Paris in pale, golden light. I took a moment to admire the croissants' doughy perfection. They got another egg wash while the oven preheated, then went back into the oven to bake.

When the timer went off, I pulled the croissants out and set them on the stove. As they cooled, I appraised them from every angle. Try as I might, I couldn't find fault. They looked beautiful. But, of course, the proof was in the eating.

I plucked the plumpest-looking croissant from the tray and took a bite. The golden-brown crust crackled, and the airy inner layers nearly melted in my mouth. The taste of it sent me back to all the thousands of croissants I'd eaten over the years: at breakfast with my mother, at school, on stilted dates, quickly while waiting for a train to arrive, late at night from a greasy paper bag, in strange new countries, in my own home.

I chewed slowly, savoring every bite. When the croissant was gone, I licked its buttery remnants from my fingers.

"That was very good," I said aloud to my empty apartment. For a few moments, I soaked in the quiet feeling of pride.

"Alright," I sighed. "What should I make next?"

So, as it had all my life, baking pulled me out of the depths of despair. In the days that followed, I baked everything I knew and found new recipes when those ran out. I baked squashy eclairs, rainbow-colored macarons, and baguettes by the ton. I baked maple pecan sticky buns, tarte au citrons with candied lemon, tiny petit-fours scented with rose and lavender, Cornish pasties filled with beef and onions and cheddar, apple strudels, chocolate chip biscotti, banana honey nut bread with a crackly top.

Of course, I couldn't eat all this, so everyone I knew found themselves gifted with the bounties of my labor.

"Again, chérie?" Madame Blanchet asked, looking at the miniature apple pie I was holding out to her. She took it with a strained smile. "Well, I'm glad you're keeping yourself busy."

Work brought a surprising bright spot: There was another proposal, and not one we'd been told of ahead of time. Its unexpectedness made it all the sweeter.

Malcolm and Lily were at one of my tables along the windows. As I was walking toward them to clear their table of the pasta course, a jittery Malcolm shoved a small box across the table toward his girlfriend. I stopped in my tracks.

Lily only looked at the box bemusedly.

"Um. You should open it," Malcolm said.

Still frowning, Lily did.

Her eyes bulged. I was several meters away and had to crane my neck to get a better view of the ring. Rose gold setting with a sapphire center stone. A very nice choice.

Once the ring was revealed, neither Malcolm nor Lily moved.

Come on, I silently urged the proposal gods. *Let this one go right.*

Lily looked at the ring for several seconds (during which I was genuinely concerned Malcolm might pass out). Then she looked at Malcolm and burst into tears.

I heaved a sigh of relief. Very quickly, Malcolm and Lily were both crying, Malcolm was putting the ring on Lily's finger, and Lily was trying to hug Malcolm while wiping her face. I gave them a few minutes, then came over with champagne and my congratulations. I took the photo they requested, checked the rest of my tables, then asked the kitchen to hold Malcolm and Lily's next course for a few minutes. There are many moments in life that are the perfect moment to dive into a plate of short ribs, but immediately after your engagement is not one of them.

The two of them were so obviously bursting with happiness as they admired the ring, and each other, and crinkled their noses as they drank the champagne. They were the final table to leave that night, and I wouldn't have let anything in the world hurry them. I knew how rare it was to have a moment in your life when you felt so completely happy. Life is hard and full of moments you think will break you. You need to hold on to those shining moments as much as you can.

***

"Want to grab a quick bite?" Yasmine asked after our shift ended. "Anywhere you want."

"You know when you say that I'm going to choose McDonald's," I told her.

"To the Golden Arches it is."

"The proposal seemed like it went well," Yasmine said as we walked along the dark street.

"It did."

"They seemed very happy."

"Oh, they were."

"You seem miserable though."

I stopped abruptly on the darkened sidewalk. "What do you mean?"

Yasmine raised her eyebrows. "Margot."

I started walking again, quickly now because I was uncomfortable. I should never have taken Yasmine up on this outing. Even McDonald's wasn't worth this.

Yasmine hurried to stay alongside me. "Margot, I'm your best friend. I know how you're feeling."

We were in front of the McDonald's now. I took the opportunity to go straight to the counter and place my order of a double cheeseburger with fries and a milkshake. A lot of people think you can't supersize your McDonald's order in France, but I know firsthand that if you ask them to do it while looking really sad, they'll shove a bunch of extra fries in the container for free.

We took a seat in the least sticky-looking of the booths. Yasmine hadn't spoken again, but she was watching me closely.

"Do you ever think about moving on from Le Jules Verne?" she asked finally.

I blinked, startled at this new line of discussion.

"Leave the restaurant?" It was almost funny. "Yasmine, that place saved me five years ago when I was barely able to function after my mother died. Do you remember what a wreck I was when I started working there? Making people happy gave me a reason to get up in the morning. I'm up to one hundred and ninety-one proposals. *I* did that. I helped those people have one of the happiest moments of their life."

"But Margot, you never *became* one of those happy people. You've spent the last five years always smiling, always solving problems as you chased happiness for guests, but you haven't figured out how to get it for yourself."

I looked away. I couldn't believe I was getting attacked like this, and in McDonald's, of all places.

"Have you—" Yasmine hesitated. "Have you considered applying to pastry school again?"

"Yasmine, I can't think about this right now. It's just too much, with the gala coming up, and ending things with Laurent..."

"But why not?" Yasmine pressed. "What's a better time to change your life than when it's at its worst? What if this is your sign to really go after what you want?"

I remembered Laurent's words the day we broke up, how he'd accused me of giving up on my dream.

He wasn't wrong.

But still.

"Why should I be good enough for pastry school?" I said heavily. "I've already failed at it once. I'm not even good enough to be a girlfriend. I'm back to being as single as ever."

Yasmine rolled her eyes so hard I thought she'd crick her neck. "Margot Delcour. You are not going to sit here and tell me you won't start living your life until someone tells you you're good enough. Don't give them that power. Sabine thinks you're the worst baker to have ever walked the Earth? Make your gala desserts so good that she cries herself to sleep. You want to go back to pastry school? Finally finish one of those applications you've been littering your wastebasket with for years, and get back to it. Only this time, go to the school *you want* to go to, not the school your mother wanted you to go to.

"And if you fail again? I mean, that's a great story. Who fails pastry school twice? As for Laurent, he can go cry himself to sleep in Berlin. You don't need someone to choose you, Margot." Yasmine's eyes were blazing. "You choose yourself."

The fluorescent lights of the McDonald's smeared and blurred as my eyes filled with tears.

"Margot, I know you love the restaurant, and making people's dreams come true, but it's become your excuse to not take any risks. Just tell me this: do you still want to be a pastry chef?"

I made myself meet Yasmine's gaze.

"More than anything," I said, and although my voice was barely a whisper, Yasmine heard me.

Yasmine leaned across the plastic table. "Then why don't you do it?"

On the tip of my tongue were the lines I'd used for years: that I was fine, that everything was great, that I was *so* happy, couldn't you tell by how much I was smiling? But this time the usual words wouldn't come.

I sniffed, then said the only thing I could manage: "I can't have this conversation without a milkshake."

Yasmine hurried to get our food, and, as I pulled my tray toward me, a tear splashed onto my food. I sighed. It seemed cosmically unfair that, on top of everything else, I couldn't even enjoy crispy fries.

"I don't know if I'm up for this," I admitted. "I'm afraid of failing and letting down my mom again."

Yasmine looked as forceful as I'd ever seen her. "Margot. You didn't let down your mother. You didn't even fail. You just had a setback. It only defines you if you let it. It can just be one page in your story. It doesn't need to be the end."

"But what if I'm terrible at pastry school again, and I learn I'm actually not as good at baking as my mother thought I was?"

"I don't think that'll happen, but if it does, then your mom still has a daughter who was brave enough to try again after the hardest failure of her life. How could she be disappointed with that?"

I wrapped my trembling hands around my milkshake. My voice was small. "I don't know how to start."

Yasmine gripped my greasy fingers. "Just take one step forward."

Chapter 28

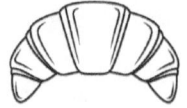

I started with baby steps. Two days after McDonald's, I booked a trip to Sicily for the end of summer. It was a place I'd always wanted to go, but I'd been waiting for a boyfriend who'd join me. But why? I didn't need a partner to go on a cycling tour of Mt. Etna wineries, walk the cobbled streets of Palermo, or stuff my face with cannoli.

Next, I finally stepped inside the animal shelter I'd walked past almost every week.

"Do you have any older cats who need to be adopted?" I asked.

"Oh, we have so many," the woman working there said. She led me into a room filled with gamboling cats and kittens. I petted half a dozen of them before noticing a small, dark brown cat in the corner, watching me.

"Ma petite chou," I said, holding out a hand for her to sniff. When she stretched out her little pink nose and crawled into my lap, I knew I wasn't leaving without her.

I named her Noisette, set her up in style in my apartment, and devoted myself to perfecting recipes for homemade cat treats. In return, she kept me company while I baked and slept next to me every night, purring softly.

It took me a full week to start taking any steps at all toward even considering pastry school. One afternoon, during the break between lunch and dinner shifts, I finally worked up the courage to venture into the kitchens. Chef La Croix was in back, sipping a glass of wine and looking somewhat content. For him.

"Chef? Do you have a minute?" Even though I (mostly) wasn't terrified of Chef La Croix anymore, I was still terrified by what I was about to say to him.

Chef La Croix set down his glass. "Yes? Get on with it."

"I...I was wondering if you had any recommendations for pastry schools to attend."

Chef La Croix raised an eyebrow. "Have a friend who wants to be a pastry chef?"

I blushed. "No. Um, it would be for me. I'd be the one going to pastry school."

"ABOUT TIME!" Chef La Croix roared. He was so loud I ended up flattened against the opposite wall.

"What?" I squeaked.

"If you hadn't figured it out soon, I was going to fire you just to force a career change."

I swallowed hard. "You don't know this, but I actually attended pastry school once, in Austria. I got asked to leave because I did so poorly."

I expected Chef La Croix to look troubled or surprised, but he just rolled his eyes. "Such stupidity I'm forced to deal with." He drained his glass.

"Mademoiselle Delcour, I have tasted your baking. You were put on this earth to be a pastry chef. I don't care about idiots you've had to deal with in your past. Now," he said, pulling out his notebook and a pencil stub. "Here is the list of pastry schools to consider."

I took the piece of paper he ripped out. "Are there any that, um, allow for more creativity in recipes? Not just making things the traditional way? That's what I've always wanted to do with baking."

Chef La Croix took the paper back and made little stars next to a few of the schools.

"There. Any of those will suit you. Now, do not look for other opinions or ask anyone else's advice. They'll all be wrong."

I took the paper back, my mind a mix of fear and hope and excitement.

Several days later, I sat in my apartment with Yasmine, staring at my computer screen. A completed pastry school application glowed on the screen. All I had to do was click "Submit."

"You know what?" I said, suddenly standing up. "Maybe this is a bad idea."

Yasmine groaned. "Margot."

"I should really wait until after the gala. To make sure I'm ready for this."

Yasmine was trying (and failing) to get Noisette's attention. "No. You don't need an external event to tell you if you're good enough. You already know that you're good enough. You'll submit the application right now."

"It's just...I always thought I'd graduate from the same school as my mom. That's what she wanted for me."

My anxiety must have been obvious because, when Yasmine turned to me, her face softened. "You're not doing it for her this time. You're doing it for you. That means you get to do it the way you want to."

I realized I was clenching my jaw and shook myself to relax. I looked at Yasmine and tried to grin. "You do realize that you've made me do so many terrifying things lately, right? First the gala, and now this. If anything goes wrong, I will hold it against you for the rest of our lives. Every food influencer who comes to Le Jules Verne will get sent to your tables for eternity, and they *will* make you take photos of them for an hour while asking if we have a secret menu we don't tell any of the other influencers about except them."

Yasmine grinned back at me. "Deal. Now send that thing."

I put my index finger on the Enter key and, squeezing my eyes shut, pressed the key down. My eyes flew open, and I watched the page turn white as it loaded. Suddenly, a black check mark appeared on screen. Submitted.

Laurent would be proud of what I'd just done.

Except I wasn't thinking about Laurent anymore, so his opinion didn't matter. In fact, I was sure I was going to stop dreaming about him any night now.

Onward.

"Oh mon dieu," I breathed. "That was awful. That was terrifying. I really need to get out more." I turned to Yasmine. "Let's get out of here."

As we pulled on our shoes and walked outside into the Parisian spring, I felt a heavy weight, one that had been around for so long I'd almost started to think of it as part of me, begin to lift. Just barely, but I noticed.

Chapter 29

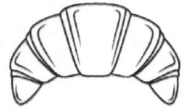

I took the two days leading up to the gala off from work to get started on the massive amount of baking I needed to complete. For the past week, I'd supervised deliveries of kilos of flour, kilos of eggs, kilos of sugar, chocolate, and butter to the kitchens. Then there were the specialty ingredients: cardamom pods, orange extract, saffron, Medjool dates...

"I should have never let Yasmine talk me into this," I grunted, dragging a giant sack of flour to my work station.

As I lugged the boxes to the appropriate places, I remembered Laurent and I joking about how much I'd baked for his family before Christmas. Something sharp twisted in my chest, but before I could even identify it, I forced the memory out of my mind. I had work to do.

The gala's graphics team had typed my menu up in an elegant script and printed out copies to have on display. I had one they'd given me to review propped against the stand mixer.

Patisserie Menu
Macarons (lemon, pistachio, fig)
Baklava croissants drizzled with honey and rosewater syrup
Mille feuilles with date paste and lavender-scented whipped cream
Saffron and cardamom crèmes brûlées
Ma'amoul cookies with raspberry coulis

The macarons needed a day or two to rest and reach the perfect texture, so I tackled them first. Yasmine herself came by at lunchtime, bearing gifts of coffee and ham and butter sandwiches.

"Look, I made it myself," she said, holding up takeaway containers. "I considered bringing dessert too, but you seem to have that taken care of," she added drily.

I'd fully run out of counter space by now, so I had a dozen trays of drying macarons spread across the floor.

"After this, I'm off sugar for the next decade," I told her, scrubbing my hands under the sink. "But look," I said, delicately picking up a macaron. "Look how good the feet look."

Yasmine surveyed the kitchens. "When I forced you into this, I didn't realize how much work it'd be." Suddenly, she hugged me. "I'm really proud of you, Margot."

I could barely take in her compliment. All I could think was that there were less than thirty-six hours until the gala. As the date had inched closer, succeeding at the gala had become inexorably linked to my self-confidence. If I could pull this off, it meant, somehow, everything else might turn out alright.

And maybe—*maybe*—if I was really good, my mother would notice, somehow, wherever she was, and she'd be proud. But I couldn't think about that too much because if I did I started crying, and saltwater is ruinous to baked goods.

***

The next day was even more harried. I started by tackling the miniature crèmes brûlées. It'd been tricky to get the brûlées' saffron and cardamom flavoring just right, but after dropping over a hundred euros on saffron and nearly setting the countertop on fire when I got too excited with the blowtorch, I was pleased with the final result.

I had a surprise guest that afternoon. I was filling the dishwasher (for the thousandth time that day) when I heard a harsh knock outside the kitchens. I lifted my head. Standing there, filling the doorway and looking as dour as Death himself, was Chef La Croix.

As with the time he'd appeared outside my apartment, I had no idea how he knew where the gala was being held or that I'd be here. He said nothing, not in greeting and not when I led him into the kitchen.

He took in the mounds of dough, bowls of jam, heaps of cracked eggs, rows of spices, and the absolute mountain of dirty dishes awaiting me. I watched him as he moved around the tables. He looked terrifying, but, then again, he always did. At the edge of my vision, I saw one of the chefs across the room elbow another. They both stared at Chef La Croix, wide-eyed.

"May I?" Chef La Croix asked, pointing to a bowl of pastry cream nearly scraped empty.

"Of course."

He tasted it, his face still expressionless. I grabbed a macaron and passed it to him. He ate it slowly. I watched his face, looking for any sign of his opinion.

When he was finished, he stared down at me, his eyes two fathomless voids.

"You'll do alright," Chef La Croix said, and he showed himself out.

Buzzing with pride, I got back to work.

The baklava croissants, with their nutty, honey-drenched filling, were nearly done. They just needed to be baked in the morning and drizzled with honey and rosewater syrup.

Ma'amoul cookies were one of the delicious desserts I'd tried at the first meeting for the gala. I'd never heard of them before, but one bite of the buttery cookie, so rich it actually did melt in my mouth, was enough to convince me it needed to be added to the menu. I'd found the woman who'd made them, and she'd happily passed along her recipe, along with her ma'amoul mold so I could stamp the traditional intricate design into them. The only change I made was to swap out the date filling for a traditional French raspberry coulis so it fit the fusion theme. Making them was my task for tomorrow morning.

That left just the mille feuilles. It was one of the trickier dishes: three stacks of flaky, buttery puff pastry sandwiched between thin layers of date paste and custardy pastry cream, all topped with ginger and vanilla icing. Made right, mille feuilles were a thing of beauty, but any slip-up could spell disaster.

Technically, they could be made ahead of time too, but the best mille feuilles have a perfect balance of crisp puff pastry and delicate pastry cream. If they sat for too long, the whole thing would get soggy and dull. I had nearly all the components ready, and I'd bake the puff pastry and assemble them tomorrow, right before the gala began.

I went to bed that night exhausted—and still a bit sticky from various caramels and custards—but happy with how everything had turned out.

Maybe I was capable of pulling this off. Maybe this event would be the start of a renowned pastry career that filled me with passion and pride until the end of my working life, leaving me fulfilled and exhilarated that I'd been brave enough to take that first step.

But enough of that. Let's just get through this party first.

Chapter 30

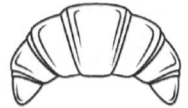

My first mistake was oversleeping. I normally wake up at a reasonable hour without an alarm, but I must have underestimated how much the preparations for the gala had worn me out. Waking up late was annoying, but as long as I hurried, I'd still make it there with enough time to finish everything.

I looked at my phone. There were three missed calls and a flurry of texts from Yasmine.

WHAT'S YOUR PLAN??? was all the final one said.

I called her back, and she picked up on the first ring.

"I'm heading to the gala," Yasmine said as soon as she picked up. "Have you left yet?"

"Not quite. But it's only two Metro stops away and I don't need to be there for an hour."

"Margot, the Metro workers are on strike."

I shot upright. "What? I hadn't heard anything about it."

"I know," Yasmine said. "Apparently everyone thought the negotiations would work out, so there wasn't much coverage about it, but talks fell through and they're striking now. It's all over the news."

I groaned. I was a proud Frenchwoman through and through, and I fully supported workers' rights, and unions, and the right to strike to improve working conditions. But why, *why* must they assert their rights on the day I really needed their services?

"How are you getting there?" I asked her.

"My mother and I are literally walking there."

"Hello Margot!" Madame Saidi called cheerfully into the phone.

"It's terrible," Yasmine said. "You know how much I hate exercise."

I rubbed a hand over my face. "Maybe I can take a taxi?"

"You and everyone else in Paris. None of the taxi companies I called were even answering their phones."

A pit was growing in my stomach. It'd take me well over two hours to walk to the gala. Maybe I could run the whole way? But I knew that feat of athleticism was far beyond my abilities. Damn my preference for reading cookbooks over hitting the gym.

I didn't know a single person in Paris who owned a car. Well, actually the guy who'd eaten crème brûlée with his hands on our first and only date three years ago had a car, but I couldn't ask him for a ride, right?

Well, maybe...

I recalled the image of him plunging his bare hands into a ramekin full of custard and shuddered.

No. I had to think of something else. And quickly. If I didn't get to the gala on time, half the desserts wouldn't be ready when the event began. I couldn't let Fatima and the others down like that.

"What am I going to do?" I whispered.

I'd been on the brink of a meltdown all month, and this was really looking like the thing that would push me over the edge. How ironic. It had taken me so long to build up the courage to bake for the gala, and when the day finally arrived, I'm thwarted by a strike.

"I can't miss this," I told Yasmine.

"You won't," she assured me. "We'll figure something out. Umm, what if you try to flag down a random driver and ask them to take you to the gala? Maybe pack a knife in case they're crazy?"

"Yasmine."

"Well, what better option is there?"

I looked blindly around my apartment, as though the answer was written on the walls. "I'll think of something. I'll call you back when it's figured out."

I hung up the phone and dropped my head into my hands. Maybe I could go onto the street, and there'd be a taxi. It was a long shot, but I was due for a bit of luck.

I quickly showered, changed, and gathered everything I needed before stepping outside.

There was nothing, of course. My street was too residential to see many taxis at the best of times, and with the strike, I was sure they'd all be in the busiest parts of the city.

What was I going to do? I stood there, frozen with anxiety, trying to work out a solution. When a voice spoke beside me, I nearly jumped out of my skin.

"Margot?" Madame Blanchet was frowning at me. "Why are you crying, chérie?"

I wiped a hand across my face. "I need to get to the gala, and the métro workers are striking, and there are no taxis, and I don't know how to get there, but I need to get there. Like, right *now*." Saying my predicament out loud made the tears come even faster.

To my surprise, Madame Blanchet smiled. "I wondered why you hadn't left yet. Come on, I'll get you there."

She started to move away, but I remained rooted to the spot. She must have misheard me. Or her age was finally catching up with her.

"Margot," Madame Blanchet said, more firmly now. "Come along. It wouldn't do for you to be late."

She took my arm, and I allowed her to lead me toward the apartment building. Instead of going inside, she made a beeline for a storage closet.

My mind was spinning. "How am I getting to the gala?"

Madame Blanchet produced a set of keys. She selected a large brass one and fit it in the storage closet's lock. With a feat of strength I wouldn't have thought her capable of, she wrenched open the door. Inside were the normal repair tools and extra supplies one would expect. But in the center of the closet, looking almost comically out of place, was a bright pink Vespa.

No. She couldn't be serious. I glanced at Madame Blanchet. She most definitely was serious.

"Madame, I don't know how to drive that."

"Of course not," she said kindly. "*I'm* going to drive it. There's plenty of room for two."

I looked again at the Vespa. I'd never seen a model like it on the streets; it had to be decades old. There was rust encroaching across the pink paint, and the basket hung sadly on one hinge.

"Madame, I don't think this is safe. It's difficult enough to drive in Paris, even when you're not driving a, a..." *A neon pink death trap,* I wanted to say, but I refrained.

"Margot Delcour." Margot Blanchet removed her glasses. Her gaze became even more piercing. She folded her arms. My tiny landlady, who spent her time crocheting baby blankets and singing arias to her dog, was suddenly terrifying.

"I have watched you bake astonishing things for nearly six years. Astonishing things that you have done nothing better with than give away to people, like myself, who don't appreciate half the time and skill you put into them. This day is your chance to prove yourself. I'm not going to let you be late."

I swallowed hard. "You know how to drive it?"

Madame Blanchet smiled, and the imperious spell she'd cast broke. "But of course I do. I learned when I was twenty, and I don't remember it being hard at all."

Please have driven since you were twenty, I prayed to the traffic gods. Madame Blanchet jammed a helmet over her head and passed another to me. Meekly, I put it on.

I scrambled on behind her, trying to hide that I was shaking. After all this was over, I was going to take a vacation. No working, no baking.

Madame Blanchet turned on the engine. The Vespa made a horrific coughing noise and emitted a billow of smoke.

And absolutely no motorized vehicles.

"We're off!" Madame Blanchet declared.

She promptly reversed into the wall.

"Ah, I always forget that," she muttered.

"You forget if you're going forward or backward?" I asked, my voice unnaturally high. I don't think she heard me over the noise of the engine. It was louder than a truck.

"Hold tight," Madame Blanchet said. As if I needed reminding.

We sputtered onto the street, nearly tipping over.

"Don't worry. It'll steady once we're going fast," Madame Blanchet shouted. A whimper escaped me.

We wove along the streets, Madame Blanchet seemingly trying to remember how to drive in a straight line.

"Awful giant cars," she grumbled, nearly clipping an SUV. I couldn't decide which was worse, opening my eyes or keeping them shut. I settled for staring into my lap, muttering positive affirmations as though they were protection spells.

"I welcome new experiences. I am open to adventure. I have released my fear and can enjoy this moment," I whispered frantically, breaking off to cough as another cloud of Vespa smoke engulfed me.

It took Madame Blanchet several intersections to remember how the Vespa's turn signals worked. Until she got it, she settled for shouting to the world at large which direction she was turning.

By the time we reached the busier roads, she seemed to have gotten the hang of the Vespa. With her increased confidence came road rage. I was shocked at the words coming out of my demure landlady's mouth.

"Learn the rules of the road!" she shouted at a man she decided had passed too close in front of us. "And your girlfriend is too pretty for you, you ugly bastard!"

"We didn't free this country from the Nazis so you could drive like a filthy connard! Casse-toi, espèce d'abruti!" she shouted at another while flipping him off, her scarf flapping in the breeze.

I did not know it was possible to be so terrified of impending death while simultaneously wishing the world would swallow me whole.

At one point, the engine made a sad sort of clanking sound and just died, right on the road. Swearing, Madame Blanchet managed to pull over while she tried to figure out what the problem was.

"J'en ai ras de cul," she said, kicking the Vespa with her heel-clad foot. "We have places to go." She kicked it a few more times, and just as I was about to say I didn't think that was an approved Vespa repair tactic, the engine roared back to life.

"Exactly. And there's more where that came from if you act up again. Putain de bordel," Madame Blanchet said, kicking the bike a final time.

By this point, I was beyond the power of speech.

But we made it to the gala as Madame Blanchet promised, on time and in one piece. I'd kept my legs so locked during the ride that I nearly fell over when I got off.

Once I was confidently on terra firma, I thanked Madame Blanchet profusely, assured her I wouldn't need a ride back (I'd crawl across Paris if I had to), and went inside. The Vespa ride hadn't done a thing to calm my nerves, and I was keyed up as I opened the doors.

When I walked into the main ballroom, I paused in pulling leaves out of my hair (There'd been a low-lying branch hanging over the road at one point, and I'd gotten a faceful of it). My eyes widened.

Gone was the bland, aging room that had looked better suited to hosting business conferences than a fancy event. The decorators had worked their magic, filling the space with glittering chandeliers, potted palms in ceramic planters, turquoise and pink rugs spread across the floor, divans with piles of cushions, and bouquets of red and orange flowers.

"Margot!" I turned to see Fatima striding toward me, energy crackling around her. In her hands was a towering stack of papers, heavily earmarked. A trio of assistants trailed behind her.

"Margot, I'm so glad you were able to get here. The strike is expected to be resolved this afternoon, so it shouldn't affect guests, but it's been chaos making sure the staff is able to get here." We stepped into the kitchens. "Do you have everything you need?"

I took a glance around my counters. "I think so. Thank you, Fatima."

"No, thank *you*, Margot. I don't know what we would have done without your talents." Fatima smiled warmly at me.

Don't thank me until this is all over, I almost said, but Fatima didn't need any more stress today.

I relaxed more once I was in the familiar order of the kitchens. I set the first trays of croissants I'd made yesterday into the oven to bake. Once they were cooking, I got to work making the ma'amoul cookies. It was my favorite type of recipe: streamlined, uncluttered. There weren't many steps or ingredients, but each of them mattered.

I mixed ghee and sugar with flour, then slowly added in rosewater and milk. I kneaded it into a sticky, sweet-smelling dough, then let it rest while I thickened the raspberry coulis until it could hold its shape. Then a piece of dough was wrapped around a bit of jam to form the cookies, and I gently pressed the mold into its surface to leave a delicate geometric pattern.

By late morning, the first batch of croissants was cooling, and the second was in the oven. When the croissants were just slightly warm, I drizzled them with a mixture of rosewater, honey, and chopped pistachios. I took the most misshapen one (although, really, they all looked perfect) for my breakfast.

Next, I spent an inordinate amount of time plating the macarons. They were the star of the pastry table, and I wanted them to look like it. I carefully arranged them on golden tiered platters, alternating colors so that they looked like rows of golden, emerald, and violet jewels.

I couldn't help but feel a little rush of pride when I looked at them. Macarons had been my first baking creation that had really impressed my mother, and they'd been the menu item that had most impressed the gala team.

A sweaty Yasmine hurried in while I was obsessing over them.

"Oh, they look gorgeous," she said, reaching out a hand. I slapped it away.

"No touching. The extras are over here," I said, directing her to a small pile on the counter.

Yasmine bit into one and sighed with pleasure.

"Incredible. Now take a break and come see where you'll be for the gala."

The dessert area was at the back of the ballroom. I was glad to see it'd be slightly removed from the main bustle of the party. The table was draped in pink and orange silk, and platters were already set up with the cookies and croissants.

"Your team did a lovely job," I said. Displayed so fancily, my desserts really did look worthy of the event.

"Didn't they?" Yasmine said admiringly. She plucked a croissant from the back of a platter and winked at me. "No one will notice. Keep doing your thing. I'll stop by again soon."

Back in the kitchens, the rest of the culinary team were busy chopping, baking, and sautéing. Laurent's dishes were all coming together.

There was buttery couscous that'd be garnished with thin slices of preserved lemon, chicken tagine with crackly, golden skin, paper-thin crepes that'd be filled with mushrooms, spinach, and melty Emmental cheese, beef stew bubbling away, heaps of salads, mountains of figs and dried nuts, ice-cold slices of melon, glass dishes of jams and preserves and—my heart twisted—a whole row of perfect-looking quiches.

Focus, I told myself. The first guests would be arriving in less than an hour, and I had dozens of mille feuilles to assemble before then.

I got to work baking the puff pastry. It took several rounds in the oven to cook it all. Once that was done, I began piping perfect circles of pastry cream onto the pastry, then stacking them three high. Next, I striped the blue and gold glazes on top of each mille feuille and dragged a toothpick through them several times to create a chevron pattern. I finished with ten minutes to spare.

In the ballroom, everything looked perfect. Dozens of candles had been lit, and the room flickered with their light. The band was setting up on stage, the bar was ready, and the first guests, dressed in gowns and tuxedos, were walking in.

I was about to turn back to my table when the main doors opened again. It was a sunny afternoon, and the figure was backlit so that I only saw a vague form. But then the person lifted a hand to smooth his curls, a gesture that was so etched into my heart that I'd know it anywhere.

Laurent stepped into the light.

Chapter 31

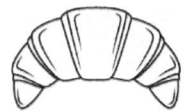

We met in the middle of the ballroom. I have no idea how I got there. One moment I was standing frozen, and the next I was beside Laurent, grinning stupidly as I looked him up and down.

He looked chic but slightly uncomfortable, the way he always did when wearing a suit. His curls were flopping onto his forehead again, and his face blazed with happiness and pride.

"What are you doing here?" I breathed. "They need you at the restaurant." My knees were weak, but I didn't survive that Vespa ride just to keel over at the gala. Without thinking, I reached a hand out. Laurent gripped it with his own.

Laurent grinned, his eyes crinkling. "Don't worry about the restaurant. I realized I couldn't miss seeing you shine here."

I had such a rush of emotions I could barely form a coherent thought: What was Laurent doing here? What did that mean for us? What about the restaurant?

Still smiling, Laurent caught me in a tight embrace, then quickly released me. "I know you have so much to do. Don't worry about me. I'll just be milling around, maybe popping into the kitchens if they need me. We can talk when the event is over."

I nodded dumbly and watched as Laurent melted into the growing crowd. I remained frozen a moment longer, hope and happiness surging inside me.

Maybe this is the day everything goes right.

Laurent's sudden appearance had left me jittery, but I couldn't think of him right now. I had work to do. I greeted the first guests, explained the pastry offerings and answered their questions. I was rearranging the mille feuilles when a wave of expensive perfume wafted over me.

I looked up to see Sabine a few meters away. She had her hair in waves and was wearing a crimson dress that drew every eye to her. At her throat was a massive ruby necklace that probably cost more than my lifetime earnings.

Rubies look terrible with your skin tone, I told myself, *So no need to be jealous of that.* Turning my back to Sabine, I concentrated on plating the last of the mille feuilles. I had just finished when there was a thunderous crash behind me.

Whipping around, I saw Sabine, a delicate hand covering her mouth. At her feet was one of the dessert platters. And all around the floor were the remains of the hundreds of macarons I'd baked. Shattered to pieces.

"Oh no," Sabine said. "I'm *so* sorry. They looked so delicious that I had to try one, and then it just toppled." She tucked a curl behind her ear.

I wanted to rage at Sabine, tell her that her acting skills were horrible, and that I'd made certain all the dessert platters were well away from the edge of the table, but all I could see was dozens of hours' worth of baking scattered across the floor. Ruined.

I'd been so proud of how they had turned out. They were supposed to be the centerpiece of the dessert offerings. They were physical proof that my mother had been right to think I was talented and that I didn't give up after setbacks. But now? They were just a mess on the floor that people were stepping around.

Someone arrived with a broom and began sweeping my creations into a dustbin. Fatima appeared at my side, assuring me everything would be fine, but she kept looking worriedly at the empty spot on the dessert table.

"Do you want me to get Yasmine?"

"No," I said, my voice sounding strange. "I'm fine. Thank you."

Fatima said something else reassuring, although I couldn't quite make out the words. Then she was gone, dragging along Sabine, who was still doing her best "horrified shock" expression. Her eyebrows were nearly climbing into her hairline.

There was a pause when no one went near my table, then a new couple walked over. I was still reeling from the macaron disaster, but I smiled as brightly as I could.

"Bienvenue. Are you interested in hearing about the desserts we have this evening?"

The couple looked at the printed menu, then at the table, obviously searching for the macarons that were the very first item listed.

After a few moments, they took two desserts each, so I guess the other options appealed to them enough. I wished them a pleasant evening, although I had to shout to be heard over the band. They were playing so loudly I wondered why Fatima or someone else didn't tell them to turn the volume down. I could barely hear myself think.

I appeared to be in the minority, though. The dance floor was filling up quickly. The well-lubricated crowd swayed and spun in time to the music.

I had a headache building behind my eyes, and when I blinked to clear my vision, I realized the polite woman standing in front of me must have asked for something.

"I'm sorry, Madame. What would you like?"

"Which are the ma'amoul cookies?"

Slowly, I scanned the table. I was feeling lightheaded now too, and I tried to remember the last time I'd eaten. Actually, now that I thought of it, all I'd had today was the baklava croissant. The day had been too chaotic to sit down for an actual meal.

"Right here," I said, lifting the tray they were on and trying to place it closer to the woman. I misjudged the distance and dropped it a little harder than I meant to. The woman flinched at the sound. My vision was slightly blurred, and I couldn't see her expression, so I just smiled widely and hoped I still looked like I was holding things together. She took her cookie and walked away. The band's music now felt like it was being pounded directly into my skull.

I should really find some water, I thought. *And sit down for a bit.*

Just as I was about to step out from behind the table, the guitarist played the opening chords of a new number.

My body reacted before I recognized the song. My vision went black. I realized I was gripping the table with both hands.

My chest heaved up and down. I wasn't getting enough air.

I took a shuddering breath, sucking in all the air I could.

It wasn't enough. I couldn't breathe. I was going to suffocate.

I took a series of desperate breaths, trying to bring oxygen into my body, but it still wasn't enough. I swayed on the spot, gasping now, trying to get any air at all. I could feel my body shutting down from asphyxiation. My ears were roaring, blotting out all other sound. My hands scrabbled helplessly at my throat. Losing my balance, I tumbled to the floor.

I'd broken into a sweat; I felt it as my hands slipped across my damp face. I was gasping so rapidly that I was close to vomiting, but still there was no air.

I whipped my head around as I continued to hyperventilate. My mouth was stretched wide in a futile attempt to get oxygen. I could barely see anything; my vision had narrowed to two pinpricks of light. All I could make out was the pink silk of the table skirt.

No one could see me here. No one could help me as I struggled to breathe. I was all alone.

Chapter 32

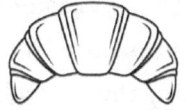

S uddenly, two hands grabbed me and roughly pulled me into a sitting position.

"What's happening? What's wrong?" a voice asked. It was sharp and angry.

The sudden movement was enough to shock my lungs out of the shallow breaths they'd been stuck in. My first real gulp of air was cool and sweet. For a long minute, all I could do was concentrate on my breathing as I trembled on the floor.

"P-panic attack," I finally gasped out. I slumped back to the ground, but the hands forced me up again. The cool rim of a water glass was pressed to my lips.

"Drink it."

I obeyed, although I half-choked on the first sips. The water gave me something to focus on, something to anchor myself to. I concentrated on how cool it was, how pleasant it was to drink. I'd been so thirsty; how had I not realized that?

Slowly, the roaring in my ears receded and my vision came back into focus. It wasn't until nearly a minute later that I realized I had enough air now, although my breathing remained rapid.

"Are you alright?" the voice asked, and now I recognized it.

Laurent, who had been so pristine when he'd walked in, now looked distinctly disheveled as he knelt on the floor beside me. Concern was vivid on his face.

"Margot, are you alright?" he asked again.

I wanted to nod and get composedly to my feet. That'd show Laurent that this had been just a moment of weakness, but that I was doing fine. Better than fine, even. Then he would be confident in my status as an independent, capable woman. All I had to do was say "yes."

Instead, I burst into tears.

Laurent didn't need any more answer than that. With a purposeful but gentle touch, he got me up and hustled me out of the ballroom. But instead of turning to the kitchens, he opened a random side door and ushered me in. I was crying too hard to see where we were, but I had a sense that we were now in a much smaller space. That was comforting, somehow.

It had been nearly two months since Laurent and I had seen each other. I was afraid that, after such a long time apart, he'd be awkward now, keeping his distance as I cried myself out.

But I need not have worried; Laurent had no such reservations. He held me as I sobbed into his shoulder, stroking my hair and murmuring my name.

When I finally shuddered to a stop, Laurent handed me a roll of paper towels. I looked around as I blew my nose. We were in some sort of storage closet, and it was absolutely filthy. I shuddered as I took in thick coats of dust and desiccated food scraps.

"I'm sorry," I said, apologizing for I don't even know what. "That song, it..." I was trembling, but my voice was steady. That was something, at least. "That song the band played was my mother's favorite song. She listened to it all the time, and I had it played at her funeral. I guess I wasn't expecting to hear it," I finished weakly.

I was looking at my clenched hands, but I felt Laurent's arm come around my shoulders. His touch steadied me. I inhaled deeply, concentrating on the air filling my lungs. I lay my head against Laurent's chest, feeling the steady rise and fall of his breaths. "I'm sorry," I said again.

"You don't need to apologize," he said softly.

Laurent handed me another paper towel. "Margot, I'm so sorry for what I said the last time we spoke. It was horrible of me. I know how much you miss your mom. She'd be so proud of you right now. *I'm* so proud of you. Look at what you've accomplished tonight."

I sniffed. "Having a mental breakdown and cowering in a closet that's littered with rat droppings?"

"I was thinking more of the desserts you baked for hundreds of people."

"The macarons got ruined. We're going to be short desserts." I dropped my head. That was a mistake because I suddenly had an up-close view of the moldy bread crusts I was kneeling on.

"The macarons are ruined? How?"

"Sabine 'bumped' them." I looked up to see Laurent's face darken.

"That little—" his jaw clenched. "Don't let her ruin this for you, Margot. Why don't you bake something else to replace the macarons? Something quick?"

"I can't."

"Why not?"

I thought about it. Why not? Why let Sabine's petty vengeance be the last word? The gala had barely started, and I had plenty of extra ingredients. What was to stop me from dusting myself off (thoroughly, this closet really was disgusting), and baking something new?

I didn't have time for macarons, but I had at least fifty recipes rattling around my head at any one time. I could just choose one of them.

I lifted my head so I could see Laurent. His face was radiant with confidence. It certainly meant something when the Earth's number one grump thought I could fix this situation.

"You're right. I'm going to do some frantic baking and save the pastry table. Thank you," I told him. "Who would have thought you'd be the optimistic one between the two of us?"

Laurent's eyes shone gold. "*You* are the only thing I'm ever optimistic about."

There was hardly any space between us. His face was so close to mine. All I had to do was lean in a centimeter, and—

A door closed sharply down the hall, startling me. In a rush, my senses came flooding back.

What was I doing, nearly making out in a dilapidated storage closet with my ex? I had baking to do.

"Let's get out of here," I said, deliberately making my voice light. "Fatima probably thinks I've been kidnapped."

Laurent pulled a rag from somewhere and wiped his face. (He's a braver person than me. This whole closet was so filthy I was tempted to schedule myself a flea dip.)

When we stepped into the hallway, it was jarring to remember where I was. I had no idea what I'd see when I re-entered the ballroom. I didn't think anyone, besides Laurent, had noticed when I'd collapsed from the panic attack. The table runner would have blocked most of it from view. But people must have seen that my station was deserted. No one would have replenished the food, and we were already short one dessert. I quickened my steps, dusting myself off as I went.

But when I entered the ballroom, what I found wasn't empty platters of food or Fatima looking bemusedly at my unmanned station.

Instead, Madame Blanchet, of all people, was at my spot behind the table, still wearing her street clothes, and with her helmet at her feet. She was passing out desserts and holding court with a group of enraptured guests.

"And these are mille feuilles with date paste and almond-scented pastry cream," she said confidently. I was the only one who noticed her reading from the menu. "Our pastry chef traveled to Morocco to harvest the dates and almonds by hand."

Well, that was patently false, but Madame Blanchet's audience seemed tipsy enough that I doubted they'd repeat the story anywhere. I went up to her.

"Madame, you didn't go back home?"

Madame Blanchet, about to begin another tale, broke off and smiled serenely at me. "I decided I'd rather attend your nice event. I told the young man at the entrance I was the Prime Minister's mother and he let me in."

I winced.

"Don't worry. I won't cause any trouble. I only wanted to see what you've been working so hard on. I've packed some crèmes brûlées to take home. I didn't think you'd mind."

She indicated a black handbag. Peering inside, I saw it was crammed with ramekins.

Madame Blanchet looked up at me. "What a lovely event. Did you see the silent auction items? I put a thousand euros down on a blue Vespa. It'd be nice to have a pair, I think. Wish me luck!" She gathered her helmet and glided onto the dance floor.

I turned to Laurent. "Can you watch the table while I'm baking? I'll be back as quick as I can." He nodded, and I was gone.

Back in the kitchens, I surveyed my options. I needed a recipe I was confident in and that wouldn't take long.

I spent a minute thinking about it, but, really, the choice was obvious. I'd make my mother's palmiers. I had all the ingredients, they'd be done in half an hour, and I could pull off the recipe even in my worked-up state.

And if Sabine thought they were "too simple?" Well, Sabine could—

Your status as a sunshiny person depends on you not completing that thought, I told myself. Sabine would just have to deal with it.

In under five minutes I had the ingredients arrayed before me: puff pastry leftover from the mille feuilles, sugar, salt, cinnamon, and lemons. I decided to add tahini for some North African flair. The steps couldn't be simpler: Mix the cinnamon, sugar, salt, and—my mother's special ingredient—lemon zest in a bowl, roll out the puff pastry so it was smooth and flat, sprinkle the mixture liberally across the pastry, fold the sides inward a few times to form a roll with tight layers, then slice the dough, creating the classic palmier "heart" shape.

Once I'd laid the slices out, I spread them with a thin layer of tahini and a little more lemon zest, then into the oven they went. When they emerged a short time later, they'd be lightly caramelized and glittering with sugar.

As I worked through the steps, the tension that had saturated my body began to ebb away.

I can do this, I told myself. *I've made palmiers since before I could reach the kitchen countertop.* They were one of the very first recipes my mother had taught me. I could see her so clearly in my mind now: showing me how to spread the sugar mixture over the dough, explaining to my toddler self the importance of the lemon zest to balance the sweetness, exclaiming over the perfect heart-shapes I made, as though I really was as talented at baking as she was.

As I plated the warm palmiers, I could almost feel her in the kitchens with me: her long, curly hair pulled back into a bun, her sky-blue apron dusted with flour, her face relaxed into a smile as she observed my work.

"These are wonderful, Margot," she'd said to me, over and over again throughout my life. For a moment, I thought I could hear her voice again, here in the gala kitchens. It was almost like she was right—

No. The moment passed. But still, I felt so close to her right now. I took a minute to savor the feeling.

The party was in full swing when I returned. I sent Laurent off, ordering him to enjoy himself, and arranged the palmiers on the stand the macarons had occupied. They perhaps weren't quite as fancy, but they looked just as appetizing. My mother would be proud, I think.

The gala was a smashing success. Hundreds of people filled the ballroom, the band sounded incredible, the bids on the silent auction items kept creeping higher and higher, the tables were laden with food, and all around me I heard people laughing and chatting.

"Did you try the tabouli salad with the mustard vinaigrette? It's incredible. Oh, and the lamb meatballs, don't miss those!" one woman said excitedly.

"Save room for dessert, though," her friend advised. "Those baklava croissants, I've never tasted anything like them. And the palmiers; they're some of the best I've ever had. The tahini adds such complexity."

I swelled with pride.

There was plenty to focus on, and the dessert area was crowded with people tasting my creations. This was France, of course, so many of them were interested in knowing how each recipe had been made and what ingredients I'd added. I was happy to tell them, and I even wrote out a few quick recipes for people who seemed especially keen.

Just then Colette, resplendent in a merlot-colored gown with a high slit, appeared with a dashing gentleman. She was giggly with champagne as she kissed me on each cheek.

"Everything is fabulous, Margot. When you become more famous than Dominique Ansel, I'm going to tell everyone I knew you back when we were servers and you were the only person who didn't yell at me when I dropped all the cutlery." She leaned in closer. "What do you think of Eduardo?" she whispered, her breath tickling my ear.

I eyed her companion, who looked very suave in his tux.

"Gorgeous," I whispered back. "Why does he look familiar? Wait, no," I said, gasping as I realized. "Colette, you are *not* dating a member of the Spanish Prime Minister's security team."

Colette giggled again. "Why not? His mother lives in Paris, and he needs a tour guide when he comes to visit her. Wish me luck!" She winked as she drew her beau back into the crowd.

Yasmine was helping her mother and Fatima, and she knew dozens of people herself at the gala, but she made sure to check on me when she had a spare moment.

"Margot, these are absolutely the most delicious things you've ever made," she said as she devoured her third croissant.

"My mother said Fatima is over the moon with how good your desserts are. You should have seen Sabine's face when she mentioned it. God, when I heard she'd knocked over your macarons..." Yasmine looked as murderous as a person could with a dollop of honey on her nose. "I'm going to find Sabine and tell her we've already decided to ask you to be pastry chef for next year's gala, just so I can see her expression," she said, grabbing a cookie for the road.

Later in the evening, Sabine reappeared. She appraised the dessert table with her lips pursed, her mouth just short of a smirk. When she came to the palmiers, already half gone, she paused.

"What's this?"

"Palmiers!" a woman next to her exclaimed. "And they're wonderful. Here, have one," she said and tried to put a pastry in Sabine's hand.

Sabine backed away, flicking crystals of sugar from her fingertips. She frowned at the palmiers, then at me, but she didn't seem to know what to say in front of all the people surrounding the dessert table. Turning on her stiletto heel, she stalked off. And I didn't see her for the rest of the evening.

As the night wore on, I was kept busy with final requests for dessert and wrapping up little packages of leftovers for people who wanted to take them home. At the end of the evening, I brought the dishes and platters back to the kitchens where a new team was already busily washing up. As I set down the empty platters, Fatima strode in, looking exultant.

"This is the most successful fundraiser we've ever had," she said delightedly. I smiled back, buzzing with pride and accomplishment. I'd actually done it: I'd been the pastry chef for a fancy event, people thought the desserts had come out well, and—shockingly—I did, too.

When I'd (reluctantly) taken this job, I'd seen it as a one-off, a taste of professional baking I could fondly look back on when I returned to baking just for fun. But why stop now? I had pastry school applications in the mail and a successful event under my belt. Maybe this gala wasn't the huge event in my life. Maybe this was me just getting started.

Guests trickled out of the ballroom as I carried dirty dishes to the kitchens. Each time I came back out, there were fewer people remaining. And when I'd dropped off the final plates, there was just one person left. He was seated at a corner table, drumming his fingers nervously on the wood. When he saw me, he smoothed a hand over his curls and smiled.

Chapter 33

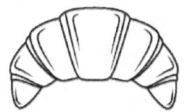

I went up to him.

"Can I give you a ride home?" Laurent asked, breaking the silence. "I have a rental car."

"Yes," I croaked. My voice seemed to have fled.

This was it. This was the moment Laurent and I laid down our cards and learned if we had enough to make a go of things.

But maybe not. Maybe he was still a workaholic. Maybe he'd decided what we had wasn't that special. Maybe he'd decided to dedicate his life to making quiches, and the only reason he'd shown up to the gala was to get my opinion on his newest attempt.

Probably not that last one, I told myself. *That would be strange.*

The pressure was enough to make me consider chasing Madame Blanchet down and taking another spin on the Vespa. But I'd been so brave these last few weeks. I wasn't going to shy away now. Digging deep for one last bit of courage, I followed Laurent to his car and opened the passenger door.

At first all I saw were glass food containers. They were stacked half a dozen high, completely filling the backseat.

"Oh. Wow."

I'd promised myself that I'd be brave, not that I'd be articulate.

"I made you some food," Laurent said solemnly.

"I'm very pleased to hear that!" called Madame Blanchet from behind us as she jammed her helmet on and struggled with the Vespa's kickstand.

That seemed to be an excellent sign to get in the car. Once inside, with seat belts fastened, Laurent and I stared at each other in silence. How did I always forget just how handsome he was? Even looking as grave and nervous as he did now, he still made my breath come faster.

"I wanted to bring you some food," Laurent said, still sounding deadly serious. "I couldn't decide what to cook, and I wanted to make sure I made something you liked. So I made a lot of things."

He and I both glanced at the backseat. The amount of food he'd brought could probably keep a small village nicely fed for a week.

"That was very thoughtful of you," I told him.

"There's the beef stew you mentioned liking a few months ago." Laurent reached back to adjust the container so it was perfectly lined up with the others.

"Oh, right. Beef stew. Thanks."

Wow, we were really bringing the passion today.

Someone behind us blared their horn. We both jumped, looked guiltily at each other as though we'd been doing something illegal, then Laurent started the car.

We didn't speak on the ride to my apartment. Once Laurent parked, we both took a mountain of food containers inside and arrayed them on my countertop. We stared at each other from across the sea of food.

"Margot," Laurent began, and the sound of my name on his lips thawed things a little.

I spoke up. "How did you get the time off?"

"Well," Laurent said slowly. "They had to give me the time off because I quit."

He grinned, looking so happy that, despite all the remaining unknowns, I found myself grinning back.

"You quit?"

"I absolutely quit."

"Why?"

Laurent grimaced. "Because that job was terrible, and it turned me into a horrible person. I was terrible to you, back in Berlin. Everything you said to me—about falling back into bad habits, about not making you a priority—it was true. I was an idiot. Hurting the people most important to me for a job that made me miserable. Again. Margot, I'm so sorry."

His words hung heavily between us.

"I'm applying to pastry school." It was the only thing I could think to say. I could barely take in what Laurent was telling me or what it might mean for us.

Laurent laughed in delight. "Of course you are. You'll blow them away."

"I'm only applying to programs that are a good fit for me. Not the one my mother graduated from."

"Do you know, I tried every dessert you made at the gala? I even grabbed one of the macarons from the garbage."

"You ate trash macarons for me?"

"Ate it and loved it. Your trash macarons nearly brought me to tears."

"That was probably because of the bleach they use to disinfect the trash cans."

Laurent shrugged. "Look, when a flavor combination works, it works."

I swallowed hard. "You were right, in Berlin, about me giving up too easily." Laurent opened his mouth to interrupt, but I held up a hand. "You were an asshole about it, but you were right. I'd stopped trying anything new in life just to try and avoid failure."

I paused. "But now I'm working on changing that."

Laurent took my hand and led me to the couch. "Tell me about it."

So I did. Slowly at first, as I explained speaking to Chef La Croix and deciding which pastry schools to apply to. I picked up steam as I told him about the trips I'd booked. Noisette crept over, and she let Laurent stroke her as I told him how I'd wanted a cat since we'd given Jacques away but had never gone through with it. As I spoke, Laurent kept hold of my hand the entire time.

"I'm so proud of you," he said when I'd petered to a stop. "Margot, I can't even put into words how proud of you I am. And I'm so completely unsurprised."

I laughed a little. "You knew I wasn't going to spend the rest of my life in shambles?"

Laurent's eyes blazed green and gold. "I knew from the moment you—rightfully—told me off the night we met at Le Jules Verne that you were a person who wouldn't go down without a fight."

"I was smiling that whole evening!" I protested. "Perfectly friendly."

"I know. And I could still tell you weren't someone to mess with." Laurent smiled his crooked smile. It had been so long since I'd seen him smile like that.

"Margot, a year ago *my* life was in shambles. I didn't think I was worthy of anyone. I figured I'd just have to struggle through things alone. What I didn't realize was that all I needed for everything to make sense was to meet a relentlessly optimistic baker who put more effort into making others happy than anyone I'd ever met."

Laurent heaved a sigh. "Every day since you left Berlin, I've known what an idiot I was for losing you. It made it very easy to quit. I'm just terrified I've done it too late." Laurent swallowed hard. "Have I?"

Again, I dodged his question. "You're done being a chef?" I didn't want that for Laurent, for him to return to a soulless office job, but I also didn't want to risk losing him to his work again.

Laurent smiled. "It took me weeks to figure things out. It's the only reason why I didn't quit the night you left. I wanted to come back to you with a plan."

He exhaled. "I'm done working as a chef for a restaurant that isn't mine. It's too easy to lose control and end up working insane hours and making food that doesn't excite me, all for someone else's vision. I'm done with that. Instead..."

Laurent paused to take an excited breath. "I want to open a small restaurant. Very small, just a handful of seats. It's a new concept, but it's becoming more popular. The space will be small enough that I'll be able to afford rent, utilities, and everything else without needing a financial backer who makes all the decisions. Instead of hiring a team, I can do everything on my own: I'll make the food in front of the diners, mix the drinks, hell I'll even be able to do the washing up. It'll be a premium experience, so I'll only need to do a few seatings a day and can keep my hours manageable. And I'll answer only to myself."

Laurent's eyes shone as he spoke, and I found myself catching his enthusiasm. "Margot," he said, turning serious. "I feel confident about this, but not if it comes at the expense of us. If this idea doesn't work out, if you ever think it's the wrong choice, I'm not afraid to step away from it. More than any restaurant, I want to be with you. I want that more than I've ever wanted anything in my life." He hesitated. "If you'll still have me."

Laurent was speaking so honestly, and his feelings so perfectly mirrored my own, that all I could do was fall forward and let myself collapse into his embrace. He pulled me in close.

"Margot, I can't offer you a perfect life. All I know is that when I met you, I finally stopped feeling lost.

That, of course, made me cry.

We stayed like that, tight in our embrace. I became acutely aware of Laurent's body pressed to mine, our tear-dampened faces touching, his lips resting in my hair.

He seemed to get the same idea. He kissed my hair first, so gently I wasn't sure if I was imagining it. But he kept going, trailing the kisses along my hairline, across my cheekbone, until he reached my mouth. I wanted him more than I'd ever wanted him before.

In a smooth motion, he scooped me up, his brawny chef arms bulging. He carried me into my bedroom and laid me on the bed. I looked at him for a moment, filling my vision with this man I loved, the man who made my life make sense. We undressed each other, and he was gorgeous in the dark.

Laurent climbed into bed and pulled me close, covering me with kisses until I couldn't think straight. But every time I looked at him, I knew that I was where I was meant to be.

Afterwards, we curled around each other and talked into the night.

"Have you thought about where you want to open your restaurant?" I asked.

"Wherever you want to live."

"I was..." I hesitated. "Well, I was thinking, after I finish pastry school, of moving back to Colmar. Whenever my mother and I moved, it was always the place I'd hoped to go back to. I've missed being home."

He pulled me close. "Then I'll find a place in Colmar, and we'll make a new home there."

In the morning, I awoke to a pale Paris dawn. I was alone in bed; I heard Laurent moving around in the kitchen and talking to Noisette. I sprawled across the bed and took a few minutes to soak in the weak sun and feeling of hopefulness that washed over me.

That's what I'd been missing for five years. There'd been moments when I'd been happy, even moments I'd bent over double with laughter. But there'd been so little hope. Now, I could feel it returning.

As I was rubbing the last bit of sleep from my eyes, Laurent came in bearing a tray laden with breakfast.

"I made the rolls myself," Laurent said proudly. "Shall we eat in the window seat?" he asked.

There was just enough space for both of us and the tray. I tried to lean my head against Laurent, but he was weirdly jumpy. I gave it up.

"The coffee's excellent," I told him.

"What about the rolls?"

I made a noncommittal noise that I hoped he'd take positively.

Suddenly, Laurent stood up, nearly overturning the breakfast tray.

"Margot." He sounded so concerned that I set my mug back down.

"Margot," he said again. "I know that you're used to this, you know, working where you do. I didn't want to do something cliché. But I also know how much you love your work and love Paris."

I stared at him, utterly baffled at where this was going.

"What I'm trying to say is..." Laurent collapsed to the floor.

No. No, he was kneeling.

"You can just see the Eiffel Tower from here, and I wanted it to be part of this moment." Laurent was actually sweating.

I followed his pointing finger and looked out my window. Yes, there was the Eiffel Tower. It looked lovely today.

I turned back, about to comment on the perfect weather, then froze.

In Laurent's shaking hand was my mother's emerald ring.

"Celine found it at her house last month. You must have taken it off when you were baking cookies with her daughters. They'd stolen it as a spoil of war. I didn't want to buy a ring I wasn't sure you would like, and when this one reappeared..." Laurent looked anxious and happy and terrified.

He swallowed hard, then took my hands.

"Margot Delcour, will you marry me?"

There was a sudden roaring in my ears. I tried to speak and found my voice had fled. I suddenly understood why so many people at Le Jules Verne were speechless when they were proposed to.

I managed to hold out a trembling hand. Laurent slipped my mother's ring on. It sparkled in the sun.

"Yes," I breathed. I grabbed Laurent's shirt and dragged him to me, nearly overturning the breakfast tray a second time.

Unlike our conversation at Christmas, when I'd clung to Laurent's mention of marriage as proof I was worthy, this proposal wasn't about validation. Instead, it was the icing on the cake. Which didn't make it any less sweet.

I kissed Laurent, losing myself in the utter perfection of the moment.

When we paused to catch our breath, Laurent looked at me and grinned. "I was driving myself mad trying to decide when to ask, and I thought the idea of a proposal over breakfast sounded romantic. How do the rolls taste? Remember, you're my fiancée now, so we have to be honest with each other."

"Honestly?" I repeated, and Laurent nodded. I looked at this man and was almost overwhelmed by the amount of love I had for him.

But I still couldn't flatter his ego about baked goods.

"They're just slightly too tough," I admitted, squeezing my eyes shut. "You always overwork the dough." I opened my eyes tentatively, then dissolved into laughter at the affronted look on Laurent's face.

"But don't worry," I said, pulling him close. "We have an entire lifetime to perfect it."

One Year Later

One month after Laurent and I got engaged, I was accepted into my top choice for pastry school.

Leaving Le Jules was harder than I expected. Of course, once I had made the decision to leave, all the diners behaved perfectly, as happy as I was to be in the Eiffel Tower. I still drop by every month or so to see Chef La Croix and Luc and everyone else.

I'm nearly finished with my nine-month *Diplôme de Pâtisserie* program. It's been hard, but I've never doubted it's what I'm meant to be doing.

Once I have my certificate, I plan to work in a bakery for at least a year to find my feet. After that, I may keep going with that job or try to open my own shop. Either idea makes me feel overwhelmed with happiness and excitement.

Laurent and I found the perfect spot to open his new restaurant in Colmar. It's a tiny space, just enough for six seats, exactly what Laurent wanted. The grand opening went off without a hitch. Laurent did everything from cooking the meals, to pouring the wine, to, yes, washing the dishes until they sparkled.

We've been traveling between Paris and Colmar on our days off to see each other, and as soon as I finish my program, I'm joining him in our new apartment.

Yasmine got accepted into EHL's hospitality program, left Le Jules Verne right before I did, and is throwing herself into her courses in Switzerland. Leïla took over as head server at Le Jules Verne and, by all accounts, is doing perfectly. Even Chef La Croix says so.

I see Chef almost more than I did when he was my boss. He stopped by my apartment once to see how I was doing and ran into Madame Blanchet on his way out. I don't know what they spoke about (with them, truly the possibilities are endless), but he now stops by to see her at least once a week, a bag of homemade dog treats clutched in his hand.

Laurent and I were married two months ago. We had the official ceremony at the town hall in Colmar, just the two of us. Our reception was a week later, at Laurent's parents' house.

We spent the week before the wedding preparing all the food ourselves. Laurent made the main courses, and I baked a four-tiered lemon poppyseed cake with vanilla buttercream frosting. Yasmine and Noelle helped me put up decorations. There were fairy lights in the garden and strawberries in the champagne. Luc manned the speakers, and people danced in the grass as the sun went down.

Before the night ended, I ducked into the shadows for a moment to soak everything in. Here we were, on the cusp of our new careers, surrounded by our friends and family before we began our new life together. I couldn't have pictured a more perfect wedding.

And the food, of course, was delicious.

About the Author

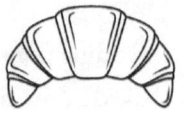

CHRISTINE DESALVO has been publishing fiction and nonfiction for over a decade. She drew many of the ideas for FROM PARIS, WITH BUTTER from the two years she lived in France—and the three days she worked as a waitress (a story for another time). She lives in San Francisco, California, with her family and two spoiled cats.

You can follow her on Instagram @christinedesalvoauthor and on Substack at https://christinedesalvoauthor.substack.com/

www.ingramcontent.com/pod-product-compliance
Lightning Source LLC
Chambersburg PA
CBHW020136120726

47903CB00007B/2286